PRAISE for GERALD DUFF

"Duff's transcendent prose swings and sways, whoops and moans in pulsating cadences reminiscent of the King."
—Publishers Weekly (starred review)

"Gerald Duff has an unerring ear for Memphis dialect."
—The Washington Post

"Duff writes lean, straightforward prose well enough that each paragraph conveys even more than the background which the words supply."
—Tennessean

"Gerald Duff is among the best fiction writers working today and I anticipate that he will go on to become one of the great names in American literature."
—Nashville Life Magazine

"Brilliant..." *—The Boston Globe*

"A serious writer about not-always-serious topics."
—The Dallas Morning News

"Here is a writer that shows us a well-controlled comic touch. Gerald Duff is a new name in contemporary fiction."
—Newark Star-Ledger

"Fasten your seat belts...the tale unfolds like a tornado in a Southern storm."
—The Orlando Sentinel

"A serious literary work of fiction in the Southern tradition..."
—Tulsa World

Memphis Ribs

Books by Gerald Duff

Novels

Indian Giver
Graveyard Working
That's All Right, Mama: The Unauthorized Life of Elvis's Twin

Poetry

A Ceremony of Light
Calling Collect

Non-Fiction

William Cobbett and the Politics of Earth
Letters of William Cobbett

Memphis Ribs

Gerald Duff

SALVO PRESS
Bend, Oregon

MEMPHIS RIBS

Copyright © 1999 by Gerald Duff

Salvo Press
61149 South Hwy 97, Suite 134
Bend, OR 97702
www.salvopress.com

Cover Designed by Andrew and Scott Schmidt

Library of Congress Catalog Card Number: 98-87928

ISBN: 0-9664520-1-1

Printed in Canada
Second printing 1999

For Carroll and Dan Mayfield
best of Memphians
sliced, chopped or pulled

For more than 125 years, Tennessee law has fixed the maximum penalty for stealing a hog at fifteen years in prison—three times greater than the penalty for involuntary manslaughter. No other element in Memphis society more effectively bridges the gaps of race, sex, age, socioeconomic status, religious belief and political philosophy than barbecue.

John Egerton in
Southern Food

"This is a slow operation," he said, as he checked a rack laden with dark brown shoulders. "You can't rush it. You have to know how to wait, and when to act—and when the time comes, you have to move fast and then wait some more. It's too tedious for most young people—they don't have the patience for it."

James Willis, Senior Cook
Leonard's Barbecue
Quoted in *Southern Food*

1

Midnight on Front Street in Memphis, and Franklin Saxon was leaning up against the grill of his father's Lincoln Continental, watching five members of the Bones Family attack a Union Planter's Bank ATM with two sledgehammers. The stand-alone machine was newly installed and located in a part of the Bluff City away from the center of downtown. Franklin wondered if the executive in charge of that division of Union Planter's had guessed right about its profitability. It would probably do well in the daylight hours, nothing after nine p.m., of course, and pick-up again each morning when the sun rose to shine on the Hernando DeSoto Bridge over the Mississippi. It was worth a try, probably, and Franklin wished the bank well in the venture.

Franklin Saxon did hope the Bones Family would get the ATM cracked open, though, soon, so he could finish his business with them and leave that deserted part of the city and get back to Midtown. The drinks he had had in the Peabody Hotel before, during and after his keynote speech to the medical equipment convention were dying on him, and with each bang of a sledgehammer against the face of the ATM, he was realizing how careless he had been to agree to meet with the Bones Family here.

It had seemed droll at the time when their spokesman, one T-Bird, had said they needed to make a withdrawal, but now all Franklin Saxon felt was not amusement but rising impatience and a hint of growing anxiety. This first deal with the Bones Family was off to a twisted start, and Franklin felt a twinge begin just at the top of his nose between his eyes. It started to move up and into his forehead, and he stepped away from the front of the Lincoln and looked up and down Front Street, beginning to scratch at his temples with both hands. Not a headlight was in sight in either direction, but a deep need to move was rising up from Franklin's viscera with each clang of the sledgehammers.

"Gentlemen," he called from the shadows where he had parked, "that hammering's not going to do it. I'll give you two more minutes, and then

I will consider our deal to be off."

"That's all we be needing," the one called T-Bird said. "We just prizing up the bottom now. Flash, he getting the forklift to tear it loose. See yonder?"

"Tear it loose?" Franklin Saxon said, hearing an engine crank as he spoke and then, turning to look, seeing a forklift approaching from a construction site just behind the ATM, an area he had not noticed previously. "Look, this is not the way I want to do business."

"We be putting the machine in the pickup bed," T-Bird said, pointing toward a Toyota truck parked on the sidewalk. "Then we give you the cash over yonder on Jackson behind the Piggly Wiggly store."

"Oh," Franklin Saxon said. "I see. It's got to be quick, though. I'm leaving, and I'll drive by there in thirty minutes. One-half hour from now on the dot. Understand?"

By the time he had said that, he had taken a couple of steps toward T-Bird and when he turned to get into the Lincoln, he saw a man staggering toward him on the sidewalk in the shadows of the building beyond the car. He was white and balding, carrying a sportcoat over his shoulder. He was obviously drunk and holding out one hand in front of him as though to tell Franklin to wait, don't tell me your name, I almost got it, it's right on the tip of my tongue.

"Saxon," the man announced in a tone of triumph. "I know you. You're Mister Saxon."

"No," Franklin said. "You're mistaken, I'm afraid."

"Oh, yeah, sure," the man said, stopping and beginning to look toward the swarm of Bones Family members around the ATM, two with their backs turned to the machine, pushing hard against it, one directing the fork lift driver, and another preparing to slam a sledgehammer one more time against the lawful property of Union Planter's Bank.

"You talked to us tonight at the convention, remember?" the man said. "About business conditions in the Delta. There in the Peabody." The man gave Franklin Saxon a big sales grin and paused as though waiting to be recognized. At the sound of a particularly well-placed sledgehammer blow from across the street, he turned to look at the ATM. "What're they doing over there, Mister Saxon?" he said. "That bunch of boys?"

"Conditions in the Delta and here in Memphis are a lot worse than I led you to believe, I'm sorry to say, my friend," Franklin Saxon said, opening the door of the Lincoln. "Tell you what. Why don't you discuss them with my colleagues?"

"T-Bird," Franklin went on, calling toward the Bones Family at work, "this gentleman wants to discuss economic trends with you and your group. See he learns what he needs to know, all right?"

As Saxon pulled away in the Lincoln up Front Street, he could see through the rearview mirror the conventioneer beginning to run toward the buildings across the street with two Bones Family members following at a trot.

He headed the car toward the next intersection, telling himself to be careful and to watch for drunk drivers on the way to Overton Park with its winding roads and dark stands of trees. Hardly the time for a fender-bender now.

"Cool and calm," he said aloud, hearing the phrases his father had repeated to him each day of his life, "slow and steady does the trick. One step, then another." After this part of it tonight, he thought, Mister Barry Speed of points east will fly into the Delta, and that will be the next bit of new business I'll have to tend to. Right now, though, I'll get to Overton Park, he promised himself, park by the twelfth hole under those big red oaks, and give myself a little boost before I have to meet that bunch again.

The old man was right about one thing, Franklin reflected as he drove up Madison, the speedometer steady on forty-five through the deserted streets of downtown Memphis, every new thing's a learning experience.

2

The heat and humidity of May in Memphis had put a tight seal between the door and the frame again, so J.W. Ragsdale had to try twice before he could break loose from his house into the morning light. The weather started doing that sometime in the spring every year, and every time J.W. noticed the trouble he had getting outside the house on Tutwiler, he promised himself he'd borrow a chisel from somebody at the station and take care of it.

But by the time he got back home each night, he'd forgotten the fact that water and sun were trying to entomb him in a rent house in Midtown and he just got a drink and went on to bed.

I'll ask Delbert today, he told himself, and stepped out onto the porch to pick up the *Commercial Appeal*. Delbert Jackson liked to build birdhouses and whatever else homeowners in White Haven did on the weekends, so he was bound to have a spare chisel to bring into the division station in the big brown briefcase he always carried.

The news girl had thrown the paper where she always did, just at the point when the sidewalk joined the porch, but this time it had landed up against a cardboard box positioned right in front of J.W. Ragsdale's front step.

When J.W. leaned over, he saw that the box was filled to its top edges with dead magnolia leaves and buds that had blown from the big tree in his front yard over into the one next door.

Mrs. Stoker had also left him a note fixed to one flap of the box with a clothes pin. J.W. dropped the wooden pin into his shirt pocket while he read the neighborly message. "Here's some of your trash, Sergeant Ragsdale," Mrs. Stoker said in a small even hand, "for you to dispose of properly. A police officer ought to know a good neighbor maintains property values. Handle your own trash."

J.W. thought two things. First, he imagined himself knocking on Mrs. Stoker's door, the box in hand, waiting for her to open up so he could pour the dead leaves and magnolia buds over his neighbor's head.

Second, he wondered if the old lady would be willing to enter 2319 Tutwiler and do some more picking up and boxing away of what she found there.

Instead, he reached into his pocket and pulled out a ballpoint pen. On the reverse side of Mrs. Stoker's note, he printed in large letters GOD IS LOVE and stuck it between the screen door and the locked wooden one to her house. He figured he'd save the clothes pin to use to close up a package of nacho-flavored Doritos lying on his kitchen counter, a domestic trick he had learned from his ex-wife, one of two she possessed. The other was keeping opened cans of coffee in the freezer compartment of the refrigerator.

The sun already as hot as it was reminded J.W. of the way the bolls would be firming all over the cotton fields of Panola County, Mississippi, this late in the spring. Later it would look like a field of snow to a man who knelt just right and looked out over it at the perfect angle. Reckon the government planted cotton or soybeans this year on the old place, he wondered. And whichever one it was, how much acreage did Uncle Sam allot himself this time? Better get on downtown, he told himself, don't get started on that.

It wasn't until four years ago that J.W. had finally lost all the Ragsdale farm, when the government and the banks foreclosed on the last forty-nine acres, but it had been being chewed away at even before he got out of the army and came back home to Mississippi to plant and work it.

He had been with the Memphis Police Department for twelve years of driving back and forth on I-55 between the Delta and the city before the recession and the banks and the foreclosure had finally focused his mind for him on one subject: urban homicide in the Bluff City.

Now and again he still felt what a lady lawyer he had been involved with for a while called "rural twinges," but he tried to keep those pushed down.

"Hey," she'd say to him. "Do you think you want to take your stand one more time? Are you sensing an attack of the agrarian coming on?"

"When I do," he'd say, "I just think about the rain coming when you didn't want it and not coming when you do. And then I think about Memphis and how regular the cuttings and the shootings and the pay rolls are, and I just hunker on down."

It had been easy to joke about it with the lady lawyer, but J.W. was glad the old man was gone by the time the last of the Ragsdale place was eaten up in the foreclosure. He would have tried to find somebody to shoot.

Memphis was like Cuba, J.W. reflected as he drove down McLean toward the Midtown station. Hot, humid, dark-complected, and full of huge outdated cars from Detroit. He had to drive around two stalled vehicles, as the morning-drive DJs called them in their traffic reports, on his way to work. One was a '73 Olds still occupied by its female driver and nosed halfway into an intersection, and the other was an earlier model Cadillac Fleetwood. Its passengers had left it and moved to seats on the sidewalk while they waited for somebody with jumper cables to stop and get their luxury automobile moving again.

Neither obstacle was having much effect on the traffic moving downtown, so J.W. didn't feel guilty about not stopping to call in help. Memphis drivers had grown used to such scenes as the city's fleet of GM, Ford, and Chrysler products aged. Japanese, German and Korean cars were flowing around the Detroit clots with hardly a horn-honk.

J.W. waved at the sidewalk sitters as he pulled his '78 Buick around the Cadillac, and they all lifted a patient hand in return. "We built this city," sang the Jefferson Starship through his car radio, "on rock and roll."

"Some lady been calling you, J.W.," said Tyrone Walker, looking up from his side of the desk the two shared in one of the cubicles in the single floor of the Midtown Station. "Twice in the last fifteen minutes."

"What did she want?"

"Wouldn't say. Asking for Eagle, she kept saying."

"Oh, hell," said J.W. "Hope it was long distance. A way long distance."

"Could be a local call, I don't know. She just said 'Eagle' every breath she drew. Why she call you that?"

"Well," said J.W. pointing toward a package of Salems in Tyrone's shirt pocket, "because I used to always holler like an eagle whenever I came into the cafeteria back in high school."

"Like a eagle? How'd you know how to do that?" Tyrone took out one cigarette and held it toward J.W. and then put the package into the inside pocket of the coat hanging on the back of his chair.

"Saw it in a picture show and practiced how to do it chopping cotton. Something to do."

"She wouldn't leave a number. Gonna call you back, she said. Somebody from Batesville, I guess."

"I imagine," said J.W. and then, going on the offensive, "you look like you better get you some ice cubes and hold them to your eyeballs. They's so red I expect you're fixing to bleed to death through them any minute now."

"Twins kept us both walking all night," Tyrone said. "Me and Marvelle both. Squalling and carrying on."

"That's the advantage of having them two at a time. Each of you got one to deal with."

Tyrone looked back down at the stack of paper in front of him and lifted both hands to his forehead. His manicure was perfect. J.W. could see a half-moon at the base of each nail looking as it had been designed by an architect and glowing palely against the blueblack of Tyrone's skin.

"That lady calls again," J.W. said, "tell her you don't know where I am and when I'm coming in."

"Lord God," said Tyrone. "I'm so glad I'm a married man not getting no sleep at night."

"You laugh. You don't know how hard it is on a middle-aged man flung back into the single life in his forties."

"I imagine it's hard as a rock on the man."

"Hard as a hoe-handle," J.W. said and sat down to his side of the desk to begin going through the file he had left there the night before.

What it contained was a patrol officer's report of a crime from two days before, two slips of paper with telephone numbers written on them and an address that had been underlined, written over, and crossed through. All of this had been fresh only a few hours before, but J.W. knew it was rapidly becoming as cold as the body of the deceased involved, one Tollman Blevins of Columbus Grove, Ohio.

Mr. Blevins had been on the program committee of a medical equipment convention meeting for four days at the Peabody Hotel. According to the official program, a copy of which J.W. had obtained from a cute little blonde in the hotel's public relations office, the theme of the meeting was business opportunities in the New South, and the keynote speaker had been Franklin Saxon, CEO of Delta Pride BarBQ. On the last night of scheduled activities, Blevins had left the lobby of the Peabody, where according to received local opinion the Mississippi Delta begins, and proceeded by foot and by free trolley down Mid America Mall. His destination was Mud Island where Wayne Newton was scheduled to appear, but did not, it developed, because of scheduling problems. Had Wayne showed, J.W. reflected, he probably would have saved Tollman Blevins' life as well as delighting several thousand fans of "Daddy, Don't You Walk So Fast" and "Danke Schoen."

Disappointed by Wayne Newton, Mr. Blevins stopped for music and beer in several establishments along the Mall and on Front Street. Patrons of Blues Alley, the Sidebar, and Prince Mongo's later identified him from the medical examiner's photograph as having been a happy member of their number, drinking Mexican beers with lime quarters stuck in the mouths of the bottles, offering to dance with various young women and behaving generally in the time-honored way of Ohioans temporarily out of state.

Around midnight he ran out of cash and then, a few minutes later, out of luck when he decided to visit a money machine on Front Street by the river. A native Memphian wouldn't have done that at that time of night, J.W. thought, unless he was knee-walking drunk or felt in deep need of being that way.

What Tollman Blevins ran into sometime between 12:15 and 12:45 a.m. was a group of men at work, number uncertain but prints at the scene indicated at least three, laboring to free the ATM from its moorings in the cement of the sidewalk where it was attached by six bolts.

A hot-wired forklift from a nearby construction site was used to push the ATM over far enough to get the tines of the lift under its front edge, and then the whole thing was torn loose and carried off.

Most likely they stopped what they were doing to knife and club Blevins before they got the ATM broken loose, J.W. figured. He thought that because a couple who were parked a block away from Front Street told the investigating officer that they heard sounds of metal tearing and motor revving, then a break for a few minutes, and a return of the sounds later.

Probably upset the demolition crew to have to stop and tend to the fool who wanted to get cash out of the ATM with a credit card, J.W. reflected, rather than trying the direct method they were using.

They got double duty out of their screw driver and sledgehammer, though, judging from the medical examiner's report. The one with the hammer had been especially enthusiastic in his job. Somebody had missed a bet, though, because Blevin's wallet was still on his person.

"Tyrone," J.W. said across the desk, pawing at the shirt pocket where he used to keep cigarettes. "You ever heard of them taking the whole ATM before?"

"That's a new one, J.W., far as I know. Usually they just beat the shit out of it until they hit the jackpot. Looks like they moving up technologically nowadays."

Tyrone Walker looked pointedly down at J.W.'s shirt pocket.

"Just an itch," said J.W. "Scratching."

"Uh huh. I hear you put a little pinch of Copenhagen between your gum and your lip, it'll take care of that craving."

"That stuff'll turn your teeth all brown. Make your gums recede and get cancer. Women won't French-kiss you no more."

"Say all that on the surgeon-general's warning, huh? Side of the package where all that warning stuff is?"

"I don't suppose they found that empty ATM yet," J.W. said.

"Oh, yeah, they did. Meter reader saw it off Jackson in a culvert. Somewhere in the 800 block, empty as my bank account."

"I guess I'll go out there this afternoon and poke around some. See what things look like."

"I don't think you'll see much. The Bank's done reclaimed the ATM and put up a new one where the first one got tore loose."

"That's a crime scene, damn it," said J.W. "They got to wait until we release it."

"Not when Memphis is getting ready for the barbecue festival," Tyrone said, leaning back in his chair and putting on a big fake grin. "Got to get things cleaned up and looking good for the tourists and the TV people. Put on a happy face. Sing a cheerful song of my people."

"Long as you ain't the one singing it," J.W. said.

3

J.W. spent most of the rest of the afternoon poking around the crime scene off Front Street where the Ohioan had interrupted the construction crew at work on the ATM. Tyrone Walker had been right. There wasn't much to see. The bank had erected a new ATM, this one set directly into concrete with its bottom flange buried below ground level with no bolts showing. A member of one of the largest black gangs in Memphis, the Bones Family, had got to the concrete before it dried and cut the emblem of the group into it. Crossed bones and a skull above the letters BF.

J.W. knew that didn't necessarily mean the Bones Family had stolen the ATM and killed Mr. Blevins in the process, anymore than just one dog marked a boundary tree with his scent. It would be interesting to check back in the next couple of days to see what other gang insignias would be added and to notice what forms it took, though.

If another gang, say the Beale Street Boppers or the Gents, inscribed their mark more prominently and also took a hammer and chisel to the Bones Family sign in an attempt to wipe it out, maybe there'd be something to be learned from the scene. J.W. wrote himself a reminder in the notebook he carried to check next week to see who'd pissed harder.

Then he got into the Buick and drove out Jackson to see the culvert where the ATM machine had been dumped.

The ditch the cement culvert lined ran next to a row of small rent houses near the old Dixie Belle ice cream plant, a monument from the time of manufacturing on Jackson Avenue. The Dixie Belle building still stood, though roofless, windowless, and spray-painted beyond recognition of its days when something edible was made there. But the walls were thick and well built and looked likely to stand until somebody took dynamite to them.

There were even two carcasses of burned-out ice cream trucks in the old parking lot, J.W. noticed as he pulled up and stopped, one of them sporting a painting of the Dixie Belle herself on its side panel, her parasol perkily held above her blonde curly hair. Some fairly good artist had recently provided her a pair of long legs, tipped with high heels widely spread to receive the huge sex organ the artist had thoughtfully drawn in with his spray can. J.W. hated to see the Dixie Belle treated that way. Panama Freeze, one of the specialties of Dixie Belle Ice Cream, had been his mother's favorite. It had had too many suspended fruit pieces and nuts for J.W.'s palate as a kid. He wondered if he'd like it now.

Three children, from four to ten years or so in age, were squatting in the cement culvert where the ATM had been dumped. They looked up when J.W. approached, and one of them, the older of the three, said something to the other two. They all stood up and turned to face the white man coming toward the ditch.

"Howdy," said J.W. "What y'all doing? Playing in the creek?"

"It ain't no creek," said the oldest boy. "It uh culvert. Creek got fish in it."

"That's right. You got me."

The youngest child, the four-year old wearing a Batman T-shirt from a couple of fads back, volunteered a comment.

"We ain't playing. We looking for money." He said this with such pride and emphasis that J.W. had to look off to keep from grinning.

"How you boys gonna find money in a ditch?" J.W. said. "I didn't know it came from culverts."

"Apple," said the little one, "he say it was money in the culvert. Right there." He patted the ball of his right foot on a spot on the concrete and then bent over to look more closely at it, as though a picture of Andrew Jackson was likely to pop up at any second.

"Did Apple find him some money to buy some ice cream and candy?" asked J.W. "Out of this culvert?"

"Naw, fool," said the oldest boy, "Apple would a bought him some rock. He be a grown man, eighteen year old."

"Nuh uh," said the middle child, breaking his silence, "Apple be seventeen."

"Apple be his brother," the Batman fan explained, pointing for J.W.'s benefit to the child beside him.

"Looky here," said J.W. reaching into his pocket for his wallet. "If I's to give you boys a dollar apiece, what would you buy with it?"

"Snicker bar," said the middle child and held out a hand, the other two quickly following suit.

When they dumped the ATM into the ditch and busted it open, they maybe missed some in the dark, J.W. thought. Wonder if Apple just come along later, or did he maybe see them making their withdrawal? "Say," J.W. said to the little brother, "What's Apple's last name?"

"You children come up out of that ditch! And you, mister, get the hell out of here."

The commands were coming from a large woman built wide and low to the ground, advancing on J.W. from the rear. She carried a hardware store yardstick in her left hand and a look of deep and permanent disgust on her face. She was moving fast for a woman of her size and weight, and she was almost by J.W. before he could respond.

"Ain't no reason to get mad at these boys, ma'am," he said. "I'm Sergeant Ragsdale with the Memphis police department, and we was just talking about Snicker candy bars and ATM machines."

"I don't know nothing about that mess," the woman said, cocking her left arm as she advanced on the boys, but slowing her pace a step or two. "You can't never tell what's going to happen to these children these days. White mens coming up here, trying to toll them off somewheres, do something nasty."

"Mama," said the youngest boy, tears welling up as he scrambled out of the culvert, "we wasn't doing nothing bad."

"Your boy's right," J.W. said and flashed his badge holder toward the woman. "Tell me, you know where Apple stays?"

"I don't know nothing about nothing, 'cept these boys got to get on back in the house."

J.W. watched the three children trot briskly toward the row of houses lining the culvert, staying just out of range of the yardstick and cutting looks back over their shoulders at the woman herding them along. I'll ask Tyrone to come out here and find Apple tomorrow, he thought, and right now I believe I'm going to swing by the Dairy Queen on Summer and get me a Butterfinger slush.

4

There was no moon, and the pilot of the Stearman had been feeling his way south by keeping the glint of the river to the left and level with the dark line of the wingtip. He had had to swing fifteen miles to the west when passing Memphis to stay out of range of all the lights, at the insistence of his passenger, and now he was coming up on Hughes, Arkansas. Time to head it east to cross the river and work his way down into the Mississippi Delta at about two-hundred feet just above the cotton and soybean fields.

As he saw the red light winking on top of the Hughes water tower, he felt the man behind him lean forward from the space he was crammed into and tap him on the right shoulder. The passenger said again what he had said at least thirty times since they had taken off from the airstrip south of Cape Girardeau, Missouri.

"Remember, now, old buddy, you let me know at least a mile or two before we enter the Delta. I've got to have time to change tapes."

Ray Hubley lifted his right hand with his thumb extended and jabbed it toward the top of the Stearman and the stars above. Even with the engine and the wind noise, he could hear the whispers and percussion sounds coming from the earphones of the Walkman behind him. It had been a steady drone since they left the earth in Missouri. Ray couldn't recognize any of the songs and didn't want to, but from what he could tell second hand from the earphone spillover, they all had in common a bunch of field hands hollering.

The Stearman crossed the Mississippi just south of Horseshoe Lake, and Ray twisted to speak over his shoulder.

"Coming up, Mr. Speed," he said. "Them car lights up yonder is on U.S. 61."

"Jesus," said Barry Speed, hitting the eject button on his Sony Walkman and slipping in a tape he had been carrying in his shirt pocket for two hundred air miles, "Highway 61, the Delta highway, the blues road."

"You like that old honky tonk stuff, huh?" asked Ray, trying to get in a word before the next selection began.

"Shut up, you, and fly," answered Barry Speed, punching the Sony Play button. "I'm listening to Robert Johnson sing the blues, as I'm coming into the Delta itself. There's a hellhound on my trail."

Yeah, and there's a New Jersey asshole in my cropduster, Ray Hubley thought to himself and banked the Stearman toward Tunica, upping the airspeed a notch. I can't wait to get this tin bird on the ground, get this man and his package unloaded, and someday, maybe, get back to spreading malathion on green inch worms.

Outside of Tunica, the mercury vapor lights the pilot was looking for shone reflected in the farm pond beyond the main house and the out buildings of the plantation below. Four miles or so south of the pond would be the stand of trees which had gone uncut for over a hundred years, a rare sight in the Mississippi Delta and a signal to Ray Hubley to cut his airspeed, drop to a hundred feet and look for the car headlights to flash on and off two times.

Coming over the tops of the bank of red oaks, he eased back on the throttle and felt the Stearman sink a few feet like falling into a pillow, and then he picked up the double flash ahead. At that, he tapped the switch to the Stearman's running lights once, a quick on and off, and somebody on the ground, two somebodies, switched on flashlights to mark what they'd picked out as a runway for him.

Hubley knew he ought to fly over it once and circle back after a look-see before making a landing approach, but wouldn't it be a kick in the ass to get Mr. Sony Walkman's undivided attention. He put the nose of the Stearman on the dark spot between the shafts of light and came in hot, the engine bubbling like a percolator.

The ground came up in a rush, the Stearman's wheels touched, hopped and teetered, and Hubley cranked down the wing flaps and kicked the rudder to the right. One of the flashlights jerked, yawed and vanished as the man holding it sought the high grass to the aircraft's right, and the Stearman yammered and spun a full 180 degrees as Ray brought the machine to a dead stop in the middle of a dark soybean field. The air was full of insect sounds.

"Jesus Christ," Barry Speed was yelling in a high voice from his space behind the pilot's seat, "Jesus Christ, did we crash? Did we crash?"

"A little bumpy," said Ray Hubley, "sorry about that, but it's kinda hard to set her down in the night time when it ain't no lights."

"I believe, Ray," said one of the men waiting on the ground after the pilot and his passenger had crawled out of the Stearman, "That's the most economical use of runway I ever saw."

"Well, I didn't know how much there was of it to use. Didn't want to take more than my share."

"You sure weren't greedy. I'll give you that."

"Hey, guys," said Barry Speed, moving closer, the headphones to his Walkman hooked around his neck and dangling. "What is this, old home week? Who's here?"

"This here's Mr. Speed," Ray Hubley said, "and this gentleman is the man you come to see, Mr. Speed."

"Welcome to the Delta, sir. I'm Franklin Saxon." The man held out his hand, and for a second or two, Barry Speed didn't seem to notice it.

"Oh, right," he said then, and stuck just the tips of his fingers in Saxon's grasp. "You people do this handshaking thing to death, don't you?"

"Well, we hope it doesn't reach that extreme, Mr. Speed," Franklin Saxon said, "but I'll keep your impression in mind. From what you say, I believe you must want to get down to business."

"That's the reason I'm here, but there's something else, too, I want to do."

"What might that be?"

"You see, Frank, ordinarily I'd never be involved with this part of a business deal. I mean, schlepping out to BWI, flying to St. Louis, driving way the hell out in the country to Hicksville, you know. Climbing into a crate like that without even a real seat to sit in, trusting my life to some pilot who probably learned to fly by bombing gooks in Vietnam twenty-five years ago. And all that grief just to be a delivery man. Hoo, boy. Not my thing. Nuh uh."

"I wondered a little why you chose to come yourself."

"You did, huh?" said Barry Speed, pleased. "A guy my age, my level. You say, whoa, why's Barry Speed himself losing sleep, eating road food, being a delivery boy, for Christ's sake? What, he's run out of guys to do the heavy lifting? Can't get anybody to answer the phone anymore? Can't find the zipper to his own fly? Am I right?"

"That's the general idea, I suppose."

"Well, I'm going to tell you. Put your mind at ease. You ready? I personally came all the way from Baltimore to Mississippi by way of St. Louis and a Japanese what-do-you-call-it kamikaze pilot because of the blues. The Delta blues."

"You mean the old negro music?" said Franklin Saxon, pronouncing the word nigra, although he would have spelled it the other way, if asked. "You don't mean rock and roll?"

"That shit? Fuck, no," said Barry Speed, shaking his head so hard his earphones thrashed back and forth. "I'm not talking this commercial trash dummies listen to. Top forty, heavy-metal, and this rap crap. What

I mean, Frank, is the original blues. What was invented right here in the Mississippi Delta."

With that, Speed spread his arms slowly to full extension and looked from one side to the other, as though surveying a mass audience in the soybean field around him. He then tilted his head back, opened his mouth wide, and let a slow crooning sound well up from deep within his two hundred and sixty pounds. The Murphy brothers and Ray Hubley, over by the Stearman passing a 1.75 liter bottle of Jack Daniel's back and forth, jerked their heads around to look for the source of the sound.

"That's a blues moan," said Barry Speed to anybody in earshot. "You hear it in cuts by all the great ones. Johnny Shines, Little Boy Blue, Elmore James, and especially my man Robert Johnson."

Nobody said anything for a space, except for one of the Murphy boys clearing his throat. The choir of cicadas and June bugs droned on in the nightly performance of Delta midnight, and from across the fields came the howls of a couple of dogs at somebody's place.

"You seem to have learned a lot about this music," said Franklin Saxon in a polite voice. "I guess you've made it a study."

"If you got to study it, Frankie," Barry Speed announced, "you'll never learn it. It's something you know in your guts and your balls. It's a feeling."

"I see. Well, do you want to go over here to the car and talk about our business?" Franklin Saxon gestured toward an Oldsmobile 98, blue black in the moonlight and angled parallel to the makeshift runway where the Stearman had landed.

"No problem," said Barry Speed. "I'll tell you how we're gonna work it. Then I want to see about one of your boys taking me around tonight and tomorrow. I got to find the crossroads, look into a juke house, locate Son Thomas. Poke, you know, around."

"We'll be pleased to accommodate you as best we can, Mr. Speed. Did you need anybody to fetch anything from the aircraft?"

"Not on your life. I got it all with me." Speed patted the Chicago Bulls sports bag hanging from his shoulder by a strap, the pinky ring on his left hand glittering in the moonlight.

After the two men had gotten into the back seat of the Oldsmobile and closed the doors against the mosquitos, the pilot of the Stearman and the Murphy brothers continued their work on the Jack Daniel's.

"That fat Yankee boy was howling at the moon," said Pick Murphy, "you hear him giving voice?"

"I believe he said it was his balls talking," Ray Hubley said, reaching for the bottle Pick was holding.

"Me or Vance one is going to have to take him on a tour," Pick said, "judging from what Mr. Saxon told him."

"Maybe we can lose him in the woods," Vance said. "Let some tree limbs snap back in his face."

"He talks crazy," Ray said, "like a tourist would. But I wouldn't fuck with him. He comes out of that bunch all up in there in Baltimore and New Jersey and Miami. All of them spells their names funny. They been doing this shit for a long time."

"You mean buying crack?" asked Pick Murphy. "By the shitload?"

"Well, it's crack now all right," Ray said. "It was whiskey way back yonder when. Whatever folks want to put in their head that the law won't let them. Them people like him have been around for a while, doing business. Always, always on the job."

"Don't worry, Ray," said the older Murphy. "We'll keep him happy. We'll see if we can't find him some of these here singing field hands to talk to tomorrow."

"Ah oo," said the other Murphy and took a long swig of the sour mash.

Less than an hour later, Vance Murphy was counting six cars and two pick up trucks parked near a one-story building located where two cotton roads came together and crossed. The building was covered for the most part with sheets of corrugated metal, though here and there the gray clapboard siding showed through. One hand-painted sign, a little larger than the commercially-done ones for Pepsi, Royal Crown, and Kool Kid Kola surrounding it, proclaimed the establishment to be Big Daddy's Dreamland. As Murphy drove the Oldsmobile past the front door of the building, a flash of light from inside shone on the lenses of Barry Speed's designer eyeglasses.

"Is this it?" he asked. "Have we got to the crossroads?"

"Yes sir," said Vance. "This here's where Sunflower crosses Bumblebee."

"Standing at the crossroads," Speed began singing in a high, yodelling voice that no one would have predicted to be his own, "I tried to flag a ride, didn't nobody seem to know me, everybody pass me by."

Murphy nosed the car to the edge of the gravel road past the last of the vehicles parked at Big Daddy's Dreamland and put the engine in neutral.

"You want to go in?" he said to the singer beside him.

"Oh, yeah," said Speed. "Oh, yeah. What do they sell here?"

"Barbecue all day long. You can get other stuff at night. All kinds of it."

"I got you," Speed said, opening the doors and slapping at the small of his back as he stepped out onto the shoulder of the road. "You packing, Elmer?"

"The name's Murphy," said Murphy, "and I always take my tools with me when I'm doing business, and I'm doing business most of the time."

The two men walked up on the porch of the building together, Speed a step ahead, and as they neared the door, the screen swung open and a man and woman came out at the same time, stepping in unison and so close together they looked joined at the hip.

"White folks," said the man, twisting his head to look at Speed and Murphy as he and the woman swept by together off the porch, "Y'all looking for you some hot barbecue pork?"

"You came to the right place," said the woman and leaned forward to laugh. "It's all kinds of hot stuff in Dreamland. You can get your fill."

"Hot tamales and they red hot," said Barry Speed in his singing voice and pulled the screen door open. "Hot tamales and they red hot."

The two white men walked into a wall of music, smoke and heat. Two large electric fans mounted on head-high metal stands were performing at full capacity from opposite ends of the room, but they were having little effect on the atmosphere and the crowd or the dance floor and at the tables around it, except to add a steady drone to the music being produced by the band, three men with guitars, a woman on a set of drums, and a lead singer with a harmonica wired around his neck. They were cooking. And so was somebody in the kitchen behind the counter, judging from the plates of barbecue being passed through a window cut between the rooms. The smokey reddish pork was both pulled and chopped, Vance noticed, and the plates of ribs carried Big Daddy's signature touch, two slices of store-bought white bread to each rack, good for nothing but sopping up whatever sauce was left in the bottom of the plate, but perfect for that.

Murphy headed toward the counter and Barry Speed followed at his heels, maneuvering to get around and between the dancers jumping to a tune that was on none of his tapes, though one of the wails from the harmonica sounded reminiscent to Barry of a Howlin' Wolf holler.

"Howdy, Big Daddy," Vance Murphy said to the back of the man behind the counter who was faced to talk through the window into the kitchen. When Big Daddy turned back toward the white men behind him, he had two plates of ribs in one hand and a plate of pulled in the other. The old razor scar which ran from his left hair line through one eyebrow, across his nose and down his cheek, vanishing beneath his shirt collar, looked blue in the honky tonk haze of the room. He was big around enough to have to move carefully to avoid knocking things over on the counter as he turned in the working space around him.

"Mr. Vance Murphy," he said in a voice like a bass fiddle, "you want something to eat?"

"I could stand me some ribs," said Murphy and jerked a thumb toward Barry Speed, "This man here's from up north. Says he wants to see a juke house."

"That's what folks used to call it. Not no more. I ain't heard that name in a long time."

Big Daddy Monroe looked appraisingly at Barry Speed and then spoke directly to him.

"Juke house, huh? Whereabouts up north you from? Chicago?"

Barry leaned forward to be heard over the sound from the band. "Good guess. You think Chicago because I said juke house, right? But no, I'm east coast all the way."

"Naw, I say Chicago because you look like me, like you been eating a lot of pork for too long a time."

Barry Speed threw an elbow into Vance Murphy's side. "Hey, listen to this guy. He got me a zinger, huh? Here I am, playing the dozens with a guy in a tonk in the Mississippi Delta." He threw his head back and laughed, shifting his weight from one foot to the other, like a man whose bladder was too full.

"But hey, Big Daddy, why don't you call your place a juke house anymore?"

"It's just Dreamland now," Big Daddy said, "that's all, and that's why. What y'all want to drink?"

"I don't know about the Lone Ranger here," Speed said, "but I think a shot and a beer would go with ribs."

"T Boy," said Big Daddy to a white haired man so thin he looked like he was swimming in his clothes, "take'em over yonder and set 'em down."

He pointed toward the far wall, and T Boy took off at a lope. The sound level of the band increased two notches, as Murphy and Speed followed their leader to a two-man table in a corner of the room.

"Drinks," said Speed to T Boy as he eased himself into a kitchen chair, "all around. Shot and a beer."

"He ain't going to bring you no shot," Murphy said. "Big Daddy don't pour no liquor in Dreamland."

"Oh, yeah? Why not?"

"These people ain't gonna pay for whiskey by the drink. They want them one beer at the time when they paying honky tonk prices. They'll drink their liquor outside in the car."

"So it's an economic decision," said Speed, "like everything else."

"Yeah, they funny that way."

Speed ate the ribs T Boy brought to the table neatly, like a cat, polishing each bone until it shone like an art work, and he handled a lot of them, three plates to Vance Murphy's one. He was finishing his second quart of beer when Murphy was halfway through the first one. He took a deep breath, looked up and swivelled his head toward the band as they cranked into a different number.

"What is that shit they're playing?" he said. "Don't they know any blues?"

"You don't like rap? I thought you was a fan of the brothers' music. That's all you hear in Memphis these days. That and gospel."

"That tells me something then," Speed said, dabbing at his mouth with a paper napkin and twisting around in his chair to look at the couples working the dance floor. "I've got to find one of the old guys tomorrow to hear the real thing. Red Bone Walker or Son Richards. You'll drive me."

"Whatever Mr. Saxon says."

"He'll say what I want him to say, Jack. In the meantime, tell Big Daddy I need a clean woman not more than eighteen years old. Tell him to get her out to the car in ten minutes and we'll get her back to his juke house by daylight."

"Mr. Speed," said Murphy, "I don't believe Big Daddy Monroe considers himself to be in the whorehouse business. I can't predict what he'll say."

"Look, Slim," Speed said, "tell him there's a C-note for him and one for the girl in the deal. And tell him make it a real dark one. I want one as black as Delta midnight."

Vance Murphy got up and headed for the counter where Big Daddy was doling out the plates of barbecue, and Barry Speed leaned back in his kitchen chair to listen to the band. What they were playing sounded like some country hit from several years back out of Nashville. Jesus H. Christ, he said to himself, I think it's that piece of crap called Elvira. Why can't they get something right?

"You mind if I ask you something?" Murphy said, adjusting the visor of the Oldsmobile against the rays of the rising sun as he pointed the car east on Sunflower Road. "I'm just curious, you know."

"Ask away, Jack," said Barry Speed from where he lolled in the back seat, his eyes closed against the growing light. "What you want to know? I'll give you two questions."

"Back there a couple of hours ago, you know, after I got out of the car and walked off, left y'all there in the back seat?"

"Yeah, so?"

"Well, I'm talking about all the hollering she commenced doing. I was standing at least a hundred yards off, smoking a cigarette, and she was still so damn loud you'd a thought I was sitting right there in the front seat of this here car."

"I wondered about why you left," said Barry Speed, "I was surprised you didn't stay around to watch. I know I would have."

"Well, I ain't much into that," Murphy said, steering the Oldsmobile carefully across a one lane wooden bridge. "I mean I have plugged my share of these gals, but I never heard one holler like that one did. They do carry on a lot, generally, but that gal she took the cake."

"What you don't realize, Homer," Speed said, "is you have to have the right tool for any job you tackle. Be prepared, that's the Boy Scout motto."

He stretched out his left hand and patted the athletic bag on the seat beside him. "You wondering where all that yelling was coming from, you look in my tool kit for the answer."

"What is it?" asked Murphy, lifting his eyes to look through the rear view mirror into the back seat where Speed was chuckling to himself. "One of them rubber dicks?"

"What it is is my little friend I call Pony. After I turn him loose on a cunt, she'll follow me around after it's over with for a week, all goo-goo eyed and love-struck."

"I don't believe that one will," said Murphy, "judging from the way she acted when we let her out at Dreamland. Soon as the car door-opened, she took off like a scalded dog."

"You'd be surprised, Slim. I'll lay you two to one that little Black Beauty's going to be asking for my telephone number before tomorrow night."

"Why's that?" Vance said.

"Because of what I been talking about," Speed said, " and because of that high-grade medicine I helped the child take."

Up ahead in the gravel road, two road-killed possums presented Vance Murphy with the chance to demonstrate his steering skills.

"Well," he said, swerving neatly back and forth, "I imagine Big Daddy might be wanting somebody's number, if you was to ask me. Was it coke you give her?"

"I said I'd give you two questions, Jack. You had them. Let's go find Son Richards, listen to some real Delta sounds."

In the Oldsmobile back seat, in the air conditioned coolness, Barry Speed cleared his throat, threw back his head and gave voice to his well-practiced blues moan, his eyes closed against the bright May morning.

I wish he wouldn't do that, Vance Murphy thought to himself, and I hope I can find somebody to clean up that back seat before Mr. Saxon gets a look at this Regency ninety-eight.

5

J.W. Ragsdale was sitting in a booth at the Owl Bar on Central Avenue, listening to Terry Jasper tell a story about his rural upbringing on a rice farm thirty miles south of Marked Tree, Arkansas. He was also waiting for Tyrone Walker to show up with information about what he'd learned from Apple about the ATM in the culvert. It was two o'clock in the morning, but J.W. had slept on his sofa in front of the television set between eight and midnight, so he felt primed for staying up the rest of the night, which he knew was highly likely.

Anything that involved visiting with members of Memphis's black gangs had to take place after the brothers had worked the night shift and stumbled home to their hidey holes at about sun-up, so it was a good notion to get in some bed rest ahead of time. When he had first worked homicide, J.W. had been able to drink in the Owl from six to two, hit the streets for the rest of the night remaining, and then tend to business all the rest of the next day. That had been a while back, though, and he began noticing about the time he needed to get eyeglasses he also began craving a little lie-down on a more regular basis.

"She was a nurse working for the Arkansas Health Department, see," Terry Jasper was saying, "and her name was Mrs. Ewing. She'd come around every month or two and tell us kids in school there in Holly Springs how to do right. You know, stuff like how to eat the four food groups. Or was it three of them? What'd they tell y'all in Mississippi, J.W.? Four or three?"

"Let me think," said J.W. "Count them up. It was pinto beans, corn bread, okra, and buttermilk. That's four, ain't it?"

"Naw, come on. Anyway, Mrs. Ewing come one time and handed out little bitty tubes of toothpaste to all of us there in the classroom. I believe it was Ipana. You remember that old strong-tasting kind of stuff, don't you? Like putting a chunk of hard soap in your mouth?"

"Was it red-colored?" asked J.W. and allowed himself another sip of Schlitz.

"No, it was white. You thinking about something else. Well, Miz Ewing had passed them little tubes of Ipana out to all the kids on the front rows, and they had each took one and passed the rest of them on back. She was up there drawing a set of teeth on the blackboard, getting ready to show all us little country fuckers how to do teeth hygiene, when a kid on the back row of seats started waving his hand in the air and hollering her name.

'Miz Ewing, Miz Ewing,' he was just a yelling. 'Miz Ewing.' It was one of those old cotton-topped boys, he's named Orval Hammond, and he lived so far back in the woods he'd never even seen a plane fly over.

'What is it, Orval?' Miz Ewing finally said right in the middle of drawing them teeth on the black board. 'What do you want?'

'Miss Ewing, Miss Ewing,' old Orval said. 'I done et my salve.'"

By the time Terry Jasper had finished laughing at his Arkansas story, even some of the drunk off-duty police officers at the bar had turned around to see where the voice was coming from.

"Oh, hell," said Dwayne Smiles, the second oldest patrolman in the Memphis Police Department. "It's just Jasper, talking to himself again."

"That's the only one that'll listen to him," said Shallawene Lawson, a black policewoman sitting two down from Smiles.

"Fuck you, Shallawene," Terry Jasper yelled from the booth. "And your old grand-daddy sitting up there, too."

"In your dreams, Terry," Shallawene said.

"Now, wait a minute," Dwayne Smiles interrupted. "Speak for yourself, Shallawene. Maybe me and Terry can work something out here."

The door to the Owl opened, and Tyrone Walker stepped in and looked immediately toward the booth where J.W. sat with Terry Jasper. He pulled a chair around from one of the tables and drew it up to the booth.

"I done et my salve," J.W. told him.

"You have?" said Tyrone. "Well, that's a relief. Have you done drunk your beer, too?"

"First one tonight," J.W. said, tapping his Schlitz bottle against a salt shaker. "Did you find our lucky little friend over yonder on Jackson?"

"I did, I did. How's it going, Terry?"

"Y'all fixing to go to work, I'm going up there to the bar, talk to some people that know how to act at two in the morning." Terry took his bottle and headed toward the stool next to Shallawene Lawson. Seeing him coming toward her, Shallawene made an exaggerated shrinking motion with her shoulders as Terry approached.

"You have any trouble locating where my man Apple stays?" asked J.W.

"Naw, I didn't, J.W.," Tyrone said. "I know right where he lives, and

I know something else, too. He's a Bones claimer. That finger's crooked as a snake."

As part of the initiation into the Bones Family, a wannabe had to break the little finger on his left hand while the claimers watched. Most of the acolytes did the deed by smacking the fingers with a hammer or wrench or something equally heavy, J.W. knew, and the result was an unmistakable sign of membership in the group, a crooked lump.

"So he's been broke, then," J.W. said. "You find that out in the file?"

"It's in the picture gallery, along with the rest of them we been having pose for us," Tyrone said. "And speaking about been broke, look like you claim the Bones Family somewhere in your evil past, judging by that ugly old busted-up couple of fingers you got there."

"I caught them boogers in a cotton picker," J.W. said, lifting his left hand for inspection. "And when I did it, I hadn't just finished smoking two PCP dippers and drinking a quart of Schlitz Malt liquor, neither."

"I bet after you done it, you headed for something to suck on, though," Tyrone said.

"I remember doing something like that. Who you figure we ought to go visiting first, Tyrone, in that Bones bunch? Not Odis Free. He's downtown now, ain't he?"

"Odis is waiting trial on a whole shitload of stuff now. He was out on parole on a rape charge, violated that, did another little number on a woman in the Vance projects, and beat her mama's head in when she tried to interfere with his fun. Then the bitch up and died on Odis."

"You don't say. I guess they ain't making mama's heads like they used to."

"Yeah," said Tyrone, "so the Bones Family is undergoing the process of selecting a new main man, and I expect it's gonna be hard on Memphis folks until they get through the primaries."

"So you figure Apple's in the running for big boss man?"

"I believe Apple man may be willing to pick off a rival or two, maybe, and I think we ought to pay him a visit at home. See what he might tell us when he's just been roused from slumber."

"Where's Apple stay?"

"He's been cribbing down off Decatur on a little short street called Baby. You know it?"

"I believe so. Yeah."

"He'll be sleeping the sleep of the just tonight, I imagine."

"Well, let's go give him a wake-up call," said J.W., looking over at the Stroh Beer clock mounted above the door to the Owl Bar. "In about an hour and a half. If you can stay awake that long."

"Eye Hop," said Tyrone as J.W. Ragsdale pulled his Buick out of the parking lot onto Jackson just at 5:00 a.m. "Best coffee in Memphis."

"Highest octane anyway," J.W. said, "it'll sure knock your eyelids apart all right."

He drove east on Jackson for several blocks, hooked left on La Grange to come in on Decatur closer to its intersection with Baby, and slowed the car to a crawl.

"Say, Tyrone," he said, "back in the Pancake House, did you happen to see the set on that working girl that left when she saw us come in? Real healthy looking rig for a lady her age."

"Now, J.W., you know I'm a married man. I don't look at strange women."

"Shit," said J.W., stopping the Buick just short of the Decatur and Baby intersection. "I used to be married myself. Twice. I know better than that. How far down on Baby do the brother be sleeping?"

"There ain't no numbers, of course, but it's the one on the right side with the Mr. Hog Wanted sign nailed on the front of the house. I checked it out yesterday about supper time."

"I didn't know the Bones Family has got into Muslim stuff. I figured these boys'd like their ribs and pork chops."

"I don't know if they mean it," said Tyrone, "probably just dissing the beanpie eaters. Seeing what they can stir up."

The small houses in the area had all been built around the same time and had been intended to serve the needs of returning veterans and their families. They had done that task well, right up to the period of the murder of Dr. King and the resulting massive flight east of all the whites who could afford it. Urban renewal had wiped out great blocks of old Memphis after that, just as it was meant to do, and the scene J.W. saw around him was not one ever dreamed by the builders of the 'forties and 'fifties.

It put J.W. in mind of what he had seen in parts of Beirut when he had visited that fair city at the expense of Uncle Sam several years back. Burned out car bodies, shell holes in the street, what looked like bomb craters in most of the yards, barbed wire wrapped around tree trunks and threaded through the posts holding up porch roofs, and here and there a child's wheelless tricycle or a beheaded doll.

The only thing it doesn't have that Beirut did are some goats picking through the garbage, he thought, and then he heard a nanny goat neigh from somebody's backyard.

"Just a little friendly talk this morning," Tyrone said, "with Apple Jefferson. No big deal."

"That's right," said J.W. "See what he knows about that ATM he saw lying in a culvert."

He turned the corner onto Baby Street and began studying the hous-

es on the right, weaving the Buick back and forth to miss as many pot-
holes as he could.

"You ain't got no shocks on this thing, do you?" said Tyrone as
J.W.'s car bottomed out in a hole that couldn't be avoided. "Goddamn,
riding in this thing'd give a ballet dancer hemorrhoids."

"What you know about ballet dancers' assholes?" J.W. said. "There
it is. There's your sign."

J.W. pointed to the next house up where a four by six foot sheet of
plywood was nailed across the top half of one of the two windows on the
narrow building. Someone with some real artistic flair had painted the
head of a ferocious looking hog at the top of the sheet of wood, including a cigarette hanging out of the beast's mouth and two averted eyes
which conveyed somehow the impression of deceit.

"That's real good work," said J.W. "What does the writing under-
neath him say?"

"Put on your glasses, Sergeant, you want to see something."

"I don't need them, except for reading fine print. What does it say
about the hog?"

"It says Wanted for Murder, Mr. Hog. AKA Pork Chops, Bacon,
Ribs, Barbecue. Shoot the Inslaver on Sight."

"Everything I like 'cept beer," J.W. said. "Let's go knock on the
door. See who's gone beddy-bye."

J.W. parked in front of the house behind a cherry red Camaro sporting an expired temporary Tennessee paper tag, and the two men stepped
up onto the porch, avoiding a broken-through top step. From down Baby
Street came the low grumble of somebody's boom box chewing through
a rap tape, but the dwelling in front of them was completely silent.

"Apple be enjoying the sleep of the pure at heart," said Tyrone
Walker and began hammering on the top panel of the door with the heel
of his hand. The thin panel boomed like a drum.

After almost a minute of Tyrone's sustained pounding, somebody
fumbled at the lock and the handle on the inside and opened the door a
crack. From where he was standing on the porch, J.W. could see the glint
of one eye trying to focus on whoever was making all the noise with the
door so early in the morning.

"Apple, my man," said Tyrone. "Good morning to you on this bright,
sunshiney day."

"What you want?" Apple said, trying to push the door closed again
but having trouble making headway against the weight Tyrone had
leaned against it. "I ain't go talk with you."

"Now, Apple, ain't you going to ask me and my friend here, Sergeant
Ragsdale, to come on in the house and sit down with you? Swap some
stories back and forth? Cause if you don't be polite, we gonna have to

come back again with a paper from the judge and a whole shitload of blue knockers. And we gonna have to bust everything all up and seize red cars and put out the word on the street that Apple Jefferson be an informing motherfucker for the Memphis Police. You know, stuff like that."

Tyrone Walker delivered most of what he said to the man on the other side of the door in a calm and quiet voice. It wasn't until he reached the part about "red cars," J.W. noticed, that his tone changed and his voice rose and he began to get that wide-eyed look J.W. first witnessed in E.H. Crump Stadium in the All-Mississippi versus All-Tennessee football game over twenty years ago.

J.W. had been an All-State linebacker from Batesville, and Tyrone had represented Central High of Memphis as the All-Tennessee tailback. It was the first time J.W. had played against a team with blacks, and he and his fellow white Mississippians and especially the coach hadn't known what to expect.

"Defense," Coach Bobby Herbert had warned them. "I don't know what to tell you boys about this colored tailback. He's a big'un. Y'all just all try to hit him at the same time. Just hope he ain't toting no razor."

Tyrone Walker hadn't needed a razor that afternoon in Crump Stadium. The one time J.W. got him down on a solo tackle, he had ended up helmet to helmet with Tyrone and got a close look at his eyes. They were as wide and staring as stones.

Apple Jefferson on Baby Street responded the same way J.W. Ragsdale had twenty-five years earlier. He blinked and backed up, and Tyrone and J.W. stepped through the door.

"Poo wee," said Tyrone, "it stink in your house, Apple. Ain't you never heard of room deodorant like what the TV set says all the time?"

"I ain't here much," Apple said, "out, you know, on the job a lots."

"We should have brought some lime to sprinkle around," J.W. said and looked around him. "That's what you do when you got more hogs living together than the pen will hold."

The furnishings of this Bones Family member's home were minimal. Other than an expensive entertainment center set-up of a television, a VCR, a CD player and assorted industrial sized speakers, the only pieces of furniture in the room were a badly stained mattress in one corner, and a sprung sofa against one wall. Bits and pieces of electronic parts, empty Mark II quart bottles and Budweiser cans, shoes and articles of clothing were scattered like the fall-out from a small explosion or, as J.W. thought to himself, like a mad monkey's shit.

Two women were peering at the police detectives from where they lay on the mattress, one a blond white woman tattooed from the side of her face that J.W. could see down to where the markings vanished beneath the cover she held across her upper body. From what he could see of them, the tattoos appeared to J.W. not to be pictures of animals or scenes from nature but a design of whirls and circles and what looked like lightning bolts and comet tails.

The other occupant of the mattress was a younger woman, truly black in color and the possessor of buttocks so large that her share of the quilt was having little luck in covering them up.

"What you looking at?" said the black woman to J.W. as she caught his gaze resting on her most prominent feature.

"Well," he said, "I was looking at your girlfriend's pretty designs, but now I'm looking at your great big beautiful butt."

"Hush up, LaQuita," said Apple Jefferson. "You and Peachie get on in the back of the house."

"Don't tell them to haul ass," Tyrone Walker said. "It'd take two trips."

The three men watched LaQuita and Peachie leave the room through the door in the center of the back wall, both tugging at their common quilt until the tattooed body won the contest and wrapped the cover around her on the way out.

"Damn, Apple," said Tyrone. "You like a whole lot of butt on a woman, don't you? I know I do."

"Nuh uh," said Apple in affronted tone. "Peachie she care a whole lot more about all that ass on Laquita than I do. She do a lot more with it."

"Don't tell me no more," J.W. said. "Leave me a little something to dream about."

"All this is real nice," Tyrone said to Apple Jefferson, "but we didn't come out here to Baby Street to talk about your domestic arrangements. Me and Sergeant Ragsdale want to discuss a little Bones Family business with you this morning."

"That's right, Apple," J.W. chimed in. "We want to ask you about that financial transaction your family made over on Front Street a night or so ago. That little withdrawal from the ATM over yonder. The one you been talking about. And then something else that happened after that."

"Took the machine," said Tyrone. "The whole damn thing. Guts, feathers and all. And then one of you Bones claimers took a sledgehammer to a man's head. Beat his brains out 'til he died. You done drew me a picture of that."

"Don't forget about the dude with the screwdriver," J.W. said. "Give the man credit."

"Listen here," Apple said. "I don't know nothing about no ATM machine and no killing. It wasn't no Bones Family brother done that.

And the Apple man sure wasn't no part of that mess."

Tyrone Walker slapped Apple Jefferson on the left side of the head with enough force to rock him back on his heels.

"Don't never say 'listen here' to me, motherfucker," Tyrone said. "I ain't your grandpa. And don't you start lying about what I already know. You were talking about the ATM the morning after the deal went down. You were probably right there in it."

"You going to arrest me, you got to give me my rights," Apple said, rubbing his face. "You got to let me call up my legal counsel, Mr. Ronald Sharp. I wasn't nowhere around that mess."

"We ain't here to arrest you," said J.W. "We done told you that, Apple. We just want some more information from you 'cause we already know you know what happened that night on Front Street. And if we don't learn some good stuff, we going to fix it so your own family's going to kill you."

"Ain't no Bones boy gonna do nothing to me. We be blood."

"Shit, bro, you know better than that. Way things working now, it's some of your own just looking for a reason to blow your ass away. Odis Free has done said bye-bye to the Bones Family for good. And you're looking to take over his job."

"Apple ain't the only man running for office, neither, Sergeant Ragsdale," Tyrone said. "What I hear, it's a wide-open primary. And them other candidates, they looking for a way to get the edge."

"Politics," J.W. said, "is compromise, Sergeant Walker. You give me something, I give you something. You tell me a thing I need to know, I keep quiet about a thing you don't want nobody else to know."

"If I was to hear a couple of names," Tyrone said, "this early morning from Mister Apple Jefferson, I believe I'd be able to pick out which candidate to support in the election coming up."

"Otherwise you might throw your support to another man," J.W. said. "That's what you're saying?"

"I'd probably hold what you call an informal press conference," Tyrone said. "Tell folks everything I know right now. Who's been running his mouth, who's been talking to the Memphis police about Bones Family business. You know, stuff like that there."

Apple Jefferson looked down at his feet and then up at a spot on the ceiling directly above his head.

"Nobody listen to y'all, not to no knocker," he said to the spot.

"Just test it on out," said Tyrone. "See how your luck be running."

"I need me a Camel Light." Apple pointed toward a pile of clothes at the foot of the mattress. "Out of my shirt. It help me think. Maybe I remember something somebody said."

"Get you a cigarette," J.W. said. "Bring me one, too."

6

Dear Eagle," began the note taped with a neon-green bandaid to J.W.'s front door, "you don't seem to ever be home. Or at work neither. I have been calling you both places. So I guess I will have to surprise you and just show up in person! You better call me if you don't want me to play a trick on you in front of your police buddies. Love, Jackie."

J.W. groaned and put his key in the lock and then read the P.S. Jackie had written on the other side of the piece of paper. "Batesville Elementary is closed for Thursday and Friday next week. And I will be in Memphis hoping to see you at the Barbecue Festival. You should remember my number, but here it is again. I will not take no for an answer, Eagle! Jackie Jack."

That's what I get for laying a second grade teacher, J.W. said to himself. I ought never to get drunk around a convention of elementary school educators.

What made it worse about Jackie was that she was the little sister of Pert Tullos, a man he had gone to high school with, and she knew him from way back. J.W. had not remembered her from high school. Hell, she had been four years behind him in class, but he had lied that night in Captain Bilbo's down on the river and told her what he thought she wanted to hear. It was true what the Baptists say about alcohol. It is a mocker and a deceiver and it'll take your mind.

"I have sinned," J.W. said out loud and stepped into the living room of his rent house. "And been caught short," he continued, directing his comments toward the blank face of the TV set. "As God is my witness, I'll never fuck a desperate woman again."

That was easier said than not done, he knew. In fact, thinking back, J.W. Ragsdale couldn't remember being with a woman in the last several years who wasn't in some state of desperation, drunkenness, despair, or a combination of all three.

Jackie Tullos Sparks (now Jackie Tullos again since she and Jimmy

Sparks had split the sheets) was a good example of the way J.W.'s sex life had been running for longer than he liked to consider. He had gone down to Captain Bilbo's on a weeknight for the free happy hour buffet and the one dollar a cocktail price, doubles between six thirty and seven o'clock. For only five dollars apiece he and Lon Anthony had managed to get full of cheese and crackers and dip and catfish fingers and so drunk that J.W.'s lips felt numb all before the magic hour when the dollar doubles turned into three-dollar singles.

It was at that point when Jackie came up to him, called him Eagle, and told him she had always wanted him back in Batesville even before he had married Lady Leah Lafargue from Memphis and way yonder before the second much shorter term he had served with Wanda Montgomery, the real estate selling queen of Raleigh.

J.W. had let all the good work he had done with his personal economy go to pieces then. The appetizer-based meal and the solid drunk he had put together for five dollars soon dominoed into a bar bill so large he had to slap plastic for it. Sunk that far in front of Detective Sergeant Lon Anthony, he let his pride push him into leaving with Jackie so Lon could see him doing it, and he ended up with her in a room at the Peabody Hotel, rented she told him later at a really good convention rate.

And after all their clothes were off and the air conditioner was turned up to high and Jackie had gone in to the bathroom to do whatever women do when they go into the bathroom naked and then had come back and got into bed with him, Jackie had told him, "Now I got you, J.W. Ragsdale, and it sure has been worth the wait."

The next day she had sent him a ceramic eagle wrapped in a sheet of inflated plastic bubbles for insulation against breakage. J.W. had popped each bubble one by one as he watched the Cardinals lose to the Mets on television, and the next morning on the way to the Midtown Station, he handed the ceramic eagle to a panhandler who came up to his Buick at a stoplight asking for spare change.

"What I'm gonna do with this?" the panhandler asked.

"Listen to it," J.W. had said, "It'll tell you things."

J.W. wadded up Jackie's note, noticing as he did that she had written it on some kind of off-yellow kid's construction paper. She probably got it free at Batesville Elementary School and used it to economize. She probably saves up every cent she can, J.W. thought as he walked into the kitchen and threw the note toward a green plastic barrel in one corner of the room, and puts it all toward running back and forth to Memphis. Keeps I-55 hot.

The freezer of the refrigerator held two boil-in-a-bag meals of only three hundred calories each, one a Chinese and the other a stroganoff flavor. One of them, a can of Hormel chili with beans, and a section of saltine crackers would do him for the night, J.W. considered as he looked into the swirling mists of the freezer section. He remembered with a sudden lift that there was a six pack of Buckhorn Beer in the lower portion of the refrigerator, one of the economy brews he had yet to sample. If he ate fast enough, he could drink four or five Buckhorns while he watched the eleven o'clock rerun on channel 54 of the Rockford Files. Maybe Angel would be in this one. Whistling, J.W. rattled those pots and pans.

7

The next morning at eight o'clock J.W. Ragsdale was just sitting down at his side of the desk, two paper cups of coffee before him, when the telephone lit its button and buzzed at him. He opened the first cup and took two sips of coffee before he lifted the receiver.

"Yeah," he said.

"You're supposed to say your name and then your division assignment," said the woman on the other end, Irma Ray Black, a thirty year veteran of switchboards and interoffice communications.

"O.K., Irma Ray. I'll do her. You want me to hang up and you call again or can I just go on from here on this same nickel?"

"For future reference, Sergeant Ragsdale, of course. Do you think I'd waste time by calling back again on the same matter?"

J.W. said nothing and waited for Irma Ray to get to the meat course.

"The dispatcher got a 311 call at seven thirty two on a individual that Captain Willis has got your name listed by on the case docket."

"What's the name?" J.W. asked.

"Aires Saxon, 11 Carr. Body discovered by housemaid shortly before her call. Blood, blood, blood she said."

"You mean *the* Aires Saxon? The daddy of this year's Maid of Cotton? Mr. Delta himself?"

"I guess that's why Captain Willis is got your name there. That's where you come from, idn't it? Down yonder in that old flat country. Besides, I don't know no othern named Aires Saxon, do you?"

"No, Irma Ray. I'm gone," J.W. said, putting down the receiver and finishing the first cup of coffee in two swallows, hot as it still was. He'd take the other one with him.

The flag that announced that this year's Maid of Cotton lived in this house right here was waving from a polished wooden pole attached to the roof of 11 Carr as J.W. pulled up behind one of the police cars parked in front.

A patrol officer with his cap pushed to the back of his head was standing in front of the open gate to the Saxon house, holding a spool of yellow crime-scene plastic tape in one hand and looking about him as though he had lost something.

"Don't worry about trying to mark it off," J.W. told him. "Just close the gate and hang a strip on it."

"Thanks, sergeant. I was wondering where to tie the ends of it."

"And square that lid up," J.W. said, looking at the patrolman's hat. "You're in the eye of the public."

The outside wrought-iron door was open, and the heavy wooden one behind it was swinging back as J.W. approached the house. Jay Sarratt greeted him as he stepped through the entrance.

"Sergeant Ragsdale," said Jay, a formerly handsome man who looked like he'd been blown up with an air pump. "Long time no see. Come in the house."

"I see you got here quick, Jay. You have to leave in the middle of your breakfast?" J.W. pointed to a yolk stain on Jay Sarratt's tie, but the Assistant Medical Officer didn't look down.

"That's from two or three weeks back, J.W.," he said. "I keep meaning to dip all my ties in acetone someday in the lab, but I can't seem to get around to it."

"Both of them?"

"It's three now. My daughter give me a new one Christmas before last. Real pretty."

"What we got here?" J.W. asked. "And where can I view the remains?"

"It's over yonder in the den or the study or library, whatever you call it," said Sarratt and flipped open the notebook in his hand. "But he was dressed for the bedroom. Wearing pajamas and a robe and like that."

"Guess Aires Saxon heard somebody rummaging around and came down to look. Surprised his man and paid the price for it."

"I don't know nothing about that," Sarratt said. "I don't do no crime reconstructions. I just look at what all's left over."

"Ain't your job, is it?"

"You got it, J.W. A man's got to stay focused."

"What was it got the job done on Mr. Saxon?" J.W. asked and waved at a patrolman and a plainclothes officer who had just walked into the room from the hall leading to the rear of the house. They nodded and spoke.

"You want it easy or you want it hard?" said Jay Sarratt. "You want me to show off my education or do you want to understand it?"

"Get it on down to where the hogs can eat it," J.W. said. "You talking to a foreclosed cotton farmer."

"Well, then," Sarratt said, looking at his notebook. "The usual. One slug that took the right thumb off. Another one just above the center point of the collar line, and then, bingo, lights out, one that entered the right eye and exited the back of the skull carrying a whole bunch of stuff with it."

"Large caliber," said J.W. "Take that thumb off."

"Not necessarily. It was just the first joint."

"Still."

J.W. walked into the study where three or four people were watching one technician dusting surfaces with black powder. Books, brass fixtures, leather sofas, and heavy dark furniture filled the room, leaving very little space for the body lying along the edge of a mostly maroon oriental rug. One foot was crossed neatly over the other one, as though Aires Saxon had purposely lay down on the floor to take a nap, J.W. noticed. One more step brought him to a point from where he could see the upper part of the body, though, and there was no mistaking why Saxon was on the floor. The face was blue, and the splatters of bone, brain tissue, and blood reached from the floor, up the back wall, and all the way to the patterned paper on the ceiling.

"Goddamn," said J.W. "Dude used a cannon."

"Forty-five," said one of the men watching the finger print technician and dangled a clear plastic envelope back and forth between his thumb and fingertips. "This here's the one Gene dug out of the wall. Hit right in the middle of a two by four stud."

J.W. looked at the wad of metal in the envelope, gray on the side and streaked silver on the other. "That's the only one you got?"

"So far."

"How'd he get in the house?"

"Come in through a window in the kitchen. Got a real clear footprint of a big old Nike in one of them sinks."

"That'll narrow it down," J.W. said. "There ain't but two million pair of that kind of shoe in the Midsouth."

"You suppose Bo knows forty-fives?" said the fingerprint technician, looking up to see if anybody would laugh. Everybody in hearing range gave him a chuckle, and J.W. spoke again to the police detective holding the slug in the envelope.

"Is anybody here in the house that lives here? Mrs. Saxon? A son or daughter?"

"The wife is over in Little Rock, visiting some folks. Probably on her way back now. The youngest daughter, the one that still lives at home, is upstairs with some people tending to her." The man paused, looked around the room as though checking for eavesdroppers, and then leaned toward J.W. "And sergeant, them Maid of Cotton people didn't just go by the pedigree this time." He extended his right arm out to the side, cupped his hand and made a rapid up and down motion for several strokes.

"Oh, yeah?" J.W. said. "She comes with all required attachments, huh?"

"I'd go barefooted all winter," the detective answered.

"Where is that big black body guard you always see with Mr. Saxon everywhere he goes? Looks like an All-American nose tackle from Notre Dame. You know. The one that's in the newspaper pictures with him all the time."

"He's either a Oscar winning actor, or he's real broke up about his boss getting it. Last time I saw him, about twenty minutes ago, he's in a room in the back there, hitting himself on both sides of the head with his fists all balled-up. Just carrying on."

"Well, he missed a blocking assignment. Coach don't like that." J.W. reached into his coat pocket for something to write on and found to his surprise that he did have a small notebook there. "What did he say to you?"

"Said he fell asleep with earphones on, listening to some jazz music, and didn't hear nothing until Cameron woke him up, hollering and knocking on his door."

"I'll need to talk to him in a little while here," J.W. said. "The daughter now, Cameron, huh? The Maid of Cotton. Irma Ray said the housekeeper called it in. Why'd the daughter wake up the bodyguard?"

"I imagine everybody was hollering at everybody else for a while there this morning. That's all I know about it right now, Sergeant."

"I'm going to go up there and meet Miss Cameron Saxon," J.W. said, jerking his head toward the stairs. "Catch her before too many more people talk to her."

The staircase was wide, deep, and polished to a high gloss, and the dark green rug runner was fastened to the steps with metal clips that glowed silver in the morning light. Every surface in this house had been brought up to the highest level of preparedness, J.W. thought as he mounted the stairs, place ready for all those Cotton Carnival parties and receptions and brunches and masquerades and mint julep sippings. Everything here's right up to snuff except for that mess in the reading room.

A tall woman close to J.W.'s age opened the door to his single knock. Her blonde hair looked like it had already been worked on for an hour by a professional, as early as it was in the morning, and the jewelry at her throat, wrists and ear lobes said East Memphis way beyond the interstate loop.

"May I help you, sir?" the woman said, after giving him a sweeping look that moved from his tie to his coat lapel to his eyes. "This is not a good time for conversation."

J.W. felt like flicking his fingertips on the shoulders of his sportcoat to knock off anything organic that might have fallen there. He was sure there was a stray hair or two or some other kind of nastiness open to plain sight.

"Yes, Ma'am, I know it is," he said. "But I need to talk to Miss Saxon about what she saw downstairs. I'm Sergeant Ragsdale in charge of the investigation, and I have to learn all I can from her."

"Is that the Delta Ragsdales, Sergeant? Around Batesville?"

"Yes, Ma'am. That's us. Was us."

"Must it be now, Sergeant Ragsdale? Cameron is in a dreadful state of shock and grief. Why don't you wait to ask your questions until later?"

The blonde woman ended every statement she made with an uplift on the last word, but J.W. knew she wasn't being timid or uncertain. She had spent her whole life just learning how to sound that way. Everything she said was an order and had been since her second birthday.

"It's gotta be now and later," J.W. said, moving a half-step closer to the woman. "Sometimes we can learn something that'll help us right after a terrible thing like this happens that if we wait too long people will forget about or misremember."

The woman didn't budge except for a little flicker at the corner of one eye. What if I was to lean over and bite her on the end of the nose, J.W. thought, or just lick her on the cheekbone?

"Aunt Connie, I'll talk to the Sergeant," said a voice coming from deeper in the room. "I want to do anything I can to help the police catch the man who did that to Daddy."

"Well, darling, if you feel up to it," the blond woman said and made the first sign of retreat. "You mustn't feel you need to push yourself if you aren't able."

"I'll be as quick as I can," J.W. said, stepping through the door. "I appreciate the situation."

Miss Cameron Saxon was sitting near a window in a chair covered with material in what J.W. remembered his second wife calling flame stitching. Wanda Montgomery had explained such details of furnishings to him often and at great length over the whole period of that marriage. J.W. never did understand why.

This year's Maid of Cotton was still wearing what she had had on for some function the night before. J.W. didn't know the name for the dress, but he had seen it many times before on rich women in the Bluff City. It was a light colored garment that started loose at the bottom, suddenly began getting tighter above the knee and increased that process until it couldn't possibly get any closer to the woman inside it, and then relaxed into a burst of looser material at the top. Seeing how this example of the type looked on Cameron Saxon, J.W. could understand why the police detective downstairs had made the jacking motion a few minutes earlier.

The young woman got out of the flame-stitched chair and walked smartly toward J.W., her hand extended toward him. When J.W. took it, she squeezed and shook it like a man, almost like a Rotarian.

"Sergeant Ragsdale," she said. "I'm Cameron Saxon, and I want to help you catch the scum that shot my father."

She sounded the way she must have during the interview portion of the Maid of Cotton selection process, firm in voice, eyes fixed directly on those of the person she was addressing, and well-prepared to discuss the topic in question. Of course, then the subject had been something like the "role of cotton in balancing the U.S. trade deficit" or "cotton, the true miracle fiber: an historical analysis of a marvelous plant." This time the Maid of Cotton had been handed an assignment that ought to stop even a Memphis debutante in her tracks, or at least slow her down a little. But Cameron Saxon had on her game face and was ready to play.

She had big hair, J.W. noticed, the kind that most women in Memphis tried to achieve when they were wanting to look good, which was most all of the time, and when Cameron Saxon moved her head briskly from side to side, the hairdo got a little behind and had to hurry to catch up. It made for an interesting thrash of movement and curls. Watching that action, J.W. understood for the first time the reason for a particular female hairstyle. He felt like he had learned something.

"What time did you get home last night, Miss Saxon?" J.W. asked.

"Very late. I'd been at three balls, making appearances in connection with my responsibilities, you know, as Maid of Cotton, and to relax, I'd gone with a bunch of my girlfriends and boyfriends to a place to be by ourselves and dance a little bit."

"Can you give me an approximate time? Was it two? Before two? Can you narrow it down any?"

"About two, I guess," Cameron Saxon said. "A little after, maybe."

"Uh huh. So you just let yourself into the house without letting anybody else know you were home?"

"Yes, I didn't want to wake anybody up it was so late and I was so tired. Danny Magee let me out in front of the house and watched me go in, and I waved good bye through the gate and then came on in."

"Didn't notice anything that looked funny to you in the house?" J.W. said. "Didn't hear nothing?"

"No sir. The light was on in Daddy's study. I looked at the bottom of the door, but I was real quiet and didn't knock because he goes in there to read and nine times out of ten he goes to sleep in his chair." Cameron's voice wavered, and she looked away from J.W.'s eyes for the first time since she had started talking.

"Oh," she said, "he used to."

"Cameron," said the blonde woman and moved toward her. "Darling child."

"I'm all right, Aunt Connie," Cameron said, returning to her Central Gardens voice. "I want to get through this on the first try. Don't get me started."

"You know I would never do anything to upset you, dearest girl," Aunt Connie said a little huffily as she sat back down, "I was only trying to be supportive."

"Then you came on up to your room," J.W. said to Cameron, "directly after you saw the light under the door."

"Yes, I did. Very quietly, and I went to sleep right away and I didn't wake up until I heard Mindy screaming."

"Thank you for talking to me this morning," J.W. said. "I know it ain't no easy thing." The blonde woman began to make rustling sounds in her chair, and J.W. turned toward the door.

"One more thing before I forget," he said. "You got a older brother and a sister, haven't you? They live in Memphis?"

"Franklin is my half-brother. He lives down close to Batesville and runs the farms and the franchise business. And my half-sister, Caitlin, is living in New Orleans now." Cameron Saxon paused and put her hands up to the sides of her head, touching her temples as though they were painful. "My daddy's been married three times. We've all got different mothers."

"What's that sister's last name?" J.W. said. "Still Saxon?"

"Well, it might be," Cameron said. "It was LeBlanc up until the divorce became final. I don't recall what name Cat's using now."

"I'm certain you can determine all these little details later, Sergeant," said the blonde woman called Aunt Connie in a tone that took J.W. back to memories of his first years as a Memphis police officer when he'd had to manage traffic control at fundraisers at the Brooks Museum and the Pink Palace. Memphis society ladies always sounded like that when they were telling you to get the fuck out of their way.

"I'm going to need to talk to you too, Miss uh..." J.W. said. "Later."

"Taylor. Connolly Taylor."

As he left the room and walked downstairs, J.W. wondered why it was that the money folks in Central Gardens forgot all the girl names for female offspring and had to settle for labels like Cameron and Connolly and McLean. He fully expected to meet some woman in Midtown any

day now with a name slapped on her something like Weimaraner or
Doberman Jones.

At the foot of the stairs the police officer who had earlier expressed
his appreciation of the reigning Maid of Cotton stood looking up at J.W.,
trying to catch his eye. When he saw that J.W. had noticed him, he
looked quizzical and made his rapid motion with his right hand again.
J.W. nodded at him, but made no answering move. Be damned, he
thought to himself, if I'm going to jack back at him.

Lawrence Glide was sitting in a chair next to an end table stacked
high with books and magazines, and his eyes were closed as though he
were in prayer or meditation. The upholstered chair looked two sizes too
small for him, and when J.W. knocked on the door facing to get the
man's attention, he jumped as though someone had poked him with a
stick, hard enough to cause the legs of the chair to make a scraping
sound on the waxed hardwood floor.

"Mister Glide," J.W. said. "Didn't mean to surprise you. I'm
Sergeant Ragsdale, Homicide Division. I'd like to ask you a few questions."

"Certainly, Sergeant," Glide said, standing up to face J.W. "I can't
tell you much about this terrible thing, but I'll do what I can. Do you
want to sit down?" Glide asked and gestured toward the chair he had just
left.

"Naw," J.W. said. "I'll stand here. Tell me, if you will, Mister Glide,
what it is you do for Mister Saxon."

"Aires Saxon," Glide said. "I didn't do enough, obviously. God, it's
awful."

"Uh huh. What's your job?"

"I was hired by his son, Franklin Saxon, on a short-term basis, to be
Mister Saxon's protector."

"Protector? Like a bodyguard?"

"Not exactly, no. Mister Saxon, Aires, I mean, is getting on in age,
and he and his wife and daughter are here in this big house in Midtown.
Franklin Saxon was concerned with all the hoopla involving the daughter's becoming Maid of Cotton that a lot of attention would be directed
toward the family. More than usual, I mean. And Franklin lives out of
state. And it was to be just a short-term thing, like I said."

"So you're supposed to sort of look out for the wrong kind of folks?"

"I thought it was over-reaction on the part of the younger Mister
Saxon, myself, Sergeant," Glide said, making a gesture with both hands
as though to push open a set of closed curtains. "But I was ready for a
short stay in Memphis, and Mister Saxon persuaded me to sign on for a
few months. Just to be a presence, you understand."

"Wasn't no over-reaction, though, was it?" J.W. said. "When you come right down to it."

"No," Glide said. "God, no. I'll never get over it."

"You say your job, the reason for it, had to do with the daughter getting to be Maid of Cotton this year. How long has she known she's the one to win it?"

"It wasn't completely that," Glide said. "She has been in the contest for a while, but her doing that just intensified the concern Mister Franklin Saxon was already feeling. I think she learned she was selected a couple of weeks ago. Maybe longer."

"I guess I see," J.W. said. "Can you tell me what you were doing last night when the shooting took place?"

"Listening to Coltrane," Glide said and pointed toward a music system set in a corner of the room that looked to J.W. big enough to announce baseball games over. "With headphones, of course."

"Headphones?"

"Yes, yes, and I'll always have that to have to live with. I like to hear every nuance, and of course not bother anybody in the house with the volume level. I had them on, the system turned high, for, I don't know, two or three hours, right up to the time Miss Saxon opened the door to my room."

"The wife?"

"No, Cameron. Miss Saxon. She came in screaming and crying and that's when I knew something terrible had happened."

"What time was that?"

"Let's see. I'll have to try to figure it out," Glide said and looked at the floor. "I had fallen asleep with the headphones on. Not sound asleep, but, you know, dozing. And I had noticed it was getting late, after one o'clock, before I dozed off. So it must have been about two, I guess. Around there."

"Two, huh? You didn't hear anything before then?"

"No, just Coltrane. And then poor Cameron."

"Do you make a profession of being a protector, I believe you called it, Mister Glide?"

"Oh, no," Glide said. "This thing began as just something to do. I met Mister Saxon, Franklin, in Chicago through the Delta BarBQ franchise business he runs. I was doing some motivational speaking at a convention he attended. He sought me out."

"Motivational speaking," J.W. said. "Like telling people what to do, how to act?"

"How to think positively, Sergeant," Glide said. "How to get up for a project. How to will yourself to succeed."

"Where'd you learn that?" J.W. asked. "In college or somewhere?"

"By living, by focussing," Glide said. "It applies to any and everything, I believe, but in my case it came out of athletics."

"Is it a Fellowship of Christian Athletes?" J.W. said. "One of these prayer things you see all these jocks doing?"

"No," Glide said. "It's personal. It's existential."

"Uh huh," J.W. said. "Well, I'll want to talk to you later again. Or somebody else will. Thanks for your time, Mister Glide."

When he left the room, Lawrence Glide had sunk back into his undersized chair and closed his eyes again. Probably focussing, J.W. told himself, trying to get positive one more time. Wonder if that line of work pays good? And who did Franklin Saxon think was out to get his daddy? And why would he hire a retired motivating jock from Chicago to watch out for him? Give him one thing. Mister Lawrence Glide is sure big enough for the job. If only he could stay awake.

8

"heck this out," Stone Job said stepping to the window and letting off four rounds from the nine-millimeter Glock in his left hand. "Listen to her rip. Sound like my grandmama's sewing machine."

"Don't be shooting into no buildings, fool," said T-Bird. "Blue knockers be getting calls, coming round here, fucking with us."

"I aim up at the sky. Shoot a hole in the motherfucking moon."

"Can't reach no moon with no bullet," Leatherman said, pausing after every word like a bad tape on a boom box. "Moon too high."

"Me, I'm gonna be higher than the moon I get this rock crackling," Flash said and fiddled with the glass rig he was loading. "I be getting ignition and lift-off soon's this pipe be working."

"Ain't you, ain't nobody else gonna be getting fried too done right now," T-Bird said. "Everybody get just one little bit before we go over yonder Baby Street, do the deed. That's all you be getting. Beside, you ain't suppose to be using up all your own merchandise."

"Shee-it," said Stone Job. "Sheeit. Merchandise. Why you call it that?"

"Fool, that's what it is. That's what we be buying and selling. Why you think we done made a withdrawal from the ATM other night?"

"To pay the white man the money for the rock. That's why."

"Right, you getting it. That be the Bones business. Buying and selling, just like the business man do."

Stone Job and T-Bird slapped hands in a high, then a low and then a middle five, while Leatherman and Flash watched as though to observe and critique the transaction.

"We pay him, he pay us," T-Bird said. "The white man do for us, and we do for him. Free enterprise, motherfucker."

"I need me one strong little hit," Stone Job said. "See, you know, do what we be selling be good. The right thing, you know, before we go out there do our business."

"You heard me, motherfucker. We gonna be sharp, we gonna be

tight, we gonna be slick."

"We be Bones Family," Leatherman said in low gear, "be take care of business first."

"Then we burn some rock," Flash said. "Light up some pebbles."

"After we do Apple, we light up some motherfucking boulders," T-Bird said, "big as Leatherman's head. Then's the time we smoke up a taste of what Bones be selling."

Outside in the dark street, easing away from the curb almost soundlessly, Stone Job at the wheel, the Buick Park Lane headed up Esplanade toward Napoleon. The car would take Riverside Drive up to the foot of Jackson Avenue, skirting downtown Memphis and encountering only three stoplights on the way.

"What kind of car you pick out for me tonight, Stone Job?" said Flash. "This thing be a old fat honky businessman car."

"It a big car," Leatherman said. "Be a black car."

"I know what color it be, nigger," said Flash. "Goddamn, I be talking about the name of the machine."

Leatherman turned slowly from where he was sitting in the front seat and began to lift his left hand.

"Nuh uh, Leatherman," T-Bird said. "Flash just be running his mouth."

By the time T-Bird got the last word out, Leatherman had already backhanded Flash on the side of the head. The sound the blow made was not sharp, like that of a slap, but more like a five pound sack of corn meal dropped from chest high onto a cement floor.

"Shit," Flash said, nursing his head with both hands. "Motherfucker's crazy. Why he do that?"

"You lucky he wasn't holding something in his hand when he hit you," T-Bird said. "You be spitting Chiclets."

"Car be big," Leatherman said, looking back out the windshield and pointing to the hood. "Be black."

"Drive at your legal speed, Stone Job," said T-Bird. "Everybody lean back, be cool, think about the job."

At the intersection of Riverside and Union, two Memphis police cars were parked nose to tail so that the patrolmen inside could speak to each through their open windows. Stone Job proceeded at the thirty mile speed limit through the green light, and neither policeman looked up as the Park Lane passed by. The surface of all three cars glowed wet in the three a.m. streetlights.

In less than three minutes the Bones Family members were stopped at the turn into Baby Street, listening to T-Bird give directions and inspecting the tools they had brought with them for the night's work.

Stone Job left the engine running, the lights off, and he stayed behind the wheel with gears in neutral as the three others left the Buick and started down Baby Street toward the house with the Mister Hog sign nailed to the front wall.

As the three men stepped up on the porch together, the lights in one of the small houses across the street went out, and T-Bird and Flash stepped aside to give Leatherman room in front of the door. He lifted his right leg, reared back, and brought his foot down and forward into a collision with the middle of the door before him. The lock on the left side held, but the wood tore away from the metal it was supporting, and the hinges on the right burst free from the frame as though they had been dynamited. The slab of wood flew into the room and skidded across the floors with a scraping, chattering sound, and Leatherman was right behind it, T-Bird and Flash at his heels.

Apple Jefferson, lying in the middle of the mattress in the corner of the room, raised up and started screaming before the women did.

Halfway back down Riverside Drive to Napoleon, Flash was still asking Leatherman and T-Bird if they had seen how the Glock performed.

"This little motherfucker," he said, "just chewed Apple's ass. You see how he be jumping, T-Bird? Look like he was trying to climb the wall behind his bed mattress. He just be hollering and jumping, hollering and jumping. Motherfucker be going crazy."

"Yeah," T-Bird said, "he be jumping and carrying on while that nine millimeter work his ass, all right. But Apple lie down real quiet when I put this iron on him." T-Bird lifted a .45 automatic above the level of the seat back so the glare of the streetlights could shine on it as Stone Job drove at a steady forty-five miles per hour up the wide boulevard paralleling the Mississippi.

"This motherfucker say cut out the shit, it be nap time, motherfucker."

Leatherman spoke up for the first time since he and the others had piled into the Buick Park Lane after doing Apple and the two women on Baby Street. "T-Bird," he said, and the other three instantly hushed to let the Leatherman get something else out if he wanted to.

"T-Bird. It be two womans in bed with Apple."

"Yeah. That old ugly white woman and that big old fat-ass mama."

"Apple, he be fucking two womans in bed? Why he do that?"

"Apple Jefferson," Stone Job said. "He bump uglies with a police dog, somebody hold it down for him."

"Apple, he ought not be doing that," Leatherman said, dropping the words one by one like stones. "Two womans in bed."

"Apple, he used to be doing a lot of things he ought not to be doing,"

T-Bird said. "That's why we had to take the nigger's ass out. He be
messing in Bones Family business. He done be telling blue knockers
what we be buying and selling. He give away all our trade secrets." At
that, T-Bird and Stone Job exchanged another hand shake, this one less
elaborate because of the confines of the Buick. "He think he be running
the Bones Family," Flash said. "Apple think he gonna be the man."

"Shit," T-Bird said, "See, Apple he make it hard to keep doing the
deal with that white man. Get him all scared up. Apple he can't keep his
motherfucking mouth shut."

"The white man said Apple come to him, wanting to cut his own deal
with the crack business," Stone Job said. "Claim he had a thing to sell,
something the white man want to know."

"That white man knows who makes the money in the Bones Family,"
Flash said. "That's where Apple make his big mistake."

"Apple Jefferson he ought to be careful who he talk to," T-Bird said.

"Apple be careful now," Flash said.

"He ain't costing us no more money," T-Bird said. "Apple be bump-
ing uglies with the devil's wife now."

"His mouth be sewed up with wire," Stone Job said. " It shut now.
Real tight."

9

J.W. Ragsdale reached all the way to the back of the long drawer on his side of the desk in the Midtown Station, going by feel over a pile of papers, a snarl of paper clips and rubber bands, something mushy that gave when he touched it, and finally off at the far end, up in one corner, the slick feel of cellophane enclosing a cigarette package. There were two Kools, as he had remembered, left in the package when he had pushed it far back into the drawer several months before.

When he lit the least damaged one, the tobacco was so dry the end flared up as though he had put a blowtorch to it. He smoked it anyway and then fired up the second one. He leaned back in his chair, went over his notes and thought about Aires Saxon.

When J.W. first knew of him, Aires Saxon had just made his move from the big house in the middle of all that acreage in Panola County north to Memphis. After he had got shed of that first wife, the one from New Orleans, J.W. believed it was, though he couldn't be positive, being only a kid at the time himself, Aires had decided the quiet life of the Delta couldn't handle him and the new one. Probably got tired of keeping Highway 61 hot and decided to stay closer to the cotton brokers who handled what was left of his money in Memphis.

He had kept the farms going, though, and J.W. remembered his father speaking approvingly of that fact, but Aires focused on knocking around the Bluff City with that bunch from the Memphis Country Club and the University Club and God knew what other club clear on through the second and into the third marriage.

"Long as there's a cotton boll in Panola County, there'll be Saxons and Ragsdales trying to beat the rain and the weevils and the drought and the government," J.W. had remembered the old man saying.

The last Ragsdale is gone from the Delta, J.W. thought, smoking his second Kool down to the filter, and now with this killing, more than likely the Saxon name will be nothing more than a few words on some road signs not too long from now. All that's left is that Delta Pride BarBQ franchise Franklin's got halfway going and not over two hundred acres in cultivation on what's left of the farms.

The murder scene on Carr Avenue had all the characteristics of a typical break-in gone wrong in Midtown Memphis. Entrance through a space that only a circus freak or a Memphis burglar could squeeze through, a few things missing that were easily convertible to cash, and a panicked shooting of a householder dumb enough to stick his head up.

The kind of dude that did this was either going to start flapping his mouth about burning down somebody or he was going to become a victim of his own success when somebody on the street put the word on him. He'd be easy to sell one way or the other. All J.W. had to do was shake a few branches and see what bird flew up. Probably.

The desk shook, and J.W. looked up from his notepad as Tyrone Walker sat down across from him.

"Smoking them old nasty menthols, I see," Tyrone said, picking up the inverted lid from a large 7-11 coffee take-out cup that J.W. had used for an ashtray. "Poo wee."

"You handle that thing like it was a ripe rat turd," J.W. said. "I was going to get rid of it."

"It's poison, my friend. I done told you about the body being a temple."

"That's what they told me back in Sunday school," J.W. said. "I knew that was just a lie."

"Here's something that ain't no lie," Tyrone said, sitting down and pushing a sheet of paper across the desk. "They did Apple Jefferson this morning."

"No shit?"

"Yes sir. Before the sun rose on Baby Street. Him and the two women we saw with him, but one of them ain't dead yet."

"Where they got her? Regional?"

"Yeah, the sister with the attitude about her behind. She ain't expected to make it. Phasing in and out, they told me on the phone." Tyrone got up and started for the door to the hall. "I though you'd want to come with me."

"Let me tell Wee Willie's little helper I'm gone and I'm going to be coming back to see him."

"Right," said Tyrone. "And he can PENCIL YOU IN."

J.W. said the last part of Tyrone's sentence in unison with him, as he headed for Captain Willis's office, matching his voice word for word.

In the car on the way over to the Regional Medical Center on Madison, the two police detectives discussed Captain Willis, Major Dalbey, the failed World Football League of which the Memphis Showboats had been a member, the Canadian Football League Mad-

Dogs, the new Vietnamese hole-in-the-wall restaurant called Indochina on Southern Avenue, and ended up with speculating about how the Bones Family had gotten on to Apple Jefferson so quickly.

"He hadn't even got up the nerve to say much yet," Tyrone said. "He wasn't even ripe yet. I hadn't even gone by to thump him again, see what he sounded like by now. But I know the Bones Family did the ATM killing."

"Apple'll be sounding busted wide open now," said J.W. "We done fucked up and missed the picking season."

"Maybe his girlfriend can put us on to who did him, if she ain't all leaked out yet."

Tyrone parked the car in a slot near the main entrance to the hospital marked Physicians Only, and he and J.W. rode the elevator up to the intensive care area. The oversized elevator also carried two orderlies attending an oriental man on a cart with tubes and wires running in and out of every opening on his head, including one that appeared to have been made with a drill bit.

"He gonna make it?" J.W. asked one of the orderlies, a tall blonde man in his early twenties who was engaged in tapping on the bottom of one of the containers of liquid hanging from a metal stand on the cart.

"Huh?" said the orderly, looking up from what he was doing to the containers. "Him? I don't know. Ain't up to me."

"Damn good thing," J.W. said and stepped out of the elevator onto the sixth floor of the Regional Medical Center.

"This is Sergeant Ragsdale, Ma'am," Tyrone said to the nurse who turned toward them as they proceeded to the central desk. "And I'm Sergeant Walker. We're with the Memphis Police Department and we need to speak to LaQuita Jackson."

The floor was laid out like a wheel with the desk at the hub and five corridors leading off like spokes from the center. The nurse on desk duty, a Miss Elena Jabbour according to a large plastic name tag pinned to her scrubs, looked down the corridor to be sure she was right before she spoke.

"I'm sorry, officer. LaQuita Jackson is near a comatose state and can't possibly respond to anything you may want to ask her."

Miss Jabbour was a young woman, J.W. noted, and leaning forward to look into her eyes, he thought that she still might have enough heart left to consider LaQuita Jackson a human being if he put it right.

"That girl down there in 611," he said to Nurse Jabbour, reading the room number upside down from where the woman was still touching it with her index finger, "was brutally gunned down by a bunch of vicious men who didn't notice her when they did it. She wasn't more than a bottle cap to them. Something they'd just step on and never ever know it."

"She's just a sideshow," Tyrone chimed in, shaking his head back and forth and looking down at the floor. "Never even registered in their minds. Nothing to them."

"Well, sergeant," Elena Jabbour said after looking at the name beside the number 611 on the list before her, "if you're very quiet and quick about it, you may look in on her, but I don't think you'll get any response from the patient at all."

"Thanks, Ma'am," J.W. said, and he and Tyrone walked down the corridor and stepped through the half-open door to 611.

There were two beds in the room, one stripped of all coverings except for a clear plastic envelope encasing the mattress and the other one, closest to the window, holding the large black woman J.W. and Tyrone had seen in the house on Baby Street.

LaQuita Jackson was lying on her right side, facing the door, and she had the usual array of life support machinery and monitors attached to her bodily entrances by tubes, wires, and tape. It put J.W. in mind of the way his Buick looked hooked up to the diagnostic instruments of the Jiffy Tune franchise he took it to whenever he started to feel a spell of car fever coming on. LaQuita looked like she was never going to run again.

She had one eye open, though, and that one blinked twice when the police detectives came into the room and walked over to her bed. Tyrone kneeled down, took LaQuita's hand in his, and spoke quietly to her. As he did, J.W. kept his eyes fixed on the I.V. run into the back of the hand Tyrone was holding.

"Baby sister," Tyrone said. "Who did this to you and your man? Can you tell me?"

LaQuita's mouth opened reluctantly, like a child being forced to take a spoonful of bitter medicine, and at the sight, an image of Tommy at age three swam into J.W.'s mind. He jerked his head back and forth twice to get his son out of it, and leaned forward to hear anything LaQuita Jackson might say.

She made a low sound like someone trying to recite the alphabet phonetically, and then she repeated it, a little stronger the second time.

"What's that, sugar?" Tyrone said. "Can you say it again, sweet-heart?"

"Leather," LaQuita suddenly said in a clear voice and then closed the one eye she had had open.

"Leather?" Tyrone Walker said and twisted around to look at J.W. "She say Leather?" His eyes blazed as he spoke.

"She sure did."

"I know that motherfucker," Tyrone said, turning back toward LaQuita.

"Was it Leatherman, sweet girl, that shot you all up?"

LaQuita's eyes stayed closed, and her mouth collapsed as though she had just dropped off to sleep, but the hand with the I.V. taped to the back of it twitched in Tyrone's grasp.

"You gonna make it, girl," Tyrone said to her, "Just rest and get your strength up. Don't worry about nothing."

As he and J.W. left room 611, a long snoring sound came from the bed behind them, but neither one looked back. Elena Jabbour was waiting in the corridor outside, a look of resolve on her face.

"That's it, officers," she said. "I shouldn't have let you in in the first place."

"You don't know how much good you done us," J.W. said. "We appreciate it."

"I doubt the patient appreciated it," Miss Jabbour said, pulling the door to 611 closed. She stood watching J.W. and Tyrone all the way down the hall to where they turned for the elevator.

"That little nurse is mad at you," J.W. said to Tyrone as they waited for the car to arrive at the sixth floor. "She's finally seen right through you."

"Huh," Tyrone said. "She just wondering why a professional like me is running around with somebody dressed the way you are."

"What's wrong with my sport coat?" J.W. asked and shot his cuffs, "I sewed that button back on the front of it."

Back in the Midtown Station house, both men began poring over files and making notes for follow-up. After about the third time J.W. Ragsdale had read his notes from the conversation with Lawrence Glide to try to come up with a better reason for Franklin Saxon to have hired him to protect Aires than the one Glide had given, he heard a commotion behind him coming from near the entrance to the long room devoted to the ranks of officers below lieutenant. Sudden loud noise and outcries of grief and rage were not unusual in the area, but this sound had an element in it which triggered something in J.W.'s memory. He turned and looked.

Coming toward him down the aisle formed by two rows of desks, tables, and chairs was a female clown carrying a small sheet of plywood under her right arm. The head of every patrol officer, sergeant, and clerk swivelled to watch as she made her progress toward J.W.'s end of the room.

The clown was wearing an oversized pair of men's overalls with only one strap fastened, polka dot shoes a good two feet long, and an orange wig of curls that looked to J.W. big enough to fill a bushel basket. The face was painted dead white except for two perfectly round balls of red on the cheekbone areas and a tennis ball-sized nose attachment of deep purple.

As the clown neared J.W.'s chair, stopped and laid the sheet of plywood on the floor directly in front of him and stepped up on it, he noticed that she had oversized white canvas gloves on her hands, the kind ladies wear when they dig holes in the ground to stick flowers in.

The clown put the fingers of those gloves together in front of her chest, threw her head back briskly so that the great mass of orange curls rustled like a bucket full of rattlesnakes, and opened her mouth to speak. All the police officers in the room, the clerks and the mailman who happened to be there, three black informants and one Hispanic being questioned, and a Domino's Pizza Delivery woman began to scramble for good locations to watch. The sounds of chair legs scraping the floor, pencils being thrown on desks, and people eagerly asking each other what was going on came to J.W. Ragsdale in a wavelike combination, much the way the crowd murmured before the opening pitch at a Memphis Chicks baseball game.

"I am Boo Boo the clown," the clown began to chant in J.W.'s face, and he immediately felt all his insides give way and begin a dive to his pelvic region as he recognized the small eyes beneath the layers of makeup and heard the little-girl quality the speaker was ladling into her voice. Jackie Tullos, Jesus Christ.

"I don't mess around. I lay my little dance board down, and then I really go to town."

With the last words of her rhyme, Jackie went into a frenzy of taps, jumps, and poundings of her big shoes against the plywood sheet she had lugged into the room for her performance.

"Get it, Boo Boo," chanted Tyrone from over J.W.'s shoulder and began to clap his hands together in a fancy syncopated beat which the rest of the audience immediately joined.

"And when I come to Memphis town," Boo Boo chanted, "I'm gonna dance the Eagle down."

With a final three or four percussive slaps of her shoes against her wooden stage, Boo Boo the Clown stopped, bowed with a great flourish, grabbed J.W. by the lapels and kissed him full on the mouth, working her tongue against his clenched teeth as she rubbed her purple fake nose back and forth across his face.

It was all J.W. could do to keep from dropping Boo Boo with a left hook.

Instead, he broke her hold, turned her 180 degrees and with his right arm firmly around her shoulders, began a brisk retreat toward the door to the world outside.

"Yeah, Boo Boo," chanted the Pizza woman. "Woo, girl."

"Foxy lady," one of the informants said through his dreadlocks as J.W. and Jackie swept past. "You be a dancing mama."

"Eagle," Jackie said to J.W. and continued saying all the way out of the Midtown station, "Eagle, you forgot to let me get my little stage. I want my little stage."

J.W. didn't say a word back to her, afraid if he did he'd never be able to stop.

10

"I ain't going to the Owl Bar," J.W. said to Tyrone Walker in the parking lot of the Midtown Station six hours later in the day. "You just go on by yourself."

"Now, J.W.," Tyrone said in an overly solemn voice, "why you saying that?"

"You know damn well why. I'd have to whip somebody's ass or get mine whipped, one, and I just ain't up to it tonight."

"Oh," said Tyrone, "you mean because of Boo Boo the Clown? Why, J.W., lots of men like to dress women up in different kinds of costumes before they fuck them. Ain't nobody gonna hold that kind of thing against you. It's a natural desire. Can't nothing bad come out of the act of love. Said that on Oprah."

"Shit," J.W. said, getting into his Buick and leaning forward to crank it up. "I'll see you in the morning, asshole. We got a lot going on."

"Uh huh," said Tyrone, leaning down to speak through J.W.'s window. "Right. But, listen, partner. If you like your pussy to sing and dance and carry on first, I ain't gonna begrudge you that small pleasure. Trust me on this thing."

"Fuck you, married man," J.W. said and tapped the accelerator. He could hear Tyrone laughing behind him all the way into the street.

J.W. drove east on Union Avenue intending to turn back north toward home on East Parkway, but when he reached the intersection, he felt a sudden depression at the thought of going to bed, tired as he was after the long night before, and instead steered the car south toward the collection of restaurants, honky-tonks and showbars on Winchester. Cliff Ballard would be working the bar at Danny's Twilight Lounge, and they could swap some lies about their old days as patrol officers together back when Memphis still had a downtown all lit up at night.

Besides, Cliff poured shots of bourbon with a heavy hand, and he tended to lose count of how many J.W. had had, and always on the low side.

The parking lot at Danny's Twilight was about a third filled, slack time between "attitude adjustment hour" and the crowd that came after midnight, and J.W. was able to pull in almost next to the door. He made sure all the car doors were locked before he went in, not that he was afraid somebody would want to steal the '78 Buick, but in memory of the time that some bastard he must have rousted once recognized J.W.'s car, opened the unlocked door, and pissed all over the driver's seat.

J.W. had had to let the car air out in the Midsouth August sun with all the doors opened for three days before he was able to stand to drive it again. He still thought he could smell ammonia on muggy days.

The crowd inside Danny's Twilight was sparse. A table of salesmen and secretaries that had stayed past the cheap drink time-limit were jabbering at each other in one corner of the room, three or four pairs of men dressed in short-sleeved white shirts were talking excitedly about computer capacities, and along the bar against the far wall sat a handful of singles, looking back and forth from the drinks before them to the mirror behind the rows of liquor bottles on the shelves.

As J.W. walked past one of the tables of computer freaks from Federal Express or MCI, he heard the phrases "stand-alone," "mainframe" and "batch" plus a garble of letters from the alphabet, and he wasn't in ear range for more than three seconds. He stepped a little livelier toward the bar, raking his gaze down its length for a sight of Cliff Ballard. Black Jack, don't fail me now.

As J.W. eased onto a stool, a man behind the bar bent over doing something straightened up to face the new patron. He was a young one, late twenties with a little mustache and a razor-cut helmet of hair.

"Yes sir," he said and let J.W. see his teeth. "Can I get you?"

"Double Black Jack, water back," J.W. said. "Cliff ain't working tonight?"

"Cliff Ballard? No sir. Not since last month when he got married."

"Married?" J.W. said. "Who to?"

"Well, Cliff's funny, you know. He calls her the widow woman from Horseshoe Lake. I don't know the lady's real name. You want ice in that water?"

"No, no," J.W. said, thinking about Cliff Ballard sitting on Horseshoe Lake in a boat with a casting rod in his hand. He watched Cliff flip his right wrist and the filament play out from the rod tip into a line of silver over the water. "And, uh, second thought. Make that the house bourbon instead of Jack Daniel's. What're you pouring?"

"Heaven Hill."

"Yeah, shit. Make it Heaven Hill."

The bartender moved away to do his business and J.W. lifted his gaze to the mirror behind the row of bottles, joining the rest of the stoolsitters in their consideration of themselves. Cliff Ballard married to a widow with a lake house, he thought, looking hard at the face staring back at him. You got to find you a new place for a quiet drink, buddy-ro, much less every other double Black Jack free.

The hands of the kid bartender appeared in front of him, setting the two glasses of brown and clear liquid on little paper coasters. The Heaven Hill looked like it had been measured by a mainframe stand-alone with resource sharing/time sharing capacities. It was one shot, straight up and down.

J.W. Ragsdale lifted it to his mouth for the first sip, took it and then called for ice.

As the bartender fetched it, J.W. looked again at the mirror and caught a flicker of something off to his left, a flash, eyes looking at his. He shifted his gaze to an angle.

She was curly-haired, eyes a little popped, and she appeared to be ten to fifteen years younger than J.W. But he always found ages of women hard to tell, particularly in dim light. Get one out in the bright sun now, light at the right angle, and every year would announce itself. He had discovered, though, in the last five or six years, that he was becoming increasingly grateful for every day of experience women around him showed. It seemed more and more worth the trade-off.

This one here in Danny's Twilight Lounge, he knew, was on the young side of predictable, and he almost fixed his gaze back on his own washed-out eyes in the mirror. Then the helmet-haired bartender asked J.W. if he could hurt him again with a Heaven Hill, and an image of Cliff Ballard in that boat swam up and settled into his mind. "Yeah, son," J.W. said and turned his head toward the woman down the bar on the left.

Her name was Linda Votaw, she was from Mount Vernon, Ohio, where she was a dental receptionist, she was in Memphis to do an Elvis tour, and she was drinking vodka tonics.

"Do you know," she asked J.W., "that where we are sitting right now this minute used to be the Hideaway Club back in the early fifties?"

"Is that right?" J.W. said and knocked back a quarter of the Heaven Hill in his glass. "Right here where we're sitting?"

"Yes," said Linda Votaw, widening her eyes even further and speaking in a confidential tone. "And you know what happened here in this room in 1953?"

"I hadn't a clue," J.W. said, knowing what was coming next and also knowing that the Hideaway Lounge was out on Brooks Road and had burned to the ground in 1968 during the riots after Dr. King's murder.

"Elvis sang here, that's what. See, he would come out here to the Hideaway and do solos between sets of the headliner. And you know who that was?"

"Was it a hillbilly band?"

"Almost as bad. It was a lounge singer named Tony Preston. You know, like the one Bill Murray used to do the take-off on the old SNL?"

"SNL?" J.W. said, truly puzzled.

"Saturday Night Live," Linda said, her eyes shining. "Elvis sang right in this room, and nobody ever knew who they were listening to."

"You sure know your Elvis," J.W. said and signaled for another round. "It's sure funny for me to learn something about Elvis from a lady from Ohio."

"You're just too close to it," Linda said kindly. "A person never looks at where they live. It takes distant eyes to do that."

"Distant eyes," J.W. repeated. "That's got a ring to it. Listen, something I do know though. You ever been to the Vapors?"

J.W. and Linda Votaw both drove their own cars from Danny's to the Vapors Supper Club, J.W. in his Buick and Linda in her Ford Tempo rental from Alamo, neither one ready to trust the other to deliver them back to where they started if things went wrong.

J.W. pulled around to an open spot on the side of the cement block building and walked back to where Linda sat in the Tempo next to the steel posts supporting the Vapors sign. She had the motor still running.

"I don't know where to park," she said. "There's just that one little space and I don't want to get dinged. On the agreement form, it says they do a walk-around inspection on the car after it's returned. Alamo does."

"Pull up in between these iron things," J.W. said, slapping one of the posts. "That'll take care of it."

"Is that him?" Linda said, craning her neck to look up at the foot high letters on the sign marquee. "Lance Lee?"

"In a tribute to the King," J.W. said. "Everybody tells me he's the best in the business."

"All right. I'm so excited. Let me just get it parked."

She eased the nose of the Tempo into the space between the posts, backing and hauling two or three times until she felt satisfied and then got out with a big smile on her face.

"Does Lance Lee do a young Elvis or a Vegas one?" Linda asked, looking up at the letters. "I hope it's not the Hillbilly Cat."

"He sings all the big songs," J.W. Ragsdale said. "From what they say. I don't know how he dresses up."

Inside, the bandstand was empty except for a drum set and two banks of speakers, but the open floor was jammed with couples dancing to the Eagles on the jukebox. J.W. found a table with two chairs just outside a wrought-iron fence surrounding the dance floor, and he and Linda got seated just as "Witchy Woman" drew to a close.

That seemed to be a signal. As the crowd of car salesmen, secretaries, housewives, and besuited mechanics and clerks headed back to
their vodkas and wine spritzers, two men carrying guitars and one with
drumsticks climbed up on the bandstand and began tuning up.

"Just in time for the eleven o'clock show," J.W. said and waved at a
passing waitress.

"I hope Lance Lee's good," said Linda. "I can't wait. Vodka and
Tonic, please."

About then the drummer hit the bass two loud licks, the lamps lining
the walls went down, and a baby spot being operated from somewhere
in the back of the room raked its beam up and down an aisle from the
bandstand to a door on the far side of the building.

As the spot wavered back and forth a time or two across the door and
then settled dead on the middle of it, the lead guitarist began to pick out
a wailing version of a tune that sounded strongly familiar to J.W. The
drummer increased the speed and force of his beats on the big drum in
concert with the guitar, and J.W. had it. The theme from that space
movie, 2001, the one with the monkeys fighting at the start of it and then
gathering around to look up at a big, planed-off rock like they were in a
church.

The door in the center of the white light swung open, and two men
dressed in white shirts and bow ties came through it, one throwing up a
hand to shield his eyes. About four steps behind them appeared a single
figure, the sequined jump suit he was wearing alive with rainbow colors
as he stepped into the full beam of the baby spot. Aztec suns of gold and
red shimmered on each shoulder.

"Ladies and gentlemen," a voice boomed over the bank of speakers,"
Mr. Lance Lee, in a living tribute to the king."

A woman screamed somewhere in the darkness of the Vapors ball-
room, and Linda Votaw leaned forward over J.W.'s shoulder to get a better view.

"Goddamn," she said in a guttural voice in J.W.'s ear, "He looks just
like him."

Lance Lee moved at a stately pace to the stage and then gave a little
jump which landed him right by the microphone stand. He grabbed the
mike with his right hand, pointed to the drummer with his left, spun
around on the heels of his white boots, and launched into the first words
of a pounding rendition of "C.C. Rider."

Linda let out a squeal right next to J.W.'s head so loud that he jerked
away to get some distance between himself and the lady from Ohio. She
didn't seem to notice.

Looks like Lance Lee is sure showing her something, J.W. thought
as he worked on his bourbon and ice. Might be she'll do the same thing

for me later on. Shame I ain't got access to the same bottle of hair dye he's using, though. That'd probably insure me a hunka hunka burning love.

11

"Devastated," Franklin Saxon said into the mouthpiece of the beige telephone. "Yes, the entire family is simply crushed. All we can do is ask why."

Vance Murphy leaned against a bookcase across the room from the desk where Saxon was talking. He hadn't been asked to sit down yet by Mr. Saxon, so he just shifted his weight from one leg to the other and studied the pattern in the oriental rug while he waited. It was funny, Vance considered, how all these high-dollar folks owned the whole country for miles in every direction and all that was in it, but would leave these old-looking rugs lying around on their shiny hardwood floors. You'd think they'd want their rugs to be top of the line, too, like their cars and their whiskey and their speedboats. A funny damn bunch of assholes, when you came right down to it.

"I appreciate those sentiments," Saxon was saying to the telephone. "Father and I had disagreements, of course. He was a man of great will and force, but he was the binding element for all of us. He was a rallying point for all of us emotionally."

Somebody on the other end of the telephone talked for a full minute without Saxon saying a word. Had to be some old woman, Vance Murphy figured, babbling on about how awful it was about the old man getting his brains shot out in Memphis. She's trying to break Mr. Franklin Saxon down, get him to squall a little bit on the phone for her. A man would be able to walk to Arkansas on the ice before that happened. Only thing that cold-blooded fucker would squall for is a higher grade of nose candy.

"Pru," Saxon said, "You are sweet, and I appreciate and will cherish what you've just said to me. I will relay that to my sisters and to mother, of course. Darling, we will be in touch with you constantly. Yes, dear. Goodbye."

He put the telephone down, looked over at Vance and gestured toward a chair in front of the deck. "Silly old bitch," he said. "She wears my ass out. Pull up a seat, Vance, and tell me what you know. How's my meat doing?"

"Your meat?"

"Yes, my meat. Have you forgot that we're running a barbecue operation, Vance? Does the name Delta Pride BarBQ cease to mean anything to you? It sure the fuck has to the rest of the world from all accounts."

"Oh, sure, Mr. Saxon. I just didn't have my mind on the franchising stuff lately. What with all that's going on and everything."

"Well, Vance, I suggest you learn to run your mind rather than letting your mind run you. Understand?"

"Yessir, I get you," Vance Murphy said, thinking that he wished he could see Franklin Saxon in hell with his back broke.

"Well?"

"Sir?"

"Delta Pride BarBQ. How's productivity, how're shipments? Still lower than frog shit?"

"Yes sir. A bunch of the boners and choppers didn't show for work a couple of days last week. But them women's got kids finishing up school, graduating and what not, over to Drew High School, and they'll be back soon as that business is took care of."

"Ah, graduation," Franklin Saxon said, "the eager young ready to commence a life on the processing line of Delta BarBQ or to go to Memphis, get knocked up and join the welfare roll."

He leaned back in his leather chair and laughed, and Vance joined in. "Yes sir," he said. "I reckon so, Mr. Frank."

"You're sure," Saxon said abruptly, with no trace of humor now in his voice, "that these absences have nothing to do with that union organizing activity last month?"

"You can rest easy about that," Vance Murphy said. "Me and my brother Pick encouraged that fellow to leave Panola County and go on back where he came from. He was glad to oblige, time we got through explaining things to him."

"Fair's fair," Saxon said. "We treat our people right. They ought to treat their employer right. A day's work for a day's pay. We don't need any third party involvement. One thing that would be nice is if the people we hired to do the Delta Pride entry in the International Barbecue Contest in Memphis would be able to at least place in some division. It'd do wonders for public relations if we could advertise we'd won something. Maybe we could move some pork for a change. God, some good news would be nice."

Vance Murphy wondered how long Saxon was going to rant on about Delta Pride, pork cooking contests, production problems, and a few colored women taking the day off to rest and go to Wal-Mart. It showed

how worried he was about the final deal with the old man and with the
truck coming in from New Orleans tonight. That was the thing he was
counting on, as he had told Vance over and over until it felt like Vance's
ears were about to bleed. It had to work. The only time Franklin Saxon
ever tried to start talking like a businessman was when one of his
schemes got to a dicey point. Then you'd think the way he carried on
about Delta Pride or the price of cotton or Japanese protective tariffs that
he was president of the Mississippi Chamber of Commerce.

When the real nut-cutting started, Franklin Saxon commenced to
squall.

"Get this, Vance," he was saying, "the other day Annie May Gunn
called up Mrs. Saxon and said she couldn't come in and help serve at a
tea she's giving because Annie May has got carpal tunnel syndrome.
Can you imagine that? That old doddering woman doesn't know carpal
tunnel syndrome from ExLax. Where do they get this stuff?"

"Oprah," Vance Murphy said simply.

"You think so?"

"Yessir. My wife watches that mess. That big-mouthed woman talks
about everything on that television show. Female queers. Women saying
their daddies did it to them when they were little. You name it. Oprah
just pours that garbage into these housemaids' heads. Everyday at nine
o'clock in the morning on channel six out of Memphis."

"Yeah?" Franklin Saxon said. "Really? I should try to catch it sometime."

The telephone on the oak desk began ringing, and Vance Murphy and
Saxon watched it until it stopped. After a minute or two of silence,
Vance spoke.

"Like I said, Mr. Saxon. Everything looks good for tonight. Truck's
supposed to get to the plantation about two in the morning. Man named
Tee John Doucette driving it."

"I'm going to be in Memphis for the next three or four days, taking
care of the funeral and talking to police. You know where to call me.
And I'm sure going to be in touch with you Murphy boys. This is the
first big shipment we've tried. The rest has been small potatoes. This has
got to work. It's got to prosper."

"Don't worry about a thing. It'll go slicker'n owl shit. I flat guarantee you or I'll ride a hog out of here sidesaddle."

"You are a country son of a bitch, aren't you, Vance?" Franklin
Saxon said fondly, looking over his half-glasses at Murphy.

"Yessir," Vance said. "I am that."

After Vance Murphy left the study, Franklin Saxon sat for almost a
full minute alternatively drumming his fingers on his desk and chewing

at his right thumbnail. He then picked up the telephone and punched in one of the numbers in the family home on Carr Avenue in Memphis, the one that rang in Lawrence Glide's quarters.

"Glide," a voice said.

"Is everything still being held in the road, my friend?" Franklin said. "Have you been talked to by some folks?"

"Of course," Glide answered. "I'm surprised you called to ask."

"No real reason, Lawrence. I know you feel very let-down that the precise thing I hired you to prevent has happened."

"You have no idea," Glide said, "what it is to fail at one's primary assignment. I'm just broken by the experience."

"I can imagine. But buck up. You did your best."

"I always do."

"Things will look better for you soon," Franklin Saxon said. "Trust me. They certainly do for me."

"I hope you feel my overall performance has been satisfactory," Glide said, "given circumstances."

"Rest assured I do. You've been a real protector."

"We'll need to talk when you come to Memphis, you know."

"There's no problem you're having, is there?" Franklin Saxon said, putting his right hand back up to his mouth to get at the thumbnail again.

"No, we just need to discuss my status now, the way it's changed."

"Oh, of course. All will be well, I'm sure. You'll be satisfied."

"That's what I'm looking for," Lawrence Glide said, "always," and he broke the connection.

12

Cameron Saxon, Maid of Cotton elect, was walking in small circles about her bedroom, a white portable telephone jammed between her right shoulder and her ear, as she listened to Ray Earle Sealy, chairman of the Cotton Carnival, express sympathy, support, and concern. While Mr. Sealy talked, Cameron used her free right hand to steer a silver nail file around the cuticles of the fingers on her left. She shifted expertly from one hand to the other without touching the telephone as Ray Earle Sealy began to wind down.

"I appreciate everything you've said, Mr. Sealy," Cameron said, jumping into a pause in the chairman's discourse. "I really think it's astounding how much your thoughts and mine and the family's have been running in parallel. Of course, although you've never ever hinted at any fears you may have about the effect on the carnival, you know that I'd never do anything to harm the carnival or Memphis or the cotton industry. That's the last thing my daddy would've wanted, and I'm Aires Saxon's daughter from the top of my head to the soles of my feet."

Roy Earle Sealy said something else in response, and Cameron picked up a bottle of clear lotion from a dressing table and looked around for the box of cotton balls. She found it, pulled four or five balls free, and unscrewed the bottle lid.

"Yessir," she said into the telephone, "the funeral's this afternoon, and then there are three days before the Mayor's Ball. No sir, the Governor's is the next weekend right before the Grand Procession on the River. Why, thank you. I have studied all my responsibilities, the whole list of them, as Maid of Cotton, and I intend to carry every one of them out. I know my lessons. Yessir. To the least of them and to the fullest measure of devotion and duty."

The chairman of the Cotton Carnival spoke again, at lesser length this time, and Cameron buffed a lotion laden ball of cotton back and forth across the face of each of her nails until they shone with a light that seemed to come from the interior of the fingertips themselves.

"I don't believe the good people of Memphis and of the cotton industry would settle for anything less, Mr. Sealy," Cameron said, straightening up until she stood almost at attention, her eye fixed on a squirrel perched on a branch of the tulip tree outside the window of her room. "I'm going to be the proudest and most dignified and controlled young lady throughout the entire Cotton Carnival and the year of my reign. I'm going to be the best Maid of Cotton ever for my daddy and his memory, and there will be no voluntary stepping down. Yessir, Mr. Sealy, you heard correctly. If Cameron Saxon withdraws as Maid of Cotton, it will be because the Chairman and the Board of Directors stripped her of the title because her father was murdered in the sanctity of the family home here on Carr Avenue in Memphis."

While the Chairman spoke another couple of sentences, Cameron took the opportunity to shift her white telephone to the other ear and shoulder, looking critically at the palm of one, then the other of her hands.

"Why, certainly," she said. "Publicity and media relations are all in your control, and I'm positive that our family attorney will work so closely with any of your people you think appropriate. Why, thank you, Mr. Sealy. If I'm brave it's because that's the way my daddy brought me up to be. Let's just say it's a family characteristic. I will. I'll be there with my counsel tomorrow. Good bye, and thank you for all those sweet thoughts and kind words."

Cameron put the telephone down on the table near the window and tapped on the glass with her nail file until the squirrel jerked its head around and then darted off out of sight, the branch of the tulip tree quivering in its wake.

My big brother Franklin, Cameron thought as she reached for the telephone again, the man of the family, so fucked up on crack and macho bullshit he can't even wait until the Cotton Carnival's over before he does it. I don't care how bad the family financial picture is, how belly-up the goddamn Delta Pride BarBQ franchises are going, anything can wait for a week.

Cameron looked at the telephone in her hand, paused and then reached for the Memphis directory. This whole business had her in such a state it had driven every last number out of her head.

13

"Captain Willis says you think it wasn't nothing more than a run of the mill break-in that got turned bass-ackwards," said Major Calvin Dalbey. He was sitting behind his desk turned to face J.W. The major was wearing a close-fitting white shirt that was gaping open between the buttons under the strain of his midriff. The battle he fought with middle-age spread was continual. You had to give him that, J.W. thought. For a while it was Weight-Watchers and walking, then grapefruit and something called Miracle Soup, and now he had gone to drinking diet milk shakes all day long. You could hear the whine of his portable blender all the way out into the bullpen each time he cranked it up in the office. J.W., along with everybody else who watched Tommy Lasorda babbling between innings, knew you were supposed to drink the milk shakes in place of eating, but Major Dalbey operated in the belief that the powder and milk blend was an add-on that subtracted calories from regular meals.

"What it looks like, all right," J.W. said. "We got some forty-five slugs, a Nike footprint in the sink, and not much else. All the signs of a B and E surprised at the scene."

"No prints?"

"They all wear gloves now, Major. I ain't seen a print at a scene in five years. They can get them plastic ones at Kmart two pair for a dollar."

"Yeah, I know, J.W.," Dalbey said pensively. "All we can do is wait for him to start bragging about it and then go pick him up. I hope that don't take too long, though. We got all this Central Gardens static to put up with. Newspaper and T.V.'s just eating it up. Cotton Carnival, Memphis in May, Maid of Cotton, all this stuff rolled in together. Damn Memphis to hell. There ain't nothing going on most of the year and then everything happens at once."

"Too hot rest of the time."

"Yeah, right, right," Dalbey said. "And on top of all this stuff this fellow from Ohio gets himself killed down by the river in the middle of the night, and everybody's all over the chief's ass because of what it looks like to have a visitor offed here at the beginning of the biggest part of the tourist season."

"Least it wasn't during Elvis Week in August. They would've put that on satellite TV."

"Tell me about it, J.W.," Dalbey said. "What was that Ohioan doing at midnight in that part of town anyway, Goddamn it?"

"Getting some money out of the cash machine," J.W. said. "Putting it back into the Midsouth economy."

"He ought to've known better. Everybody ought to know better than that."

"He was in a strange city, and he was drunk, I reckon," J.W. said. "And he naturally wanted to get drunker."

"I guess so," Dalbey said distractedly. "Thing of it is, Aires Saxon there in Midtown was in his own house reading a damn book when he got done, and he has either done business with every big dog in Memphis or else felt up his wife and French-kissed his daughter. Them kind of Memphians don't like it when one of them gets his ticket punched. They don't want to buy the idea that just some stray can come in off the street right into a big house in Central Gardens and blow them up."

"Yeah," J.W. said. "But you know, the first officer on the scene did find Saxon's wallet on the floor with no money in it. So it looks pretty clear."

"Ordinarily, yeah, but that's too thin a story for us to lean on with this thing. We got to look busy until the brother that did Saxon starts in to tooting his own horn. And we got to catch that bunch that knocked that Ohio fellow in the head."

"I reckon," said J.W. "What you want me to do, Major, until the crop gets ready to pick?"

"You tell me, sergeant. You the one runs down these bad boys."

J.W. looked at a photograph hanging on the wall behind Major Dalbey's desk of the major standing between Johnny Cash and George Bush. It had been taken at a Midsouth Republican fund raising dinner during the 1992 campaign, and J.W. knew that every Memphis police officer at the rank of captain and above who had been in attendance had the same memento from that night of photo opportunities. He studied the expression in George's eyes and then Johnny's before he spoke. Both men looked suspicious.

"I tell you what, Major," J.W. said. "You know I got a reason to go to old Aires' funeral. One I could dummy up anyway."

"You mean all that Delta family connection bullshit."

"If you want to use the scientific term for it," J.W. said. "Right. See, let me go on and do that and make it clear I'm there for the services for Aires Saxon, and that's all. You know how these people are. They're going to be convinced that I'm using the old Panola County background as just an excuse and that really what I'm up to is investigating some kind of inside family thing or something."

"Hmm," Major Dalbey said. "You might be onto something, J.W. Word'll get around that we're putting out a cover story about some ordinary B and E that went strange, and what we're really up to is trying to close in on somebody that had a real reason."

"Yeah," J.W. said, leaning back to watch Dalbey's eyes dart around the office as he considered the nature of Memphis mentality, particularly that predominant in old family Midtown. "You know how they never want to believe nothing that's true on the face of it," J.W. added. "First story's always got to be wrong."

"Everything's always got to be an angle. Everybody's lying to everybody else, and they all know they're doing it the whole time."

"The trick," J.W. said, "in dealing with a Memphian is knowing what level of horseshit you're operating at. Then you can figure out where you stand."

"Part of the time," Major Dalbey said. "At least, you hope. Yeah, J.W., go on out there to Saxon's funeral. Talk a lot about how much that name has meant to the Delta over the years. How much, you know, you've always looked up to him and what he stood for and where are we headed now that this kind of thing's happened and all. If that don't convince that damn bunch we're working all the angles, I don't know where the Peabody Hotel's located."

"Consider it done," J.W. said. "I'll take Tyrone Walker with me, too."

"That's perfect," Major Dalbey said and began to laugh. "They'll all think Tyrone's his unacknowledged son by some house servant down there in Batesville. It'll be a hell of a scene. Little old ladies'll be looking for resemblances in Tyrone's facial structure."

"Yeah," J.W. said. "I'll see if I can talk Tyrone into breaking down and squalling a little bit. You know, right after the ashes to ashes part."

"I wouldn't push him too far, J.W.," the Major said. "He's liable to come up beside your head."

"He owes me a hoorawing or two," J.W. said. "I'll talk to you tomorrow after we get back. See how it went, where do we go from here, and all that stuff."

He got up and left the office, and by the time J.W. got halfway down the corridor to the bullpen, he could hear the whine of the Major's battery-powered blender start up.

* * *

J.W. Ragsdale stood next to Tyrone Walker at the edge of a large group of people clustered around a green canvas tent covering the gravesite of Aires Saxon. The immediate family sat in rows of metal chairs facing an Episcopal priest in vestments who was reading from what looked to J.W. like a Bible. But the words the priest read aloud to the mourners before him did not seem right to J.W. The fact that the people to whom the priest was reading were taking turns reading back to him also struck J.W. as wrong somehow.

"That ain't no real Bible," he said to Tyrone in a low voice. "You listen."

"Of course, it's not," Tyrone replied without moving his head. "I've been listening."

"I thought Episcopalians wasn't Catholics," J.W. said. "I thought they used the real Bible."

"Episcopalians are Catholics, and that's the Book of Common Prayer, J.W.," Tyrone said. "They're doing responses."

"Oh, of course," J.W. said and fell silent, switching his gaze from the priest bent over the book which wasn't a Bible to the tallest man in the first row of family closest to the casket on the platform above the hole in the ground. Franklin Saxon, son of and next in line to Mr. Delta himself, the dead man in the box. Franklin seemed to be keeping up with reading his responses to the priest with great skill. J.W. could pick his voice out of the others, deeper than the rest, which was a mixture of lighter tones, droning over their copies of the book. The man knows how to do, he's right at home, J.W. was thinking to himself, when Tyrone spoke.

"You didn't know that."

"What? About the common book of prayer?"

"That tells me all I need to hear."

"I know all about it. We used to pass them around to each other in Batesville First Baptist in between the snake-chunking."

"Don't make me laugh at a funeral, J.W.," Tyrone said. "This is a solemn occasion."

"What'd you do at church? You didn't read no responses back and forth to the preacher, I don't imagine."

"Did, too," Tyrone said. "When we weren't singing and shouting and doing backflips in front of the altar."

About then the priest seemed to reach a stopping point of some weight, and people began to rise from their metal chairs and drift away from the casket, moving in clots and singles toward the line of cars parked along the roadway between the rows of graves.

"You go talk to Franklin Saxon before he gets out of here," J.W. said.

"I think it's time for you to make your manners."

"You ever met him before?"

"I've seem him from a distance," J.W. said, "but I know he ain't never looked at me. And I don't want him to notice me now, neither. I'm going to wait over there in the car while you talk to him."

"All right," Tyrone said. "I'll tell you what he says."

"I got a reason for this," J.W. said. " I plan to meet him in the Delta, not here in Memphis."

"You are a shy little fellow around your betters, ain't you?" Tyrone said. "When you get into town. Look, he's walking this direction. See you in the car."

As J.W. walked off toward the car, Franklin Saxon was approaching at an angle, flanked by two elderly women who still knew how to apply makeup, and he appeared to be listening to what one of them was saying with great interest. He had his head so far inclined down and in her direction, J.W. noticed, that it looked like she might have been whispering some deep secret about how to achieve long life to him. Or at least offering him a good deal on a set of radial tires.

By the time J.W. had gotten into the driver's seat, Tyrone had already introduced himself to Franklin Saxon and begun to talk.

The two little old ladies peeled off in separate directions as the tall black man conversed with Franklin Saxon, and after two or three minutes, Tyrone pulled out a business card to give Saxon, shook his hand, and headed for the street. Seeing their chance, the two women closed back in on Saxon, and by the time Tyrone had reached the car, the three were leaving in the opposite direction.

"What'd you say to him?" J.W. asked. "To make them nice ladies walk off."

"Told him who I was. Said I knew he was in Batesville the night his daddy was done, and then he told me he'd been in Memphis two days before."

"Yeah, so," J.W. said. "That would be four, five days ago."

"Mister Franklin Saxon said he was at the Peabody Hotel that night making a big speech to a bunch of medical equipment people," Tyrone said. "It was the keynote address, he told me, for the whole convention."

"That must have been the same meeting Mister Blevins went to," J.W. said. "Right before that bunch caught up with him at the ATM on Front Street."

"Uh huh. I wonder who all else was at the Peabody that night. Seem like every time we turn around somebody's talking about that convention."

"I guess when you're keynoting, it's something you want to tell about," J.W. said. "It must go down on your list of good deeds for people to look at."

"They call that a resume, J.W.," Tyrone said. "For when you're seeking employment."

"I got more than I can handle right now. What else did Franklin tell you?"

"Oh, he told me how it wasn't appropriate to be talking to him here at the cemetery, and then he told me again how busy he was at that convention."

"Franklin is a busy man, I imagine," J.W. said. "Running Delta Pride BarBQ, going to the country clubs, hiring daddy-protectors, one thing and another."

"Daddy-protectors that don't get the job done," Tyrone said. "You know one thing I accomplished, though."

"What's that?"

"I gave those little old ladies something to talk about, asking Franklin Saxon questions in the cemetery at his daddy's funeral."

"You ain't got no respect," J.W. said. "I tell you one thing. The word'll get out now. That ought to muddy up the creek."

"If little old white ladies are anything like little old black ones, they're already limbering up the tom toms," Tyrone said. "Ready to broadcast."

"This little funeral trip is going to get me a vacation," J.W. said. "You watch what I'm telling you."

"He didn't want much to talk to Tyrone," J.W. Ragsdale said to Major Dalbey back at the station, "Out there in the graveyard."

"I bet he didn't," the Major said. "What'd you say to him?"

"Nothing," Tyrone said. "Just told him the chief would be disappointed we hadn't carried out our assignment, when he heard Mister Saxon wouldn't say much to me."

"Jesus, Tyrone," Dalbey said. "Why'd you say that to him? That damn phone will ring off the wall in a minute here now."

"Tyrone was real nice when he talked to Mr. Saxon," J.W. said. "I could see him just grinning up a storm."

"Well," Dalbey said and leaned back in his chair, "we wanted to let folks know we're lifting up every rock. That ought to just about do it."

"I imagine," J.W. said, and after everyone had sat silent for a beat, he spoke again. "Listen, Major. Let me run this by you. See what you think. Just to finish this maneuver off, why don't I try something else?"

"What? I'm afraid Tyrone's done enough already. Maybe too damn much."

"I might could go down to the Saxon plantation in Panola County," he said. "See how the cotton's coming. Talk to some folks. You know, in an unofficial capacity."

"Yeah, that could work," Major Dalbey said. "Make the investigation look thorough and far ranging. Leave no stone unturned."

"Look at every possible lead. See is it business related."

"You go on down then, poke around a little bit, far as anybody knows you just on vacation in the home country for a day or two. I can whisper in the Chief's ear, let it get on back to the Mayor, and everybody'll think we doing above and beyond. Meantime, while you're in Panola County, the cokehead that popped Saxon'll likely stick his neck up."

The major leaned back in his chair, beamed at J.W. and slapped the edge of his desk.

"Try to have a little fun with it, J.W.," he said. "You been looking peaked. But, hey, don't mess around and find nothing now."

"Right, Major," J.W. said, and he and Tyrone left Dalbey's office.

"I told you," he said to Tyrone as soon as they were out of earshot of the major. "Said I'd get me a vacation out of this thing."

"If you can call Mississippi a vacation," Tyrone said and headed for the door to the outside.

It would be good to get out of Memphis for a few days, J.W. thought to himself, as he wrote a note to stick under a miniature brass armadillo, which Tyrone used as a paperweight on his side of the desk. The likelihood of Linda Votaw, the Elvis freak from Mt. Vernon, Ohio, tracking him down was not great, since J.W. had told her he was a carpet salesman for Montgomery and Company out on Norbrook Drive, but you could never tell what Jackie Tullos might do next.

He had talked mean to her when she pulled the Boo Boo the Clown act, mean enough so she had cried in the parking lot of the Midtown station and swore she would never try to make him laugh again. J.W. knew that was a vow she was not likely to keep, no matter how much she had streaked her white clown make-up with an excess of tears while she stood beside her Honda Civic with half the Midtown force hanging out of windows to watch her. Jackie had cried an amazing amount. Drops of white-stained tears had fallen from her chin all down the front of her bib overalls, some even landing on the toes of her clown shoes.

Thinking of that scene with Boo Boo and about how he had taken advantage of a dental receptionist who had got all worked up over Lance Lee singing "Treat Me Like a Fool" in his tribute to the King, J.W. groaned out loud. He had simply got to stop fucking crazy women. But it seemed like that was the only kind of woman these days who would let him fuck her on short notice.

He knew that was really the problem, the short notice business. He had got so sorry he wouldn't take the time and energy necessary to get anywhere sexually with a normal woman. You had to talk to them and take them places other than just honky-tonks, and you had to listen to them describe how previous men had dumped on them, and you had to buy them cute little presents that didn't cost much but meant a lot. All that took concentration and planning and patience, and J.W. was afraid he'd never be able to suck it up enough to do things right ever again.

Down in Panola maybe he could get in some fishing on Sardis Lake or Arkabutla, get out on the water in a boat with an ice-chest full of beer, and stop thinking about running after women and chasing cokeheads armed with assault weapons. Be by himself.

By the time he got in the Buick, headed for the house on Tutwiler to pick up some clothes and his other handgun, J.W. was beginning to feel a little better, maybe even pretty good. He adjusted the car radio to an AM country station, and he was just in time to pick up an old Willie Nelson tune, "My Heroes Have Always Been Cowboys." He began to hum along as he drove.

14

The pork was going to spoil. Tee John Doucette had known that as soon as the refrigerator unit mounted on the front of the truck cab had begun to chatter just outside of Covington. Four hundred pounds of fresh shoulder were turning to a stinking mush about three feet behind where he was sitting in the driver's seat of the GMC. Not that anybody would care on either end of the journey, not in New Orleans and not on that big farm up yonder in north Mississippi. They'd all just as soon dump these big juicy shoulders on the ground and drive over them with the truck or let stray cats eat them.

What they were all in a sweat about was not pork meat, no. It's them bales sealed in plastic and duct tape sitting at the heart of that big metal container in the refrigerator cab, that sixty-four kilos of dirty white rocks surrounded on all sides, top and bottom, by those big shoulders of prime pork. That what worries them, yeah.

Mr. Kenwood Delcambre had told Tee John he could have any of that load of pork shoulders he wanted after he made the transfer in Mississippi, and Tee John had imagined himself driving the truck to a vacant lot somewhere on Lamar Avenue in Memphis and setting up shop. He would save back three or four shoulders to give to some light-skinned lady in South Memphis, make him up some fine Memphis bar-becue, spend two or three days in a strange apartment in a city not New Orleans. The rest they let him have he would sell at four dollars a pound as fast as he could shovel it into the plastic Baggies now riding in the floorboard of the truck. He had the sign already made up to sit outside of the parked truck on Lamar, writing on both its sides. "Prime shoulder pork," it said across the top, above the $4 part, and then underneath, "The Finest Fresh pork shoulder from Louisiana, Y'all."

If that wouldn't move pork for barbecuing, Tee John Doucette didn't know colored people and he didn't know Memphis.

Now, though, just passing the exit sign to Hazlehurst, Tee John heard a new sound come, yeah, to join the chatter in the refrigerating unit. It was a high whine, like metal rubbing against metal, and he knew that meant there was no cooling at all taking place in the chamber where the pork rode. And it was still almost two hundred miles to that big tin barn on the farm in Mississippi up by Batesville there, everything dark and the fields empty with no trees full of Spanish moss like home.

Tee John imagined himself pulling the GMC over at the next exit, parking at the convenience store, Jiffy or Tom, Jr. and buying two hundred pounds of ice to pour on his shoulders. He saw all the twenty pound bags lined up to tear open and to cool down and save all that sweet meat to take to that sister in Memphis and sell there on Lamar, maybe next to the Big Shoe.

And then he imagined arriving at the plantation there in the Delta, later than Mr. Kenwood Delcambre promised the man, maybe not arriving at all, because what if a sheriff or a police see him putting all that ice on the meat and want to see what else he's carrying. Poke down in there among them shoulders, hit that plastic package, and pull it out to see.

Tee John Doucette leaned forward, picked up a package of Kools from the dashboard and lit one up to clear his head. Keep percolating, he told himself, keep your head down and that foot at fifty-five miles per hour. It be plenty of pretty yellow ladies in Memphis, plenty more trips to make with the air conditioner set on high. Mr. Kenwood Delcambre don't like pork, don't like barbecue no way, him.

I ain't carrying no pork shoulder, me, Tee John told himself, remember that. Carrying rock, sixty-four keys.

At four minutes before two o'clock, Tee John pulled the GMC up to the break in the fence surrounding the big Delta farm, slowing to a crawl so he could see how the gate worked. There was not one. Instead, a cattle guard of steel rails built over a pit kept Mr. Saxon's animals from wandering off. They step in them cracks, they break they feet, Tee John thought as the vehicle rumbled over the rails onto the farm. Cows too dumb to tiptoe, them.

A flashlight came on before the truck had traveled fifty feet beyond the fence, and Tee John touched the brake pedal and squinted through the windshield to see who was shining the beam at him. As he did, the man holding the flashlight lowered it, turned off the switch and stepped up to the side of the truck.

He was a tall white man, wearing a St. Louis Cardinals baseball cap, and he had a whitish beard and thin wisps of hair hanging down to his shoulders. When he spoke to Tee John Doucette, he said his words in that way that made the back of Tee John's neck tingle.

"You got my meat, old buddy?" the man said. "Up from the Big Easy?"

"Yessir," Tee John answered. "I got all what they loaded in there in the back of Mr. Delcambre's truck."

"Pull it up yonder," Pick Murphy said, gesturing toward the huge metal barn at the edge of Tee John's low beams, "drive it on in through the doors."

Pick Murphy watched the GMC proceed ahead of him until the lights outlined Vance standing next to the opening into the building, and then he switched his flash back on and read the words painted across the back of the truck. Some Dago man's name and beneath that the slogan "That Means Fresh, Y'all." Everybody in New Orleans had to brag about what they did, always, Pick thought. They were almost as bad as the god-damned Texans that way. They never could just say something once and leave it at that. Had to put something else with it every time, trying to make you feel like they was lucky and you was missing out because you wasn't one of them.

Pick could feel something start up in his chest and began to rise up higher to where it could move out to make the burning feeling in the upper part of his arms, and he took a deep breath to slow it down, reminding himself that the little man in the truck was just driving and wasn't necessarily part of that bunch. He better watch how he talked, though, keep a polite tongue in his fucking head.

By the time Pick Murphy reached the metal building, his brother Vance was already sliding the doors shut and the driver was walking around to the back of the GMC with his keys in his hand. He was a lit-tle one, not much bigger than a jockey, and he bobbed his head at Pick as he walked into the building.

"It be a long way up here, gentleman," he said, "from down New Orleans."

"That's why we like it so much," Pick said. "Wouldn't live no place else, neither. Far as we can be from New Orleans and still be in Mississippi."

"Yessir," said the driver, looking from Pick to Vance and holding the keys out as though he suspected somebody would want to take them. "This here refrigerator unit done went out way down yonder about Covington, Louisiana. It gonna be some bad pork meat in this GMC truck, I declare to you."

"Let's see what we got," Vance Murphy said, taking the keys from Tee John. "Check out what the folks in the big city done sent to us. See where it's worth paying for."

Vance tried a couple of keys in the padlock fastened through the opening mechanism of the refrigerator compartment and then looked back over his shoulder at the driver.

"I believe it be that one," Tee John said, pointing delicately at one of the keys on the ring. Vance inserted it, the lock sprang open, and then Vance lifted the handle to open the door. The rubber gasket pulled away from the doorframe with a sucking sound and a blast of warm air from the interior washed over the two men like a breath from Hell.

"Goddamn," Vance said, staggering back and lifting the hand not holding the padlock and keys up to cover his mouth and nose. "What the fuck are you carrying in there? A ton of rotten sowbelly?"

"No sir," Tee John said. "It just be four hundred pound of pork shoulder. Used to be they was fresh. I believe they gone a little off, seem to me, yeah."

"A little off? They gone any farther off and we'd have to call in Pace Funeral Home to bury the motherfuckers."

"You couldn't use them to barbecue, no," Tee John agreed. "Be too strong."

"A man that'd eat a barbecue made from that mess would be a dead son of a bitch in a couple of hours," Vance said. "I thought I'd smelled some bad stuff before, but I'm here to tell you I was wrong about that."

Both Tee John and Vance stood looking up at the opening into the truck, backed off four or five steps from where they were located when Vance had first cracked the seal. Pick Murphy walked toward them gingerly, his head thrown back to sniff at the load that had so overwhelmed his brother and the jockey-sized truck driver. When the first announcement hit him, he spun around and retreated toward the closed doors to the building.

"I tell you what it smells like," Pick said, beginning to slide one of the doors open a crack. "It smells like the biggest pussy in Memphis done gone all the way bad."

"Wait a minute," Vance said. "Where the fuck you think you going? You got to crawl up in this truck and see if Franklin Saxon's cargo is down in among them shoulders. Come back over here."

"I'll be goddamned if I'm gonna dive down in that shit, Vance," Pick said. "And I'll whip your ass if you try to make me."

He had the door slid open by then, and he stuck his head through the opening out into the Delta night air and began drawing heavy breaths. Tee John and Vance, as though on command, stepped simultaneously toward the passage Pick had made into the world outside the barn and the four hundred pounds of evil hog it contained.

"Way I see it," Vance said after all three men had gotten outside and walked several feet away from the metal building, "until them sixty-four keys is out of that truck and setting on that cement floor in yonder, delivery ain't been made yet."

"I see what you saying," Pick said. "That GMC truck might as well still be on I-55, until the man driving it has done finished every bit of his job and got that crack sitting out where we can look at it."

The Murphy brothers fell silent and looked at Tee John Doucette. He threw his head back until he could see the patterns of stars across the Delta sky above him, many more than he ever got the chance to appreciate in New Orleans, what with all the lights of the city and the constant humidity that hung in the air of south Louisiana. The white dots of light were clear and cool and far away.

Beginning to unbutton his shirt, Tee John decided he would not strip all the way naked in front of these hillbilly white men. He would leave on his high-cut bikini shorts and throw them away after he finished plunging into the rotting mass of pork shoulders and fetching out the sixty-four keys of crack. He hated to lose the drawers, the ones with tiger stripes worked all through them, but Tee John was goddamned if he was going to let these honkies see his bare ass. I do lots of things for Mr. Kenwood Delcambre, he thought to himself as he headed for the door into the refrigerator truck, a white T-shirt tied around his nose and mouth, but that don't mean I gots to show white mens my privates, no.

15

J.W. Ragsdale had remembered to note the mileage on his '78 Buick before he pulled out of the driveway on Tutwiler (132,478) but only about a third of that was on the rebuilt engine he had put in three years ago. So he felt confident heading off into the Delta in his own car rather than an unmarked Dodge from the police fleet. Besides, he could get twenty-six cents a mile for using his car, and he knew he could make money on the deal at that rate.

J.W. was wearing a pair of Levi Dockers which Diane, the lady lawyer, had given him for Christmas two years back, a reddish T-shirt with a pocket on the breast, and the running shoes he used when he jogged in Overton Park. The shoes were not a top-of-the-line brand, and they were a little busted out with use, but they looked pretty good and compared to the black leather specials with inch thick soles he wore ordinarily to the Midtown Station, they felt just as good on his feet.

All in all, headed south for Panola County, J.W. felt rather stylish. By the time he passed Elmwood Cemetery where several Civil War generals and Boss Crump were buried, he had cracked the first can of Schlitz from the cooler riding in the floor board, and he could feel his heart lifting with each landmark he passed on I-55.

Maybe he could stretch this assignment out a little, up to a week or so if he called Major Dalbey two or three days into it and told him he had learned enough to make him need to stay longer, talk to a few more people, find somebody who was out of pocket and probably knew something relevant. Then by the time he got back to Midtown Memphis, the crackhead who had smoked Aires Saxon would have run out of the thicket and been picked up, and Tyrone Walker would have had enough time to sort out the Bones Family shooting squabble.

"Yeah, Tyrone," he'd tell his partner, "goddamn I wished I could have been home to lend you a hand, but I got so busy with checking out leads and eating barbecue and fishing and one thing and another, I couldn't follow my real inclination and get back to Memphis in time to help you out none."

J.W. laughed, reached over the back of the seat and fumbled in the floor board until he found what he wanted, a Bagley Better Baits gimme cap, and put it on his head. What I'll do, he told himself, is take the Arkabutla exit over to 61, find me a roadside store and buy just two packages of Pall Malls to last the whole time I'm in the Delta, take it slow all the way and come in the backside, way west of Batesville.

Up ahead a truck in his lane braked and slowed, and J.W. gave the Buick a little more throttle to pull around and pass. Cool air from the vent increased a little in velocity, and J.W. adjusted his sunglasses as the breezes blew over him. Two miles to his exit and fifteen to old U.S. 61, the straight-as-a-string highway through the gut of the Mississippi Delta.

The secondary road J.W. was travelling west intersected with 61 just south of Tunica. When he stopped to turn left at the T, he could look in all directions and see nothing but land as flat as a poker table, stretching on all sides until it joined a sky filled with huge, puffy clouds fed by the humidity of the river and its tributaries.

The only trees left in the Delta by the planters who had cleared it for crops were those in the towns and in the yards of the old home places, most of the buildings now levelled or derelict since the agricultural conglomerates had taken over. From where he sat in the Buick, waiting for two trucks and a pickup to pass, J.W. could count six stands of sycamores and pecans marking where farmhouses had stood. All these pieces of property were one now, surrounded by gleaming hog wire fence topped by three strands of barbs and marked every couple of hundred feet by metal plaques that said AAM Enterprises.

J.W. slowly turned the Buick south after the last truck had passed in front of him, knowing he ought to feel depressed or angry or at least down in the mouth from looking at these changes, but he couldn't muster it. Instead, he felt the way he always did coming into the Delta, driving a car down that last incline from the higher ground which marked what the geologists called the Tennessee promontory. Keyed up, a pang of a thrill in his viscera, a sense that something was going to happen, maybe, no telling what it might be, good or bad, scary or comforting, but something out of the ordinary, something you couldn't get ready for, you couldn't figure out was coming until it was here.

Once, driving down at midnight from Memphis to show Diane Edge the old Ragsdale place he'd lost to the banks, sipping from a bottle of Black Jack they passed back and forth between them, J.W. had tried to put into words the sensation he felt each time he began that long slide back into Mississippi, out of the city and the things he did for a living there. The best he could come up with to tell her was that the feeling was like you had when you were a kid, on the eve of something big about to happen, Christmas, say, or the first day of school in the fall, or right before the kicker moved toward the ball when his hand was still lifted in the air, everybody's eyes on it. Something told you you were about to be sick, you were going to throw up, your bowels were going to open, you were going to be taken over by your body, and all you could do was watch it happen while you were swept along for the ride.

Diane was a kind woman, trained to be a lawyer though she was, and she had never mentioned after that night what J.W. had said to her about himself and the Delta, and he was always humbly grateful to her for that. Right after that midnight journey, in fact, he had shelled three pounds of Delta pecans, removing all the broken pieces, and had left the whole ones in a plastic bag on her doorstep early one Saturday morning. The next Monday when he got home from work, he found a pie in a cardboard box just outside the door of his rent house on Tutwiler. That was all either one of them ever did about it.

He hadn't seen Diane in several months, J.W. realized, riding along down 61, hadn't called her or arranged to be near the court rooms where she might be arguing cases so he could run into her at the end of a session, ask her to have a drink, go get some supper. He ought to have. Every time he thought about her, he wanted to see her again, but she was always a little scary there in Memphis.

A woman as small as she was, dressed in one of those dark gray or brown or black suits with a white blouse all puffed up at her throat, Diane nevertheless often left J.W. at a loss at what to say to her. Get her off in a car somewhere driving back roads in Arkansas or Mississippi or north of Memphis, looking at the sights and talking about what was growing or laughing at how some farmer or his wife had fixed up the yard decorations around the house, now that was different. But back in Memphis, over a meal at Captain Bilbo's or a beer at Huey's or even in her bedroom in her little house on Snowden, Diane Edge was a different woman.

She said things that made J.W. uncomfortable, coming from a woman who had gone to school as much as she had and could act as prim and proper as she did most of the time. Once, he remembered well enough to play it over in his head every now and then still, Diane had described to him what had happened in court to her earlier in the day. It was after she had left her job at the DEA and gone into business for herself, tired of prosecuting drug dealers who nine times out of ten got off on technicalities. That day in court she hadn't taken the time to prepare properly for the defense of some eight or nine-time loser she was handling the case for, and an assistant district attorney had, as she put, "run the case up my ass, the cocksucker."

That bothered J.W., coming out of her mouth, as smart and ladylike as she was. And one other time, when he had asked her about her former husband, a little geek from Raleigh who sold radio advertising for WRVR, Diane had answered his question about her ex's whereabouts by saying, "oh, the little needle-dick has gotten married to some road whore."

I wonder if I'm needle-dicked to her, J.W. asked himself as he looked ahead to the point where the ruler-straight highway vanished into a mirage of water and sky at the limit of his vision. Suppose she says stuff like that about me to people? Old country boy from Panola County playing cop in Memphis, trying to get in with a lady lawyer that reads poetry and goes to the symphony and cusses like a freight-handler whenever it suits her?

Hell, I'm not gonna think like that, he said to himself, aiming the Buick to pass precisely over a killed possum in the middle of his lane. What I will do, though, is call up Diane Edge when I get back to town and ask her to go with me to a nice restaurant out in East Memphis that takes plastic. I'd like to see her, and I'm going to, by God, he vowed.

J.W. felt better for promising himself that and turned his mind back to the road he was on and the reason he was travelling it. Up ahead not more than fifteen miles was a turn off to Greed's Gap Creek and the farm-to-market road which paralleled it. If he took that route, he could be within two miles of the Saxon plantation in less than an hour. That would be getting there too quickly, in J.W.'s estimation, and he decided instead to choose a longer way, one that would allow him to drive by the old Ragsdale place.

At least he could stop the Buick and look at what he had lost from the road. Maybe if nobody seemed to be around, he could even climb over the fence and walk around some of the property, kick up some clods of dirt and see how the pre-emergent growth inhibiting chemicals were doing with the weed crop. Check out the root system on a couple of cotton plants. Think about what it would look like when all the bolls had opened.

Things had come to a sorry and a strange state when a Ragsdale had to sneak around this part of Panola County, J.W. considered. It had taken a hundred and fifty years for a man of that name to feel out of place in this part of Mississippi, but, by God, he had achieved it.

J.W. knew he really didn't have to sneak around the place. The conglomerate that had bought the Ragsdale acreage and everything else around it had also hired Curtis Platt, a Batesville High graduate in the same class as J.W., to manage it. All J.W. had to do was drive in the front gate, say hello to Curtis, and he could go anywhere on the place he wanted to and stay as long as he could stand it. The problem was he just couldn't see himself asking Curtis Platt, who used to sit in Future

Farmers of America meetings in high school with his mouth hanging permanently open, for permission to walk around on the Ragsdale place. Better instead to sneak in, act like the thief he was, if he wanted to drag around the farm and think about what didn't even exist anymore.

Besides, all that polite stuff took time, and he had to scope out the Saxon plantation, maybe look at the production end of the family's barbecue operation, and justify the time he was taking away from what he could be doing in Memphis in order to wander around the Delta for a few days. Major Dalbey would need to hear something specific about the investigations J.W. was conducting into the murder of Aires Saxon of Central Gardens, and dummying up a convincing report took time and concentration and interviewing some people.

In addition, J.W. had to be careful about how he did all this. A homicide detective from Memphis had no authority in Mississippi, particularly in Panola County, and anything he did had to be shutmouth and low profile, as Captain Willis loved to say when instructing the troops of the Midtown precinct. Dalbey had assured J.W. that he would contact Freddie Hubbard, Sheriff of Panola County, and tell him the nature of J.W.'s business and get his silent agreement to allow a Memphis cop to poke around in his territory, but J.W. knew Hubbard well enough to predict that he'd be cross and cranky about it.

"Freddie Hubbard owes me big," Major Dalbey had told J.W., smirking as he spoke. "It's a little matter involving an incident a couple of years ago in the old Tennessee Hotel when Ole Miss was playing Memphis State up here. All I got to do is mention football, and Freddie gets friendly."

Still and all, no matter what Major Dalbey was holding over Sheriff Hubbard's head, and J.W. was sure it involved a Memphis whore or somebody's drunk wife up from the Delta, he knew he had to lay low and not stir folks up as he conducted his clandestine police work in Panola County. The last thing he wanted to have to do was make a telephone call to the Midtown station in Memphis from behind the bars of the county jail in Batesville. If word got out to his fellow officers, and it would, that J.W. Ragsdale had been arrested and jailed by a sheriff's deputy in his own hometown for trying to practice police work out of jurisdiction, the dumb jokes and what passed for wit in that bunch would likely drive him to do something he shouldn't. He'd probably end up having to hit somebody.

In less than thirty minutes, J.W. was steering the Buick down a narrow lane that ran along the northern edge of the old Ragsdale place and ended up in a stand of second-growth timber and thicket that had defied the efforts of generations of his ancestors to clear for cultivation. The problem was the land was too low and swampy and subject to floods from the Cherow River to be worth the investment of time and money to claim it. Ragsdales had chewed at the edges, but never gained much ground.

That was then, this is now, J.W. thought as he drew near a level and cultivated field where the troublesome patch of water oaks, saw-vines and deep, sucking mud had been. It's a wonder what heavy equipment, a crew of men, and a couple of hundred thousand dollars will do. The sight of the precise row of cotton plants, the gleaming fence, and the levee of raised earth keeping the Cherow where it belonged was enough to convince J.W. that he had seen enough of what used to be to satisfy him for the foreseeable future.

Let me tend to business, he told himself. Get this Aires Saxon thing taken care of, go on back to Memphis and what I can count on, my cuttings and shootings and terminal head wounds, and let these people that know how to make money farming go on about doing it. This is the last time I'm going to subject myself to this kind of punishment. Any fool ought to know that the only way a sore gets well is if you stop pulling the scab off to see how things are doing. Let that sucker heal up and hair over. You got to.

Lighting the first of his unfiltered Pall Malls and feeling that good bite in his throat and nasal passages, J.W. drove slowly along a stretch of fence leading up to the main gate to the Saxon plantation. It was a big place, more prosperous looking than he had remembered, and the farm had a series of outbuildings rivalling the physical plants of the tracts of land owned and managed by AAM Enterprises, the front for the Japanese interests that had been buying into the Delta and its soybeans, cotton, catfish, barbecue and cheap labor for the last several years.

Before Aires Saxon bought most of it, the plantation had belonged to a family that had arrived in Mississippi about the same time the Ragsdales did, shortly before the war of Northern Aggression, as old Judge Caslin McKim used to call it, half in jest, before drink and phlebitis removed him from the bench in Batesville. They were the Nowlins, and J.W. had never really known any of the ones of his generation, their having all been shipped off to boarding schools and colleges somewhere in Virginia for a real education, but he had run into the old man, Fontaine Nowlin, on several occasions when he was desperately casting about for ways to save what was left of the Ragsdale place.

Fontaine Nowlin had been of no help or encouragement, and J.W. had been cheered one Sunday morning in Memphis when, sitting on his tiny front porch on Tutwiler, he had read in the *Commercial Appeal* obituaries that the old bastard had died.

There was a good chance he wouldn't run into anybody on the Saxon plantation who would look at him and see a Ragsdale. Dressed the way he was and driving the car he was in, J.W. figured he couldn't pass for a cotton or soybean factor, and he sure as hell didn't look like an advance man for Japanese money. I believe, he thought to himself, holding in a lungful of Pall Mall smoke for an extra second or two before expelling it, that I'm a crop duster out of work needing a job and that I have flown Stearmans all over Missouri, Texas, Kansas and the two Dakotas. I hear it's a need for pilots in the Delta, maybe, and I'm just asking around, see do they know anybody needing a low-level poison jockey.

J.W. turned off the road into the approach to the main gate and looked up at the scrolled letters worked in wrought iron above him. Saxon's Hundred, the sign stated. Somebody's been watching too many reruns of Dallas, he thought and steered the Buick toward a small building on the right where two men were standing near the open front door, engaged in conversation.

Both men were dressed in work clothes, khaki shirts and pants marked up with grease stains and dirt, both wore hightop, runover brogans, and each sported a black gimme cap with the letter S and the number 100 just beneath it. One man, the shorter and older of the two, made a gesture with his left hand as J.W. parked the Buick and killed the engine, and sunlight sparkled off the gold watch on his wrist, a Rolex J.W. could tell even from the distance from where he was sitting. They must pay the hands real well here at S100, he thought as he got out of the Buick and walked around the front of it toward the two men. Maybe I will just hire on, if they'll have me.

After J.W. had gotten within ten or twelve feet of the two men and stopped, they both turned their heads to look at him, as if they had only just that minute noticed that someone had driven up in a '78 Buick with a leaky muffler and heavy squeaks in the front shocks and had parked not fifty feet away.

"Howdy," J.W. said, reaching for a Pall Mall and then, thinking better of it, letting his hand drop. "How are y'all doing today?"

Neither man said anything. The taller one looked down at the other as though for directions and then back at J.W., shifting around a little to face him. He looked to J.W. to be in his late thirties, hatchet-faced and narrow-eyed with his lower jaw a little too slack to indicate much intelligence. He licked his lips with a pale gray tongue and set his mouth as if to speak, but then subsided. He was built country-strong, rangy through the shoulders, arms and legs with a solid belly carried high up on the torso. Looks like a basketball center going to flesh, J.W. thought. A real rebounder in his time.

"Fair to middling," the other man said in a planter's voice, the one you'd hear every Saturday night in the lobby bar of the Peabody Hotel all year long except for right around Christmas and Easter, the times set aside for family during which there was no escaping the Delta. "You looking for anybody in particular?"

"No sir," J.W. said, shaking his head and smiling. "Name's Dan Mayfield, and I'm looking around for work. Thought I'd just stop in here, talk to whoever I could find that'd be able to point me in the right direction, maybe, tell me where folks might be needing a man."

"We use colored during planting season," said the tall man, speaking in a high-pitched hill accent, definitely not the voice of a planter. "Our own colored. Use them in the picking season, too." He paused, looked down at the other man and then back at J.W.

"You ain't claiming to be one of them, are you, Mayfield?" he asked in what J.W. knew the man meant to be a sly tone, his eyes darting back and forth as he waited in hope for a chuckle from his boss.

J.W. gave him the laugh he wanted. "Naw, naw," he said, "I can't claim that, but I have worked like one, sure enough, more'n I want to admit. What I been doing for longer'n I want to remember is flying dusters. Turbo-thrushes, Stearmans, you name it."

"Despite what Vance suspected," the short man said, "I didn't figure you for a field hand, Mr. Mayfield. I think you might be like me, would-n't have the patience for it."

"That, and the complexion," J.W. said.

"Where's your airplane?" asked Vance, "Back at your private air-port?"

"I have owned one or two. Paid the bank every month on them, at least. But the last one I had any money on is junked just outside of Kountze, Texas."

"You fly it into the ground?"

"Same as. Clipped a wire at the edge of a soybean field and snow-balled it all over creation. Didn't get a scratch on me, though. Just broke my right wrist in two places."

"My name is Brent Perkins, Mr. Mayfield," said the shorter man, extending his right arm for the obligatory Mississippi handshake, "and I work for Mr. Saxon. I wish I could help you, but we're all full up with pilots right now. Fact of the matter is, there seems to be a real surplus of fellows looking to fly cropdusters these days in the Delta."

"Reason for that is," Vance offered, "they can't hold down a regular job. Don't want to put out the effort."

"That a fact?" said J.W., keeping his gaze fastened on Perkins so he wouldn't have to put so much thought into keeping his expression in control if he locked eyes with that narrow-headed goat-fucker.

"Yeah," Vance said, "Most of them flew planes over there in Vietnam and ain't done a honest day's work since. Think the world owes them a living."

"Well, Mr. Perkins," J.W. said, "I didn't expect you'd be needing a pilot this late in the year, but if something comes up, somebody gets sick or busted up or something, I'd sure like to talk to you, or to whoever's running that part of your business here."

"I appreciate your coming by, Mr. Mayfield," the overseer said. "I'll keep you in mind. Have you got a card you can leave with me?"

"No sir, I'm plumb out of them, but I can write my name and where I'm staying on a piece of paper. Let me get something to write on out of my car."

"Here," Perkins said, reaching into his wallet and handing J.W. an embossed business card and a Cross pen from his shirt pocket. "Just put it on the back of mine. Where are you staying?"

"Over at Oxford right now. General delivery until I get set up some-where."

"You ain't no college boy, are you?" Vance asked, showing his teeth. "You ain't no Ole Miss fraternity boy?"

"Not hardly," J.W. said as he wrote on the back of the Saxon's 100 card, "but wherever it's a college, beer's cheap and so's one-room apart-ments."

He handed the card and the pen back to Perkins. "Who is your head pilot, by the way? Maybe I could talk to him, find out if he knows any-where else around they might be needing a poison jockey."

"Ray Hubley," Vance said, pleased with what he'd been able to offer to the conversation so far. As he said the name, however, Brent Perkins's head moved quickly to the side, and he looked at Vance with an expres-sion sharply different from the bland straw boss's face he'd been pre-senting to J.W. up to that point.

"That has been true, Mr. Mayfield," he said, "as Vance says. But Ray Hubley is out of state for several days seeing to some business, and he won't be available to talk to anybody for quite a time to come. So I advise you not to depend on that bit of information."

"All right, Mr. Perkins," J.W. said, nodding and beginning to move toward his car. "Thanks for talking to me. Mr. Saxon's got a real nice set-up here, and I'd sure like to help you out, if the need ever comes up."

Backing the Buick to drive out through the wrought-iron gate, J.W. watched through the rear-view mirror as Vance cast an apprehensive look down at his boss. By the time the car rumbled over the cattleguard, Perkins had turned to face Vance and was beginning to talk. Chew that peckerwood's ass, bossman, J.W. urged. Son of a bitch flaps his loose-lipped mouth a whole lot too much, needs to have it hammered shut.

16

O nly two cars were parked at Big Daddy's Dreamland early in the afternoon, both held together by Bondo and duct tape, but a roil of thick woodsmoke was coming from the stove pipe at the rear of the building, so J.W. knew the pork was cooking. He pulled up as near the front door as he could get and was on the porch and through the door almost before the car door slammed, taking a deep breath as he entered the room. Yes, Lord. Big Daddy was cooking at the spot where Sunflower Road crosses Bumblebee.

"They ready yet?" J.W. asked the woman behind the counter who had turned her head to see who had just come through the door in such a hurry. "I hope I don't have to wait too long, but I'm ready to sit here 'till morning if I have to to get some of them ribs."

"Won't be that long," the woman said. "They be all plated up, cold and ate time nine o'clock get here."

"Glad I'm here on time, then. You got some kind of a beer there to hold me 'til supper gets done?"

"Quarts is all."

"Schlitz, if you got one."

As the woman rummaged around in a Coca Cola box for the beer, the screen door to the kitchen opened, and Big Daddy Monroe stepped through at an angle, adroitly turning his body to miss touching either side of the door frame. He was wearing a huge white apron, splashed with reddish stains and fastened high up over his belly at about mid-chest level. His skin was the blueblack shade of an eggplant, and he looked out at J.W. from hooded eyes.

"I thought I heard somebody hollering about ribs out here in the front," he said, shifting a pair of tongs that looked like oversized surgical forceps from his right to his left hand and then reaching across the counter to shake. "I figured it was you, J.W."

"You know the cure for all that hollering and carrying on," J.W. said, feeling his hand disappear into Big Daddy's paw like that of a child's in a grown man's. "It don't take much to fix me up and shut my mouth."

"Open your mouth's more like it," the huge man said, and then, over his shoulder to the woman who had found a quart of Schlitz in the ice of the Coke box and was setting it opened on the counter. "Get this man a double order of them ribs, down on the short end."

"I ain't seen you in a while," J.W. said after the two men had sat down at one of the tables near the counter. "I hadn't been in Dreamland in I don't know how long."

"Not since Jesus was a little boy."

"You been running lots of pork through the smoke? Lots of folks through the building?"

"Too damn many of them it seem like sometime," Monroe said. "Wrong kind, too, every now and then." He looked over at the counter and spoke loud enough to be heard in the kitchen when he didn't see the woman. "You might as well get me one of them beers, too, Onita."

"Starting early, ain't you?" she yelled from in the back somewhere.

"Yeah," Monroe agreed. "Make it the same brand J.W. got."

"You mean you're making too much money?" J.W. said. "Too many folks coming in wanting barbecue? I believe I'm in the wrong business, if that's what you complaining about."

"You shore in the wrong business, J.W., but that ain't nothing barbecue ribs'll cure. Take more'n that to set you straight."

Onita came with Big Daddy's beer and J.W.'s double of ribs, and nobody said anything else for a while until J.W. had finished the first rack and looked up from his plate for a breather before tackling the second one.

"You still ain't gonna give me the directions to that sauce," he said. "So I can make it up myself in the backyard when I feel the need to."

"Huh," Monroe said. "I could give you directions to write down until you run out of paper and ink, and still wouldn't nobody be able to eat the mess you'd come up with on a little old tin grill in Memphis."

"You're right, Paul," J.W. said, using the name Big Daddy's mother had given him when he was born in one of the shotgun houses on the old Ragsdale place back when his father worked shares in the property. "I just like to fool myself, dream I could have a plate of these ribs in Memphis whenever I want them."

"That's why it's a Dreamland here, side of the road in Mississippi. A man's got to come here to get that eating done."

Big Daddy stared hard at the water glass of beer in front of him, drained it in one motion and then filled it again from the quart bottle. "Charcoal bricquets," he said. "Huh."

"You say the wrong kind been coming into Dreamland here lately?" J.W. said. "What is it? Bad drunks?"

"Naw. Drunk man don't bother me. Drunk woman neither. They get to rearing around too much I just throw them out the door."

"What color is this wrong kind that ain't drunk, then?"

"I tell you what color they is, J.W. You know when the Cherow River get up in the spring, all that rain come, knock everything loose and tumble it over and over between them two banks?"

"Yeah, I seen too many of them spring floods to forget that sight."

"You know how that foam come on the water when it get to moving fast, how it a off-color, almost white, like wash water four or five loads of dirty clothes been run through? Water where the soap done give up and got gray looking? Make your stomach turn if you let yourself think about it?"

"Yeah," J.W. said. "I believe I got the picture. I see where you going."

"That's the color," Big Daddy said, finishing another glass of beer. "Best I can call it, that showed up here at Dreamland last week."

"How many of them was it?" J.W. asked. "Did you know them?"

"It was two. One of them I knowed, other'n I never seed before. But I hope I get to see him one more time, please Lord. That'd do me, suit me fine, right down to the ground."

"What'd they do to you? Hold up the place?"

"They didn't do nothing to me," Big Daddy said. "Didn't want nothing from me but some barbecue and a beer or two. It was one of them little old Odum girls they done messed up. Cherene her name."

"They rough her up?"

"Thing of it is, J.W., what bother me so much is it was my fault. I ain't run no womens since that time in Memphis years ago you helped get me out of that mess. Cherene, she just a little old girl been switching her tail around the boys here for the last year or two, trying to get up enough velocity to make it out of the Delta, get on up to Memphis or down to New Orleans one."

"I know what you talking about, Paul," J.W. said. "I see them younguns every day I work in Memphis."

"Well, like I said. I ain't in that business no more, ain't been, and don't want to be never no more."

Big Daddy paused, looked down at the table and reached forward to rearrange the location of a bottle of hot sauce near J.W.'s plate.

"You ain't gonna eat that other rack?" he asked. "Something wrong with the ribs?"

"Just resting."

"I got greedy, see, when I saw the chance to get one of them hundred dollar bills that funny-looking fellow was showing around. The othern said if I would send a real black girl out to their car, ride around a little bit with them, have a little fun, both her and me would get a hundred each. So I mentioned it to Cherene Odom, that family real dark, all of them, you remember, and she jump at the chance."

J.W. stayed quiet. He picked up the rack of ribs and tore off one on the small end and waited for Big Daddy to finish telling his story. The huge black man took another drink of beer and resumed talking. The sounds Onita had been making in the kitchen had ceased.

"Cherene, she figured it'd be nothing but a white man wanting a blowjob from a colored girl, you know. She didn't say that, now, to me, but I imagine that was what's in her head besides that hundred-dollar bill. Just a honky trying to change his luck."

"So they beat hell out of Cherene," J.W. said, carefully placing the barbecued rib back on his plate.

"Nuh uh. They done used something on her. She all messed up down there now. And another thing, too. They give her some coke, I believe. She ain't no user, and it must've been some strong shit, 'cause Cherene she still over there in Batesville in the Panola County Hospital, ain't able to talk no sense yet, last time I seed her. She didn't even seem to want to open her eyes for a day or two."

"Coke, huh?"

"That's what that doctor say. Extreme drug intoxication, he call it."

"Who was the one you said you know of the two that did it, the one from around here?" J.W. asked. "You got a name?"

"He got the name of Vance Murphy. One of a set of brothers. Other one he called Pick Murphy. But Pick, he wasn't with them. Least I didn't see no sign of nobody but them two that night."

J.W. leaned back in his chair and studied for a minute, his eyes fixed on the turning blades of a fan mounted on a metal stand and pointed to pour a stream of warm air over him and Big Daddy. It wasn't making things any cooler in the tin-roofed building.

"Only Murphy brothers I know in Panola County is that bunch over by Drew," he said. "And they ain't named Vance and Pick. But I do believe I have met the Vance you're talking about."

"Naw, you wouldn't know this set," Big Daddy Monroe said. "They come in here eight, ten years ago, just the two of them, from over close to Tunica, I hear. They staying in a trailer-house out there at Lowe's Crossroad, up in the woods somewheres yonder. And they ain't farming. Bet on that."

"This Vance fellow, is he kind of a squirrel-headed son of a bitch? Mouth hanging open like he can't remember how to close it up, six-three maybe, right at two-hundred pounds? Look like he ain't never give a man a full day's work in his life? Acts like he's trying to find a way to make whoever he's talking to want to knock the living shit out of him?"

"You have met the man, J.W.," Big Daddy said. "For shore. I bet his own mama couldn't draw no better picture of him." He laughed deeply, the sound coming up from his belly and chest, bouncing off the wall behind J.W. and filling the room for the first time since the two men had sat down at the table.

"Squirrel-headed," he said and laughed again.

"How do you know these Murphy boys, Paul?" J.W. said. "They like barbecue?"

"Sometime they come by Dreamland, yeah. Not too much. I hear about them hiring a young fellow or two now and then to tote and carry. They pays them with cash money some for what they do, some times with the white stuff."

"They got a regular supply of coke, then. And they don't work no place in the Delta you know of? Not on one of the big farms or anywhere like that?"

"Far as I know, J.W., they ain't attached nowhere permanent."

"I believe one of them is, Paul. Vance was wearing a uniform when I met him. Look like a full-time employee, benefits and everything."

"That's a curious thing," Big Daddy said. "I wouldn't have guessed that."

"What about the other one with Vance Murphy that night? The one you said looked funny."

"He ain't from around here. He ain't from Mississippi, and he ain't even from Memphis, Tennessee, I expect. Fat little bastard call Dreamland a juke house. Kept talking about Blues music like he knew everything they is to do with it, like he knowed it better than the old fellows what used to sing it."

"He sounds like a learned man," J.W. said. "He sounds to me like he's from the Eastern seaboard."

"He shore believe he don't need no help from nobody, best I can judge."

"I expect he was bossing Vance around, and I expect he was in Panola County on a business trip."

"He the boss of everybody and everything, the way he talk and carry on," Big Daddy said. "You better eat the rest of them ribs. I'm fixing to get my feelings hurt you don't finish up your plate."

"I'm gonna clean my plate," J.W. said, turning back to it. "You can rest assured of that, and you can look for me back in Dreamland in the next few days, too."

"Well, J.W.," Big Daddy said, "I was hoping to hear you say that, and I'm proud you did. Better let Onita bring you out some more of that rib meat fore you stop being hungry. See can you worry some more on down."

"You know I'm gonna fling on in there and try," J.W. said. "I'm about to get a taste for it."

17

"Cameron," said Franklin Saxon, rising from his chair in the study to walk toward the woman standing in the door. "My little sis, Maid of Cotton. You were spectacular at Dada's funeral. My God, the way you choked back the tears until finally they just burst forth through that iron resolve. You know what I kept thinking? You know what name just rang through my mind as I witnessed the scene? You know which? Guess."

Cameron walked into the room without speaking, took a seat in a straightbacked chair, and crossed her legs at the ankles. She looked directly into Franklin's eyes.

"Which?" she said.

"Jackie O. That's who. You know in all the old footage they use in the conspiracy shows on television, there's that scene at the funeral when the camera focuses on her right before John John salutes the casket? You can just glimpse her face behind the veil for about two seconds, and I swear when I saw you at the graveside ceremony right before the dirt-throwing part, you had captured precisely that look. Torn between deep sorrow and granite will, the young heiress shows her face to the world. Implacable."

"Cut the shit, Franklin," Cameron said. "You watch too much television, and your arch insights give me the bloat. We have things to talk about."

"No, really, I just said to myself, at that instant, my little sister, the once and future Maid of Cotton. She reigns."

"Right, big brother. Are you through now? Can we come back to earth here in Mississippi for a few minutes?"

"Damn, you talk unfriendly for not having seen me for so long. What, no kisses, no huggies?"

"That tacky crap was a long time ago," Cameron said in an even tone, "before I knew where to go to get better treatment. You ever touch me again, I'll have you denutted."

"Now, Cameron, you know there was a time when you couldn't get enough of your big old handsome half-brother. Remember the summers at the lake? Remember the screened porch, those nights after Dada and Mommy had drunk themselves to sleep?"

"There was a time when it disgusted me when you reminded me of that, Franklin," Cameron said. "Now you just make me tired. But I have had about enough of it, though. So I warn you, and you know I mean it. That's final."

"Oh, all right. Be that way. I'm just expressing a little high spirits now that we've come so far and the pressure's off, and the skies are blue in the Delta."

"That's what we need to talk about," Cameron said, "and that's why I postponed an appearance at the Memphis Rotary Club luncheon to drive down here. I have things I have to do, and you, Brother Franklin, have things you don't have to."

"And what, pray tell me, Maid of Cotton, are those?" Franklin asked, taking a seat behind the walnut desk and picking up a miniature bale of cotton, perfect in detail down to the metal strips binding it together. "You believe you have to give me tips on behavior and conduct these days? You believe you can tell big brother how the cow ate the cabbage?"

"Let me put it this way," Cameron said, "so that you can understand it. Unless we hold this thing in the road, you're going to be living over in Brushy Mountain, Tennessee with somebody like James Earl Ray as a roommate. If you're lucky, that is, and they don't put you in with some black dude from South Memphis with a taste for white meat."

"How colorfully you phrase things. Where did you learn to talk that talk? Did they teach it to you at Vanderbilt?"

"They taught me all kinds of things at Vanderbilt," Cameron said. "But not nearly as much as I learned at home."

"Fair enough," Franklin said, turning the miniature cotton bale over and winding the key hidden in one end. A tinkling rendition of the Gone With the Wind theme began to play as he placed the bale back on the desk and tented his fingers before him and smiled at his sister.

"Now," he said. "What's worrying you? This is no time for faint hearts."

"What it is a time for," Cameron said, "due to your inability to stay calm and to wait, is for the Memphis police to be looking at everything having to do with the Saxons with a microscope. And I don't mean just that scene in the study with Dada all over the walls. They're not just going to stay in Central Gardens. They'll be down here in the Delta the next thing you know, and they'll be into your stupid Delta Pride franchise dealing and what you're using it for now. I'm talking dope run-

ning. And they'll look at the land deal that went bad, and they'll be
establishing motive for the killing, and they'll work back from that to
you, you shit-for-brains, and that'll lead to my life."

With that, Cameron leaned forward in her chair, picked up the miniature cotton bale and twisted the key to its musical component backwards
until something broke loose inside and put a stop to the GWTW theme.
She tossed the bale back on the desk, and it skidded to rest against a silver mug full of pencils.

"Now see what you've done, Cameron," Franklin Saxon said.
"You've taken all the music out of my cotton, and those little bales are
a charity the Batesville Civitans are promoting for the Mississippi
School for the Blind."

"Which is all full up, I'm sure," Cameron said, "with a line at the
door back out to the street."

"That shows what you really think about cotton. I wish the selection
committee could see what sacrilege this year's Maid has just commit-
ted."

"What do you plan to do, Franklin? Is it going to be business as usual
while the police investigate the murder of the old man? Have you
thought about, maybe, just for a while tending to the barbecue franchises and the soybeans and laying off the crop from Colombia?"

"You know as well as I do that the whole fucking family enterprise
had already gone into the ditch well before we got into a different line
of goods. It's why I had to do it."

"The farms never went bust until after you took over operations,"
Cameron said. "I know that much well enough. And the very idea of a
new line of barbecue restaurants in the Delta. Who but you would have
imagined a niche existed for a new way to sell pork sandwiches. When
father was still spending some time in the Delta, income seemed to keep
flowing. I never heard talk around the dinner table about selling off
acreage and avoiding bankruptcy and can't we get by with fewer cars
and less help and God knows what other kind of middle-class bullshit."

"The real talk didn't take place at supper, Cameron," Franklin said,
reaching for the miniature cotton bale and beginning to pick strands
from one end and then the other, turning the object in his hands as
though searching for something hidden deep within which kept shifting
to the wrong side as he pulled at the fibers covering it. "Oh, no. That was
in Dada's study, with just me and the old bastard there together alone.
All those old shelves full of books nobody ever looked at staring at me
while he picked me apart night after fucking night."

"I imagine he wanted to know where all the goddamn money was
going," Cameron said. "Along with an interest in certain other little
habits and predilections of yours."

"Predilections," Franklin said, "predilections. You should have heard him lecture me when he figured out why I had to go to New Orleans so many times and why when I did, the books began looking so much better."

"He probably thought you were whoring," Cameron said, "like a decent Delta planter, either with colored girls or little boys or rough trade in the Quarter, it wouldn't have made any difference. But, no, not you."

"Look, Cameron, I didn't see you refusing any checks you were sent at Vanderbilt. Does that little Porsche still run all right? Did you finish your degree with outstanding college debts to pay? Will you be looking for a job come September? Maybe in an entry-level position at Union Planters bank? No, no, no, and no."

"So the old man figured you out," Cameron said. "And he had you so damned scared you couldn't handle his disapproval."

"Disapproval you call it. Would that's all it had been. I learned to deal with disapproval before I stopped nursing at the breast. I had to." Franklin seemed to be reaching the center of the cotton bale where what he was seeking had to be located, tearing out large chunks of fiber the size of cherry tomatoes and tossing them at a vase on the desk behind which he was sitting.

"No, not hardly," he said. "That old bastard, my own father, threatened to turn me in to the DEA. He was willing to see me indicted, convicted, and slammed into federal prison. And why, why? Because of the fucking name I've had to bear all my life. He would destroy me because I wasn't up to standard. Wasn't the right gauge of quality. Wasn't the right grade of cotton."

"So, what's the sentence for drug trafficking, Franklin? Eight or ten years, that you buy off half of? Instead of that, you've added first degree murder to it. They'll fry your ass in Tennessee for that. I don't know what they'd do in Mississippi if you'd done it there. Poke out your eyes with a bent coat hanger, probably."

"Look, Cameron," Franklin said, "that business in Memphis is nothing more to the police than just a stray darky needing his medicine and breaking into a big house in Central Gardens to find a VCR to trade. They'll look for a couple of weeks, pick up some habitual criminal and pin it on him. It's nothing to worry about."

"Don't you realize the attention this thing is getting? We're talking about Aires Saxon whose daughter is currently the Maid of Cotton and who's going to be riding the barge down the Mississippi in the coronation ceremony in a week's time. Television, the newspapers, all the media are hot on this. I'm going to be on the Today Show next Tuesday talking to Matt Fucking Lauer. And you think the police are going to set-

tle for the next burglar they pick up? What if they find the right man, asshole?"

"Put your mind at ease. You don't think I contracted this job out to
some Central High school dropout, do you? Really, I'm insulted. Like
any other thing I want done, I employed a professional, the best, experienced and skilled and all that good stuff. The man that fulfilled this con-
tract might be a thousand miles from here, and likely he's never coming
back to the Bluff City, Cameron."

"I don't give a shit," Cameron said. "Until my year as Maid of
Cotton is over, I want you to ground your damn air force and shut down
the coke runs. Go out to the Panola County Country Club and drink
yourself to sleep every night with Missy for a few months. Your wife
needs the company."

"Don't speak ugly about the light of my life, now. I'll think you don't
love your sister-in-law."

Franklin got up from the desk and moved toward the door, gesturing
to Cameron to follow him.

"You do have a point, though, I'll admit. I'm right in the middle of a
thing that'll take two, three, four, more days at most to finish up and then
I will take a vacation, I promise. I certainly wouldn't want to rain on
your parade. Why, Cameron you know I'm so proud of you. The Today
Show! My, my. I sure wish Daddy could have seen it."

18

J.W. had already driven eighty miles, and it wasn't even eight in the morning. The closest motel which wouldn't have charged more than the per diem allowed for lodging by the pencilnecks in the City of Memphis business office was in Oxford, a Quality Court establishment. I'll be damned to hell with my back broke before I'll pay any difference out of my own pocket, he thought to himself as he walked up the steps to the office of Delta Pride BarBQ. And the calculating bastards had even established a sliding scale for police detectives having to find a place to sleep outside metropolitan areas. The formula they had come up with was especially tough on anybody needing to bed down in Mississippi, lower in reimbursement even than in Arkansas, a puzzle to J.W. who like all native Mississippians knew in his heart of hearts that Arkansas was worse in every respect than the Magnolia State. People in Alabama said thank God for Mississippi, and the citizens of Mississippi were eternally grateful for the bottom rung of the fifty United States, the Land of Opportunity, Arkansas. The Natural State.

When J.W. had returned from his stint in Vietnam, something had crystallized for him the first time he drove across the Hernando DeSoto Bridge from Memphis into Arkansas. The feeling that kicked up just under the lower part of his rib cage was identical to the sense of dread he had experienced each time he had gone on a patrol which led across the border from Vietnam into Cambodia. He had almost caught himself looking for piles of skulls just off the exit ramps as he sailed into West Memphis, Arkansas that day in search of discount liquor.

The Day's Inn in Batesville would have been just what he needed, a new bed, cable and an endless supply of ice, but the cheapest room was twelve dollars above what he was allowed to claim, and he had ended up in a motel which filled only when Ole Miss played Mississippi State at home. The decor was so dated that, lying on his back smoking one of his five Pall Malls allotted for the day, J.W. had been able to make out a peace symbol carved in the ceiling above his head with some rough instrument, probably a beer can opener wielded by a fraternity boy from Starkville back when Nixon was taping in the White House.

Maybe he could look in the Batesville *News Trumpet* classifieds, find a room being rented out by the day or week by some widow-woman down on her luck, and save himself from driving all over creation for the rest of his assignment in the Delta. I'll do it this afternoon, J.W. told himself, when I'm eating my lunch at the Cottage Cafe, and he immediately felt a little better.

He walked into the front office of Delta Pride BarBQ with a little spring in his step, surprising the woman seated in front of a computer screen, staring at it as though it were a bullsnake. She jumped when J.W. swung the door open, but her hands remained fixed over the keyboard as if fastened by clamps.

"Goodness gracious," she said, the large silver colored earrings she wore making a jingling sound from the force of the snap she had given her neck when she jerked around at J.W.'s entry. "I didn't see you coming in. You liked to scared me to death."

"I'm sorry," J.W. said, giving the woman the grin that Tyrone Walker called 'white-toothing it,' "I didn't mean to disturb you. I shouldn't have come busting in here without knocking."

"Oh, no," the woman said, finally drawing her hands away from the hold of the keyboard and turning the rest of the way to face J.W. "It's a business office and you don't have to knock. I was just real into what this software's doing wrong. You're supposed to be able to hit F9 and return, and it goes back to the previous menu, but it don't seem to want to this morning."

"Maybe it needs some coffee," J.W. said, still white-toothing it. "Maybe it hadn't woke up all the way yet."

The woman laughed, and as she did so, lifted her chin so the lines in her neck would straighten and diminish under the strain. J.W. smiled, put most of his weight on one leg, and leaned forward toward the desk between them. He was glad he had gone ahead and put on the tie with his short-sleeved blue button-down shirt before he left the Quality Court in Oxford that morning. Diane Edge had told him several times blue shirts picked up the color of his eyes.

"What can I do for you?" the woman said. "After I get this PC its morning cup of caffeine?"

"I was hoping to be able to talk to somebody at Delta Pride about a business proposition today," J.W. said. "At least get started, that is."

"Mr. Bell, he's the processing plant manager, he won't talk to salesmen on a cold call. They got to submit a prospectus first. You know, like a letter."

"Oh, I'm not a salesman. I'm a buyer, and I don't want to talk to just the manager. I'd like to arrange to see the CEO, Mr. Saxon, if that'd be possible."

"Mr. Saxon doesn't come in every day. Sometimes just once a week. But I know Mr. Bell's here. His car's out yonder in the lot. But I don't know if he'd be able to see you on a short notice like this, you understand."

"I do understand. Maybe you could just let him know, and Mr. Saxon, too, if you could, that I'd like to come back this afternoon, if their schedules would allow it. See, I'm making a preliminary tour of meat processing operations in the Delta on behalf of a concern in Chicago. I work out of the Jackson, Tennessee office. Not Mississippi, now. Tennessee."

J.W. paused, white toothed it, and laughed, leaning further toward the desk.

"Remember that old Johnny Cash song? Goes something like we got married in a fever, hotter than a pepper sprout, been talking about Jackson, ever since the fire went out."

"I remember," the woman said. "Was that about Jackson, Tennessee? I always thought it was Mississippi."

"No, ma'am. It was Tennessee. I know the old boy that wrote that. And he's a cutter."

"I bet he is, writing something that funny."

"Anyway," J.W. said. "We are onto a project which could involve canning barbecue meat for all the upper Midwestern cities. You know, urban consumers of pork, and we're even thinking about an Asian outreach. What we want is a steady, reliable supplier, and I'm the point man on this."

"Well, I will sure tell Mr. Bell and ask him to let Mr. Saxon know. Have you got a business card?"

"No, I don't and the reason why really frosts me. Don't get me started. U.S. Air has lost two pieces of my luggage in Memphis, and they haven't found them yet and until they do, I'm working at a disadvantage. If you'd just write down my name, William Johnston, that's with a T, buyer for General Foods of Chicago, I'd really appreciate it."

"I could do that, all right."

"I've got an appointment with an operation about forty miles from here, I'd rather not say the name right now, and I'll swing back by here about two or so this afternoon, tell them, please."

"Sure thing. Maybe this PC will be all waked up by then."

"Why don't you promise it a plateful of barbecue if it'll start doing right?"

Leave them laughing, J.W. said to himself as he left the building for the parking lot. That business card thing was dumb. I sure as hell hope she don't see me drive off in the Buick. She'll think General Foods of Chicago is fixing to go belly-up and can't afford to buy the small sandwich platter, much less start canning pulled barbecue.

As soon as he got in the car and headed for Batesville, J.W. pulled his striped tie off and threw it into the back seat, making a mental note to put it back on before he rolled into the Delta Pride parking lot again in the afternoon. He didn't expect to learn anything there even if Franklin Saxon was around and agreed to see him, but at least he'd be able to report officially to Major Dalbey and the filing cabinet that he'd touched that base, too. He knew Saxon wouldn't recognize him. All he'd seen out there in the cemetery was a big black dude licensed to carry a gun and allowed to ask him questions. If he could add a conversation with Saxon to what he'd already done at the Saxon plantation, then talk to Ray Hubley, the pilot in the cropdusting operation that the bossman at Saxon's Hundred hadn't wanted him to know about for some reason, he'd be able to say he'd done all he could to follow up the far-flung business connections of the Saxon family and their dead Daddy. Maybe he'd even be able to turn something up worth thinking about.

One more thing did need attention, though, before he'd be able to look up Punk Kinkaid, borrow some fishing gear and float around on Sardis Lake for a couple of days, J.W. considered as he drove toward the Panola County seat and the Cottage Cafe just off the courthouse square. The Murphy brothers, the squirrel-headed one named Vance in particular, needed to be reasoned with. He'd make this matter unofficial, of course, J.W. told himself. He was nothing but a former resident of the county, interested in seeing that life in that part of the Delta went on in a calm and peaceful way. He would explain that to the newcomer Murphy, speaking as a representative of the old settler families, and he would do that in a language the Murphys could understand right down to the bone.

It would also be good to know just where a hired hand on the Saxon plantation was able to find enough coke to pay people to do things for him. If he asked Vance Murphy in just the right kind of way, he'd probably be glad to share all he knew about dope sources and fast-talking fellows from the East who liked to drive around to barbecue shacks and pick up black girls to give high-grade coke to. Old Vance was not likely to be shut-mouth at all, once things were explained to him in a way he could appreciate.

J.W. walked into the Cottage Cafe a little before noon, five or ten minutes ahead of the rush, which made him happy, and when he saw on the bulletin board listing the specials a line proclaiming that today the Panola County Rotary Club met in the private dining room of the Cottage, he was overjoyed at being early. The last thing he wanted to do was compete for a waitress with forty or fifty businessmen ragging each other about golf swings and sucking up to the man in the room with the most money.

He had already started on his plate of chicken fried steak, fried okra, field peas and cornbread when the first Rotarian bounded through the front door, head swinging around as though on a swivel as he looked for somebody that outranked him to talk to. His gaze fixed on his lunch as steadily as he could keep it, J.W. nevertheless could tell the first man in was somebody who knew him.

"I can't believe it," a voice announced to all in earshot. "Somebody tell me I'm dreaming. Look who's sitting there eating cornbread and beans. It's the Eagle himself, just as big as life."

J.W. took a sip from his glass of iced tea and looked up. "Hey, Ronnie," he said. "How's it going?"

"Ragsdale," Ronnie Street said, "put it there, partner, and move over and let me join you. I got a few minutes before I got to go in the back yonder and get the program started. How the hell are you doing, boy, and why don't we never get to see you down here no more? You done forgot where you live?"

"Oh, I know where I live all right," J.W. said, letting Ronnie Street try to crush his hand in a Rotarian shake. "In Midtown Memphis in a rent house."

"God, it's been a while, Eagle. Remember that time we kicked Oxford High's ass?"

Ronnie Street had been the indirect reason J.W. Ragsdale had been named All-State Linebacker and got to play in Crump Stadium in the Mississippi/Tennessee All-State High School game his senior year at Batesville. Ronnie had played such a timid outside linebacker that J.W. had to range all over Ronnie's territory in addition to his own, and in the process made enough tackles to get noticed. At least, it had earned him an early introduction to Tyrone Walker, first on the other side of the scrimmage line and now on the other side of the desk in the Midtown Station.

"Eagle, I'd love to talk to you all day, but I got to introduce the speakers at Rotary. I'm the second vice president this year. Tell you what. I know you're a sporting man, and something's going on tonight you'd surely love to see."

Ronnie lowered his voice and looked around the dining room, hoping to see somebody noticing that he'd dropped his voice and had a secret to tell. Nobody looked up or seemed to take an interest, and Ronnie had to go on with his conversation without an outside audience. J.W. buttered his second slice of cornbread and kept his head down.

"Remember that bunch of Huberts, J.W., from back down in yonder in the river bottoms?"

"I don't know if I do," J.W. said. "You mean Wilmer?"

"Yeah, that was one of them. Don't you remember how country them kids were? Always bringing in cut-off hawk's feet and raccoon dicks to school and showing them around. Brought their lunch to school in a syrup bucket. All of them quit school by the eighth grade, learned what they needed to know by the time they was twelve years old."

"That's better than most of us done in the Batesville schools," J.W. said.

"You got that right. Anyway, that middle Hubert, Leonard Ray, has come back to Panola County and he's built himself up the goddamndest chicken-fighting operation you ever saw. Breeding pens, holding pens, a country walk, a big old cockpit, he's got it all out there where that bunch of riverrats grew up. And there's a big meet tonight at his place. Cockers from four states gonna be matching them up."

"I be damned," J.W. said, cutting the remainder of the chicken fried steak on his plate into two last bites. "I wouldn't of thought that in Panola County. What time they start?"

"First pitting's around ten o'clock, and they got a lot of them on the schedule. They'll be all night. I figured you might want to be at it. I hope to see you out there, Eagle."

Ronnie Street caught the eye of an entering Rotarian about then and stood up from the table.

"I'd like to sit here and talk over old times with you, Eagle, but I got this meeting to get started. Maybe tonight."

"Yeah, go on to your duties, Ronnie," J.W. said. "It's the burden of office, I reckon. Thanks for the tip."

As he paid his check at the cash register, J.W. wondered why Ronnie Street would be so excited about chicken fighting. Maybe it was just an expanded chance to network for the hard-working Rotarian, he considered, or maybe it had got to the point in Panola County where even the respectable people wanted a little blood in their lives. As Tyrone Walker often remarked at homicide scenes in Memphis, you never can tell where a man's hot button is until you hit it.

An hour and a half later, tie knotted firmly back in place and a leatherette notebook purchased at the Wal-Mart in Batesville in hand, J.W. walked again through the front door of Delta Pride BarBQ. William Johnston, he said to himself, of General Foods of Chicago, out of the Jackson, Tennessee office. Please don't hold that '78 Buick in the parking lot against this hardworking pork buyer.

The receptionist was glad to see him, smiling at J.W. as he walked in and beginning to talk before the door closed behind him.

"Mr. Johnston," she said, "you hit it just right today. Mr. Bell said he'd be able to see you and show you around the plant, and I'm also expecting Mr. Saxon to come by in a few minutes. He called right after you left this morning, and I told him about you wanting to see him."

"Why, thank you. It's better to be lucky than good, like they always say, ain't it?"

"I never won anything in my life," the woman said. "Now, my sister, she's the lucky one in the family. She won a week at Sea Pines Resort for her and her husband out of a drawing last year. That's in Florida, down by Pensacola, Sea Pines is."

"That's the whitest sand down yonder," J.W. said. "Put your eyes out when the sun's up, I declare. Is Mr. Bell going to come on in here?"

"No, I'm gonna take you back to the line. He'll be waiting."

The woman stood up, turned a key in the desk drawer, and picked up a large multicolored purse from the floor.

"I ain't gonna leave my handbag here," she said. "You can't never tell who's gonna walk in with sticky fingers, even out here in the country."

"They'll sure take what ain't red hot or nailed down, that's a fact," J.W. said and followed her out of the building across a graveled lot toward a huge gray structure set back from the road about two hundred yards. A row of windows was cut into the wall of the building well above head height, and doors wide enough to let trucks enter were hung onto metal rollers on the near end. To the right of the processing plant were manmade ponds lined with concrete walls set with four-inch pipes. The sound of water gushing from these was fully audible, and as J.W. and the receptionist got nearer, he could see large exhaust grates at the end of each pond covered with wire mesh.

"Y'all do your butchering here? I don't see any sign of pens. Or smell any, neither."

"No, and I'm glad of that. We buy the carcasses from suppliers all over the state. Even some from Louisiana, and we're about to start getting shipments from all the way in South America. That's still a secret, though. It's not announced yet. And then we do just the meat processing here at Delta Pride."

"South America," J.W. said. "My goodness. How many of these tanks you got?"

"It's four. And they're all just full of the clearest water. It's our own artesian wells. For all the processing, you understand. But you know what?"

The woman stopped and turned to face J.W., her purse swinging smartly from its leather strap.

"What's that?"

"Mr. Saxon, he just hates meat. He won't eat it. He says he won't consume any food that comes from a creature with a face. Idn't that funny? Him being a vegetarian."

"It sure is. Nothing with a face, huh?" J.W. said. "Will he drink milk or eat eggs? 'Cause I heard of some that won't."

"He'll do that. It's a natural thing. Cows give more milk than a calf can drink, and chickens lay more eggs than we need biddies. Eggs don't have faces, neither. Don't you tell nobody I told you that, now, about Mister Saxon and meat. It might be bad for business."

"Oh, I won't," J.W. said, leaning toward the woman in a conspiratorial attitude. "Long as you won't tell I ain't never got my fill of barbecued pork yet."

"I won't, I won't," the receptionist said.

As J.W. followed the woman across a grassy area toward the main building of Delta Pride operations, he asked himself why there weren't enough hogs in Mississippi to supply a pork processing plant. Why would a man have to have meat shipped in from Louisiana and South America all the way to the north part of the state? It didn't seem to make sense financially, even to someone like himself, a man who'd had to leave the Delta because of a lack of business success. Who am I to judge a business decision, he thought. But still, probably, J.W. decided as he neared the building, I ought to drive by the Saxon plantation after dark and see if I can spot any transport licensed out of state. Put that in the report, and see how it shakes down. If I see anything.

The receptionist delivered J.W. to Mr. Bell just inside the gray building where he was standing on a raised metal platform overlooking the work area beneath him. When they walked up, he had his back turned staring out over the long conveyor belt which began at the far end of the building and snaked its way the full distance down it. A row of black women lined each side of the moving belt, dressed in yellow plastic overalls and wearing hairnets of a matching color. J.W. could see light from the rows of window flashing off the knives the women used as they worked.

"They came in that end," Bell said over his shoulder and pointed to the far reaches of the building, "laying up on that belt. Time they get to this end, my girls is stripped ninety percent of the meat off them shoulders and about all you're looking at is bone. It'll take four point two minutes for forty pork shoulders to make that trip down the belt."

"That's a nice operation," J.W. said, extending his hand to Mr. Bell. "I never seen one quieter than this."

"We don't use mechanical strippers, and we don't let the girls talk, Mr. Johnston," Bell said. "None of that jabbering, none of that singing, no rap music on the loud speakers. If a man was to hold his breath and listen, all he'd hear is knife blades clicking against the belt and meat hit-

ting the bucket." Bell raised his right hand up, as though about to conduct an orchestra in a pit. "Listen," he said.

He was right. The only sound other than the whir of the gears pulling
the conveyor belt was that of cutting tools doing their assigned duty and
the soft splat of cooked pork slapping into large white plastic containers
stationed every few feet along the line. Now and then the whump of a
larger than usual chunk would punctuate the other sounds of work.

"That's a pretty thing," J.W. said, shaking his head in exaggerated
admiration for the benefit of Mr. Bell. "It's not often you see something
like that in America anymore."

"I know it," Bell said, stepping back and peering intently into J.W.'s
face. "People doing their job and keeping their goddamned mouths shut.
And you know why it works? You understand what we doing at Delta
Pride BarBQ to keep this operation moving so efficient?"

"I'll be proud if you'd tell me," J.W. said, putting as much flat sin-
cerity into his voice as he could muster. "I'd surely love to know what's
keeping them women's heads down and their eyes on their work."

"The discipline," Bell said in a measured tone, "of speed." He
paused and looked out again over the scene beneath the platform. "See,
we keep that conveyor moving about a foot per second past comfortable,
if you get what I mean. One of them girls looks up, gets to thinking
about the boyfriend or the kids or some shit like that, and lets her attention wander, she ain't gonna catch up easy. And we pay them by the
bone. You see them white cans, all of them's marked with a number
belongs to one of the girls. Hell, I've seen two and three of them women
lock up and fight over a single shoulder bone that missed hitting where
it ought to. Just got down and rolled back and forth in the floor, clawing
and scratching, scrambling for that marker." Bell paused for a spell to
contemplate the scene before them and then spoke again. "And then we
ship that meat to the franchises and they slap some sauce on it and sell
a bunch of sandwiches. We hope."

"Thanks for telling me," J.W. said, "about how y'all do it. I bet that
was a sight to see, them women fighting over the bones. That's what we
used to call in the arm service responding to an initiative."

"You got it, Mr. Johnston," Bell said. "Let's go see if Mr. Saxon's
ready to talk to you about selling some prepared pork."

What I'd really like to see, J.W. thought to himself as he and Bell
climbed down the metal stairs to the floor level and headed for another
part of the building, is Mr. Bell starting at the far end of the line, tied
down to the conveyor belt and every woman along the way working
with a fresh-sharpened knife while they listen to rap music blasting
through the loudspeakers. You'd see some efficiency and speed then,
Buddy Ro, I flat guarantee you.

Franklin Saxon was waiting in a room that looked to be the nerve center of the Delta Pride operation. File cabinets, a long table covered with computer print-outs, and a bank of electronic machines filled most of the space. J.W. looked closely at Franklin, a lot nearer to him than he had been in the cemetery on burying day for Aires. He could see signs in Franklin's face that he'd been fathered by Aires Saxon, all right, particularly about the eyes and nose, but the copy machine seemed to have slipped when it got to the mouth and chin. The old man's lips, as J.W. remembered them, had been a thin line straight across the face, the kind of mouth you see on John Wayne in a picture when he's getting ready to wipe out a squad of Japanese soldiers or a tribe of renegade Indians. Stern, determined, filled with resolve, and stone crazy.

The artist who'd slapped on the lower half of Franklin Saxon's face had been a little less careful, a bit more hurried at the job, however, and had finished the younger man with a mouth that looked as if it were about to slide away from resolve into sneer. The lower lip was fuller than it should be on a man Franklin's age, more pronounced and a bit puffy. If it had been a portrait he was looking at, J.W. thought, he would have suspected the photographer of having performed some darkroom trickery involving an air brush, spirit gum and petroleum jelly. All in all, Franklin Saxon looked to J.W. as though he needed to get more protein into his system than his vegetarian diet allowed.

Saxon rose and came toward J.W., his arm extended. He was wearing a safari jacket, a blue denim shirt and khaki trousers, all right out of the Banana Republic Shop in Germantown, Tennessee.

"Franklin Saxon," the CEO of Delta Pride BarBQ announced himself. "How can we help you this afternoon, sir?"

I don't think this fucking tie's gonna do it, J.W. said to himself as he matched grips with Saxon, much less this short sleeved blue shirt all frayed at the neck. Nothing to do but fling on in and try, though. Throw up a barrage of bullshit and see if anything sticks.

"Mr. Saxon," J.W. said, fixing his gaze on a red vein in the left eye of the man facing him. "Thanks for seeing me on such short notice. I know you're a busy man and that this is a bad time for you. I just wanted to touch base with you on a possible business relationship between your operation and ours. Just real preliminary. We could talk more, later on, if we see any reason to."

"Maybe so, Mr. Johnston," Franklin Saxon said. "Like you say, we can't do much today."

"No, no," J.W. agreed. "I know what a tough thing it is to lose your Daddy, especially the way you have, and I wouldn't be bothering you at all now except I'm operating on a real tight time-line and didn't want to pass up the chance to talk to you folks at Delta Pride."

"I appreciate what you're saying. But like they say, life does go on. It has to."

"Yessir, that's the only way you can look at it. Are the police about to find out who did it?"

"If you read the Memphis newspaper, Mr. Johnston, you know as much as I do about it. I don't know what to believe anymore. I guess it's just another case of what's happening in all the cities in this country. A man's not safe in his home these days, much less a woman or a child."

"They say it was a break-in, huh? Somebody off the street?"

"It looks that way. I guess. That's all it could have been, unless my father shot himself and then hid the pistol."

"Savages," Bell spoke up. "You wouldn't catch me living in among a bunch of them porch-monkeys on a bet."

"You'll have to excuse my manager, Mr. Johnston," Saxon said. "He spends most of his working days trying to get a little productivity out of his people, and it leaves him a tad impatient with the African race at times."

"From what I see," J.W. said, white-toothing the other two men, "he does a hell of a good job of it, too. I never seen a slicker line operation in a pork processing plant, and I have seen a many of them."

"Well," said Saxon. "We're proud of what we do here, and I'll tell you that Jenkins Bell is a large part of our success story at Delta Pride."

J.W. smiled at the red vein in the CEO's left eye and nodded enthusiastically, thinking that from where Mr. Bell was standing it probably looked like if it wasn't for the good work that black folks did in cutting meat off of bones, there wouldn't be a reason for the whole race to reside another pay day in the Mississippi Delta. Can't live with them, and can't live without them, he bet Jenkins Bell and Franklin Saxon would say.

"Like I said," J.W. announced, "I won't take up any more of your time today. I'm staying in Oxford for the next day or two before I have to get back to the office, and I'll give you a call with your permission, Mr. Saxon, and see if you'd like to talk with me in more detail later."

"You do that," Saxon said. "I'm always interested in talking about the meat business with somebody from General Foods."

After J.W. left the building, Saxon moved to the window to watch him walk across the parking lot to his car in the midday heat.

Bell stood near his boss, peering over his shoulder to see what was drawing his attention. "He's driving a rust bucket, ain't he?" he said.

"General Foods of Chicago, huh?" Saxon said. "Shit. I wish he was what he says he is. Maybe we could sell some damn pork to some people. Somebody needs to buy some of this meat."

"I don't believe he's ever bought more than a plateful of barbecue at one time. He didn't know what to ask me when I showed him the line," Bell offered. "He just grinned and nodded while I was talking the whole time."

"He knows way yonder too much about some things, though," Saxon said, turning toward the telephone on the corner of the worktable. "Why's a damn buyer asking me about my personal life? You know, I believe Mr. Johnston, or whatever his name is, is driving an unsafe vehicle. A car like that heap of junk is just an accident waiting to happen."

"You don't believe he's union, do you, Mister Saxon? Trying to organize them girls on the line?"

"I don't know what he is," Franklin said. " But I know I don't want him around asking questions and talking to my people."

"Wonder if he drives safe?"

"I can tell, Jenkins," Franklin Saxon said, punching a set of numbers into the telephone, "by just looking at him, that that fellow is not safety-minded."

19

The house to which the classified advertisement in the Batesville *News Trumpet* sent J.W. was on a side street two blocks north of the Courthouse Square. The street was named Bamberg, and it was not one J.W. could remember from his days of steady driving in his youth. He would have sworn that he had memorized every street sign in Batesville and half of those in Oxford from his seat behind the wheel all those dead hours of midnight cruising he did between his fourteenth and eighteenth years, but this collection of small bungalows had not been on his route.

The woman who answered his first knock on the door showed J.W. the room listed in the newspaper and asked if he'd be wanting the space for more than a week.

"No, Ma'am," J.W. said, looking at the single bed made up with a chenille spread and a pillow enclosed by embroidery. "I'm just here for two, maybe three days, and all I need is a place to sleep for a couple of nights."

"I don't like to rent for less than a week at the time," the woman said, adjusting her glasses and peering sharply at J.W.'s face, "but I guess I could help you out this once."

They agreed on a prorated price, eighteen dollars for two days, and J.W. waited until the woman, a Mrs. Willie Vee Segrest, left the room before he tried out the bed. It wasn't too bad, a little springy for his taste, and J.W. knew if he went to sleep on top of the bedspread he would wake up with chenille patterns all over his face that would take a half hour to fade, given his complexion, but all in all, he considered the accommodation a great advance over the motel prices in town.

He rose from the bed, stripped off the chenille spread down to a flowery sheet, hit the High button on the window air conditioner, and drifted off to sleep in less than five minutes, unbothered by the yipping of a small dog which came from somewhere deep in Mrs. Segrest's house.

When he woke, the shadows were long on the lawn outside the windows, and J.W. noticed that the setting on the air conditioner was changed from High to Low. It had come to a pretty pass when an old woman could come into a room where he was sleeping, reduce the BTU level, and not come close to rousing him. Good thing he wasn't napping in Midtown Memphis. If the same thing had happened there, he'd likely be stripped buck naked by now with his throat cut. Maybe she was wearing tennis shoes, though, and knew how to sneak around without making any noise. Probably a B and E man in Memphis would have made a little racket and waked him up, knocked over a beer can or a stack of newspapers or something and roused him. Maybe he just slept harder in Panola County, J.W. told himself, had less reason to monitor the environment when he was unconscious. Still, though, shit.

By the time he'd taken a shower in the bathroom down the hall, reading a little handwritten sign pinned to the curtain before he'd turned the water on which said "Make Like This Is Your Own Home," J.W. was ready for a beer or three. He told Mrs. Segrest that he'd likely be back late and would use the key she reluctantly gave him to let himself in. He didn't tell her he'd more than likely be getting back at three in the morning drunk from a river-bottom chicken fight. J.W. figured Mrs. Willie Vee Segrest didn't need to know that.

Watching the cracked taillight on the right side of the Buick a couple of hundred yards ahead, Vance Murphy spoke into the C.B. microphone he held close to his mouth. A washed-out spot in the road caused the pickup to lurch suddenly and almost cost him a busted lip.

"Goddamn," Vance said into the instrument. "I guess Leonard Ray Hubert ain't never had this pig trail graded."

"What's that, Bar Bell?" a voice said through the speaker. "Come back."

"Nothing. Just ten miles of bad road. But everything's jake, otherwise."

"Hard to read you, Bar Bell," the voice said in the midst of a burst of static. "Is your man still in sight?"

"Relax on that," Vance said. "I'm on him like ugly on a ape. And I know right where he's going. We gonna dance a little bit, directly here, once we get the music started."

"Say you found him at a dance? In the bottoms? Whereabouts?"

"I'm gonna cut this radio off. You ain't reading me. See can you copy this. Tell the man the meat's in the pan, and the pork is fixing to fry."

"Ten-four, Bar Bell. Pork's frying. This here's Sweet'n Low, signing off."

Vance hung up the microphone and switched the radio off. Damn these airwaves. His brother Pick wasn't smart, but everybody knew that and made allowances and everything went on smooth enough most of the time. You give him a machine to work with, though, particularly one he could talk into like they did on television and the boy lost all touch with the real world. It don't make no difference, though, this time, Vance told himself, no matter how bad Pick might fuck up communications with the bossman back in the big house. I am honed in on that so-called pork buyer just like I was driving one of them Gulf War smart bombs.

Vance was feeling a lot better now than when the evening had begun. He had gone a little after seven o'clock to the spot where an asshole from outside of Panola County would look to go for a drink, the bar of the Holiday Inn up on the cut-off to I-55. But this Johnston hadn't been there, though Vance had waited for over an hour for the piece-of-shit Buick to show up in the parking lot. Vance drove to the Day's Inn, through Batesville three or four times, back up the highway toward Oxford, south ten or twelve miles on the interstate, trying out all the while to steel himself to call in on the radio that he couldn't find the man he'd been told to locate.

He could hear the message that Pick would relay to him from Franklin Saxon, and it was one that made his guts crawl to think about. It was the damndest thing that a weak piss-ant of a physical specimen like Saxon could make him afraid, but there it was, he did. And he did it through words, and the words showed Vance just how crazy the scared fucker was. A man who was as much of a coward as Franklin Saxon was always balanced on the edge of being terminally dangerous. He wouldn't hurt you himself, but he could and would make enormous hurt come down on you anytime he got scared himself. He would make you pay for it.

So when Vance Murphy pulled back into the Holiday Inn lot just before ten o'clock and saw the blue Buick parked next to the door of the bar, he had felt moved by a huge surge of relief. He had parked the pickup at the other end of the lot, between a new Ford van and a Honda Accord, and in about ten minutes the man with the Shelby County, Tennessee tags had come out of the building and got into his car.

Vance watched the taillights come on after the engine cranked and noted with pleasure that the right one was cracked, letting a thin sliver of white light leak through the red. He'd be as easy to track as a three-legged dog in a muddy yard.

Mr. Busted Taillight had started out like he wasn't going anywhere in particular, stopping at a J.R., Jr. on the edge of town and coming out with a paper sack that looked like it contained a sixpack, wandering up and down several streets in Batesville and slowing down to a crawl in front of two or three houses as though he was studying them. He had driven by the old high school, now the Batesville Middle School, pulled up in the parking lot of the football stadium and sat long enough to drink a beer. Vance knew that was what the so-called Mr. Johnston did because an empty can had been thrown out of the car window after five or ten minutes, and the '78 Buick cranked and rolled out on Bulldog Drive again.

After a few more minutes of what looked to Vance Murphy like aimless, bullshit cruising, the driver of the Buick accelerated to the thirty mile speed limit allowed in-town drivers in Batesville and headed west on Highway 6 at a pretty good clip. It was then that Vance turned on the CB radio and began his conversation with Pick out on the Saxon farm, and a little later he found himself tiptoeing his new Chevrolet pickup over and around mudholes and washouts two hundred yards behind the cracked taillight ahead as the two vehicles proceeded deeper into the river bottom of the Mississippi.

At the same time the brakelights up ahead came on and off Vance noticed at least two sets of headlights in his rearview mirror, and he gave the Chevy a little more gas. Mr. Pork Buyer, Mr. Big Shot from General Foods, would be pulling up into Leonard Ray Hubert's place in a minute or two, and Vance intended to be right behind him on their way to the chicken fights. Maybe if he gigged it a little, he could be at Hubert's and have business taken care of before the next fucker drove up into the lot with his high beams on.

But when Vance pulled his pickup between two water oaks and looked at the collection of cars and trucks parked randomly in the cleared-out area between a stand of trees and a barn newly constructed of unplaned lumber and corrugated metal, he could see no sign of Mr. William Johnston. The '78 Buick was there all right, at the end of an unevenly parked row of vehicles, but its lights were off, and there was nobody standing near it. Maybe Mr. Busted Taillight is just dying to see roosters fight and has run on into the house afraid he'll miss something. Maybe he had to go off in the woods to wee wee, Vance told himself. Wonder if he has to hike up his dress and squat down to do it?

Murphy was just opening his mouth to laugh at what he'd thought to himself when he felt something touch him on the left side of his head in the short hairs just behind the ear. He leaned forward a little, instinctively, to get away from the sensation, but it came right with him, insistent and with considerably more pressure, and by the time Vance was able to begin to know what it was and to start to move his right hand toward the seat beside him, the cold metal circle had changed its position and was now pushing against and into his left nostril.

"Nuh uh, Squirrel Head, just leave it alone," the pork buyer said in a voice that sounded very different from the way it did back at Saxon's

Hundred only a couple of days ago. He didn't sound like he wanted a job cropdusting or a meat processing business deal or for somebody to talk to him. It didn't sound like he wanted anything.

"What you do, see, is you cut your lights, kill the engine, and step out of the truck. And don't you get no boogers on the muzzle of this nine millimeter."

"Oh," said Vance, "Oh," doing as he was told and feeling everything in his chest and belly beginning to liquefy and surge as though all his insides were trying to gather to one point and huddle into a clot.

"Lord," he said to the man standing in the darkness. "Oh, God, please don't kill me. I ain't right with Jesus yet. I just kept putting it off."

"Ain't that always the way? You go along and go along, acting like nothing's going to change, and everything's going to be the way it is right now and forever. And then it comes like a thief in the night."

"Please," said Vance, collapsing to his knees in the mud of Leonard Ray Hubert's parking area as though someone had suddenly taken a boning knife to his hamstrings. "Please give me another chance, sir. I promise I'll straighten right up. I will, I will."

"Ask and it shall be given," J.W. Ragsdale said. "Seek and ye shall find." He gestured with the handgun toward the stand of trees beyond the line of cars and pickups. "Come on over here in the bushes, Squirrel Head. I may not shoot you after all. I may just want to question you about your taste for barbecue ribs and warn you against your unwise choice of road companions. Confession's good for the soul."

"Barbecue?" Vance said, scrambling to his feet and moving out of the light toward the trees.

"Yeah, you like your ribs wet or dry?"

"Dry," Vance said. "Dry, I reckon."

"No, not dry," J.W. said. "That ain't the right way to fix ribs. Ain't fit to eat."

"Wet, then," Vance said, "I really like them wet. That's what I meant to say."

"That's the time, Squirrel Head," J.W. said, tapping Vance on the back of his skull with the gun butt hard enough to cause a burst of white light to flare up before Vance's eyes and fade slowly like fireworks over the river. "We got something in common. I feel closer to you already. Now. You like your sauce sweet or sour?"

"Sweet?"

"Nuh uh. Sour. Something else now. Who were you riding around in that big old Oldsmobile the other night out to Big Daddy's Dreamland?"

"Big Daddy's? I forget."

"Think now, you can remember, if you put your mind to it," J.W. said, pushing the barrel of the handgun up against the back of Vance's head just where the hairline started. "Bear down on it. Call up that black girl. Cherene Odom. The one y'all gave a ride to that ended up putting her in the hospital."

"Speed," Vance said. "Barry Speed he said his name was. I didn't have nothing to do with that business. I never touched her."

"That's coming along. See I told you," J.W. said. "I bet you can tell me a whole lot more if you squeeze your eyes shut and hold your mouth just right."

"Oh," said Vance, dropping to his knees right on top of a cluster of sawvines which bit cruelly into his flesh but for some reason caused him no pain. "He's from Baltimore, I believe he said, doing some business with Mister Saxon."

"What kind of business?"

Let him kill me now, Vance heard a voice speaking deep inside his head, let him kill me now so it'll be easier. "I don't know," he said. "I just drive folks around. They don't never tell me nothing except where to go to."

"I saw a truck tonight," J.W. said, "out to the Saxon plantation, way back close to the out buildings."

"Yessir."

"Truck had Louisiana tags. Said a name on the side of it, first part of it was K. Delcambre. What's it doing way up here in the Delta?"

"Delivering meat?" Vance said. "Pork shoulders, I reckon."

"Why wasn't it taking them over to the Delta Pride processing plant, then?" J.W. said, moving the barrel of the handgun lazily back and forth across the nape of Vance Murphy's neck. "That don't make sense, does it, to take them to the plantation? Pork shoulders, now, does it?"

"I don't know nothing about it," Vance said, believing truly, as the face of Franklin Saxon rose up in his mind like stone, that he actually did not. "I'm sick," he said. "I believe I'm having a stroke."

"Well," J.W. said as Vance collapsed before him, full-face into the mud and sawvines of the Mississippi River bottom. "You got to do that on your own time. We got to talk about manners now. The way you're supposed to treat people when you're visiting in their home, you understand. How to conduct yourself, see, when you're a guest."

A little after three o'clock in the morning, two of the last stragglers from the competitions in Leonard Ray Hubert's cockpit stood looking into the bed of a dark blue, late-model Chevrolet pickup. The vehicle was parked at the edge of the lot, its nose run halfway up into a tangle of saw briars.

"Is he drunk?" one of the men said. "Just too much busthead whiskey a working on him?"

"I don't doubt he's been drinking all right," the other man said, moving nearer the truck to get a better view in the light reflected from a departing car. "Hell, we been at a cockfight, ain't we, and it's after dark. What puzzles me, though, is the way he looks."

"Boogered up a little, ain't he?"

"I tell you what it looks like to me. It appears to me he's been a running through a briar thicket in the dark, and he ain't been a holding his arms up in front of his face."

"Worse than that," said the first man. "He done run into a couple of water oaks, too, when he was looking off."

"Didn't stop him from getting up and taking another run at it, though, did it? You got to give him credit. This fellow was bound and determined to run through whatever was ahead of him."

"He acted like it was something after him," the other man said. "Appears to me he didn't want to be caught, neither."

"He'll sleep right there 'til morning, I'll lay you odds. He's done settled in."

"I got to get on to the house. I guess he'll be all right in that truckbed."

"He will if it don't come a gully-washer and fill that Chevy bed up and drown him."

"Way he's going to feel in the morning, drowning would probably be a relief to him."

"Wooee," said the other man, heading toward his car. "Didn't Little Red tear up that Louisiana Blacktop tonight? I never seen so many feathers fly."

"Them wasn't feathers. That was my dollar bills I had bet that that rooster was tearing all to pieces."

After the two men got into their cars and left, the sky in the west grumbled a little with thunder, and a lightning bolt or two struck somewhere across the river deep in Arkansas, but not a drop of rain fell all night in the Mississippi Delta bottom.

20

J.W. Ragsdale woke up a little after six in a single bed in a strange room, wondering for a few seconds where he was. It wasn't until his eyes focused on an embroidered slogan on the wall above a chest of drawers that he remembered Mrs. Willie Vee Segrest and the room's location. "I need Thee every hour," the framed slogan proclaimed in the midst of a burst of colored thread knotted into flowers and curliques.

Ain't that the unwashed truth, J.W. said to himself as he rose from his bed to prepare to seek out a head cropdusting pilot named Ray Hubley. Get that done this morning, and that's the last item on my checklist before I get to fish for a half a day on Sardis Lake and then head myself back to Memphis.

Then, J.W. thought as he cracked the door open and peered down Mrs. Segrest's hall to see if the bathroom door was open, then I got to sit my ass down at the desk and write up that report for Major Dalbey, tell him what's going on down in the Delta and hope that old Aires Saxon was just blowed away by an ordinary citizen of Memphis plying his trade and that's the end of it.

What I'd like to find out, he went on to himself sternly as he looked into the mirror over the bathroom sink, when I get back to Midtown is that the brother that offed Old Man Saxon has sung his song or that somebody has dialed him for dollars and that that package is wrapped up ready for sending. Then I could help Tyrone Walker run down some Bones Family shooters for the thing on Baby Street, and we could all go to Tom Lee Park to the International Barbecue Festival and get bad drunk and see can we scare up something strange.

But it's not going to be like that, he told himself, and I know it. It would be a thing to behold and wonder at, if it ended up being easy just one single time. A man would think that once in a while things would be what they looked like and he would be able to sit in a boat for a day and not have to be just figuring away, trying to understand what had gone on and what was fixing to go on next.

Might as well face it, something here's bad crossways, and even Major Dalbey, the most eager of men to see a case filed away and done with, is going to have to agree.

Before he went all to pieces last night out there in the river bottom, the squirrel-headed Murphy brother had coughed up enough to make part of a puzzle, and the side trip J.W. had made to the Saxon plantation after dark had added another piece of information. Murphy hadn't acted on his own. He wasn't the type to think far enough ahead to take action just because he had an immediate hatred for a man he'd just met. Franklin Saxon had been behind that assignment.

Why had he was the question, and part of the answer to that would come from beginning to learn something about Mister Barry Speed of Baltimore. Whoever he was, he hadn't been driving around in the Mississippi Delta just to mess up young black girls and feed them coke. He could do that back home with a lot less trouble and more variety. He needed following up on, and so did that truck.

The vehicle at the Saxon plantation had a name on its side and a license number, and once he got back to Memphis, J.W. knew he could enlist the aid of Diane Edge in getting further down that road. She hadn't been gone from her job as assistant prosecutor for the DEA so long she wouldn't be able to reach out to somebody there who could feed information into data banks and get stuff spit back at them in a relative hurry. Did whoever owned the truck or licensed it have a history?

Still, it was hard to believe that Franklin Saxon of the Delta Saxons would be mixed up with people like Barry Speed, who at the least was toting coke around the back roads of Panola County with Vance Murphy as an escort. And what was in the truck from Louisiana, the one with Delcambre painted on its side above a slogan proclaiming "that means fresh, y'all?" Maybe it was just pork carcasses. Maybe Speed was just a free-lance asshole, and Vance was no more than the garden variety peckerwood you'd find all over Mississippi and every damn where else around. Maybe.

The thing to do, J.W. told himself, staring into Mrs. Segrest's bathroom mirror, is to visit the landing strip where everybody swears Ray Hubley, the head pilot for Saxon, is not to be found, find him, see what I can come up with out there, and then head back to Memphis and make a beeline for Diane Edge.

"I'll tend to it," J.W. said to what he saw in the mirror as he lifted a blue plastic razor to his face. "But one thing I am going to do, and that's go fishing on Sardis Lake first."

Thirty minutes later as he drank coffee at the kitchen table with Mrs. Segrest, she asked him if he'd been talking to someone in the bathroom, maybe praying out loud before he faced the new workday, and J.W. told

her no ma'am he was just trying to remember the words to a song that
wouldn't let him alone.

The landing strip on Saxon's Hundred was located in the southwest
quadrant of the plantation, far from the central buildings of the lay-out
and screened from them by a large stand of cedars and loblolly pines.
The old logging road that J.W. remembered running along Horse Pen
Creek was still unfenced and passable, so he was able to drive the Buick
to within a couple of hundred yards of the hangar and the cluster of
biplanes in and around it. J.W. counted three Turbo-thrushes, two
Stearmans, and a Schweitzer Ag-Cat, all of which appeared airworthy,
and several parts of fuselages, tail and wing assemblies that looked to be
long grounded. Too much time in the air at an altitude of eight feet above
the ground, and too many pine tops caught in the wheelwells.

That was one of the things he didn't miss from his days in the Delta
trying to keep the Ragsdale name attached to some part of that country,
that sound of metal tearing and rivets popping and cables snapping as he
paid the price for an airborne mental error. For parts of three years, J.W.
had leased a Stearman and rented it and himself out to whoever needed
crops powdered and bugs poisoned, and now climbing out of the Buick
and walking toward the fence around Saxon's air operation, he felt a
twinge of the old sensation just below his breastbone kick up at the sight
of a stocky stub-winged Stearman. It was a combination of dread and
longing, like the change in the inner ear which came as the horizon
abruptly jerked, shifted and achieved a new level at the end of a low altitude run bordered by a bank of trees that allowed no margin.

"Howdy," he called through the hurricane fence to a man leaning
over with half his body stuck inside a Turbo-thrush engine. "How're you
doing?"

The man retreated from the engine and straightened up enough to
look over his shoulder toward where J.W. was standing by the fence. He
held a machine part in his left hand as though cradling the last egg of
some rare bird. Before he spoke he carefully placed the relic on a piece
of greasy cloth on a flat wing surface.

"Fair," the man said. "Except I got a shitload of work to do."

"I didn't want to take any more of your time," J.W. said, whitetooth-
ing just a measured amount. "I see you're down in the guts of a water
pump, and there ain't nothing more tricky than that."

"Tell me."

"I'm looking for Ray Hubley," J.W. said. "I understand he might be
out here this morning."

"He's done been up already, and he's done down, and he's in yonder
in the office on the telephone, I imagine."

"You suppose I could just walk in there on him, see can he talk to me a couple of minutes?"

"Yonder's the gate," the mechanic said and gently poked at the part he'd laid on the nest prepared for it. "Give it a try, far's I'm concerned."

"I appreciate it," J.W. said, moving toward the gate. "Good luck with that water pump."

"I'm gonna need it."

When J.W. walked around to the front of the hangar, he could see a man through the open doors staring hard at a wall telephone he still had a hand on.

"Mr. Hubley," J.W. said, "I'm Dan Mayfield. Your mechanic told me I'd find you inside the building."

"How'd you get back in here?" the man said. He was of medium build, blonde with most of the hair slid back off the front half of his head, and he had a big dab of white sunscreen covering his nose. His eyes were a hard, bright blue, and he looked at J.W. as though, to use the words of J.W.'s father, he were a bulldog looking at a stray puppy.

"You didn't come the front road down here," Hubley said.

"No, I didn't," J.W. agreed. "I got turned around backwards and fetched up on a road not fit to drive on, and then I spotted the windsock on the hangar. Thought I'd come on in and see if I could find you."

"What for? I ain't got but two minutes before I have to get up in the air and get to a place fifteen miles from here. What you looking for?"

"Oh, you don't just dust on Saxon's farm, then?"

"No, Mr. Saxon leases me out now and then. You not here looking for somebody to spread chemicals for you, by any chance?"

Hubley picked up a screwdriver from the cluttered table beneath the wall telephone and began flipping it in his right hand as he directed his unblinking stare at J.W.

"Just the opposite," J.W. said. "I'm looking to hire on, if you need somebody to help you out with all this work you got going on."

"Friend," Hubley said. "I'm not my own man in this operation, and I'm not authorized to do any hiring, even if I wanted to. Every minute I'm on the ground I'm losing money so I'm going to have terminate our little interview."

"I can fly anything you got," J.W. said, moving his hand in a circle, "carry anything anywhere and put it right where the boss wants it, give or take fifty feet. Any chemical you can name."

Hubley stopped the screwdriver in midflip and placed it back on the table, taking his gaze off J.W.'s face for the first time as he did so.

"Only chemicals we handle is the commercial products out of Monsanto and Buckman Labs in Memphis," he said, "and as I was saying, I can't talk to you about work, Mayfield. Now or later, neither."

"It don't hurt to try," J.W. said. "I'm just, you know, poking around, looking for a payday, trying to help out the economy. Keep me in mind."

Bet you one thing, J.W. said to himself as he walked back past the mechanic working on the Turbo-thrush and headed for his Buick, soon as I crank the engine, old blue-eyed Ray Hubley is going to pick up that telephone and talk to the folks in the big house. There wasn't but two fifty-gallon drums of bug juice anywhere in sight, and I seriously doubt Mr. Hubley does much agricultural pest poisoning. It appears to me they fly around stuff they don't want nobody identifying, something that'll fill the prescription for a lot bigger varmint than a green worm.

I might as well add Ray Hubley's name to my list for Diane Edge once I get back to Memphis, he said to himself as he fired up the Buick. See will it draw a hit.

"It was somebody with him," Vance Murphy said, trying his best to keep looking straight in front with his head held up high. "They must have been waiting hid in the bushes."

"Just looking at you," Franklin Saxon said, "I'd tend to agree, wouldn't you, Brent?"

Brent Perkins smiled, but said nothing. He swirled the drink in his hand so that the ice clicked against the glass, a friendly sound in the dark-paneled study.

"I never seen just one man able to handle Vance like that," Pick Murphy said, looking at his brother, "all our time growing up together."

"Shut your mouth, Pick," Vance said through his blue lips. "You ain't in this."

"I bet you wished he had've been though," Franklin Saxon said. "Why, Vance, judging from the way you been worked over, I expect probably four or five of them jumped you, and you know what else? Wouldn't surprise me if two of them hadn't been big bucks from Chicago with lengths of two-by-four, neither, just swinging from the floor at you."

"Fun's fun," Brent Perkins broke in, speaking in a measured tone, "like Mr. Saxon says, but we've obviously got a little problem building, and we've got to tend to it. Vance was outfoxed, but there'll be another time, and we've got to make sure that happens like it ought to. Now when exactly did you say our friend is arriving from points north and east, Mr. Saxon?"

"The blues expert is due at the strip a week from tomorrow," Saxon said. "Sometime after midnight in a larger craft than before, the way things look now."

"I wish he'd get here sooner. The first time out like this with these people, I'd feel a lot better if we got the whole thing took care of in another day or two, what with this Mayfield or Johnston or whoever he is wandering around the country."

"Now, Mr. Perkins," Vance Murphy said, "you needn't worry none about him much longer, I guarantee you. I'm gonna flat..."

"Cool off, Vance," Saxon said. "Before you say anything else about what all you're going to do to this fellow, tell me what he said to you."

"Nothing," Vance said. "He didn't say nothing. Just slipped up on me."

"Didn't want to ask you a thing, huh? Didn't want to know your name, what you're doing there, who you work for, nothing?"

"He didn't say a word to me," Vance said, "and when the time comes, I ain't going to say nothing to him, neither. I'm just going to do it."

"Go stick your head in a rain barrel. See if you can't bring some of that swelling down. Brent's right. It's way past time for getting it up to the brag. We've got business to take care of."

"Yessir," Vance said. "I just wanted to let you know that me and Pick is gonna cancel that fellow's ticket. Y'all just set your minds at ease."

Saxon held up his left hand toward the Murphy brothers and looked at his overseer. "I know what you're thinking, Brent, about timing," he said, "and I agree one hundred percent, but we can't move the merchandise before Speed and those people are ready to handle it. I don't know how they do their business up yonder, and I don't want to, but I do know there's no flex in the timing."

"Fair enough," Perkins said.

"We do know one thing, though," Saxon said, looking at the face of the eight-foot grandfather clock across the room. "As of nine o'clock, this Johnston's been fishing on Sardis Lake for two hours. Bobby Alford followed him in that old Buick out there. And I believe he hasn't caught a thing. And it's not going to matter who he is, quite soon now."

"I'm going over there," Vance Murphy said, "and I'm going to fix him. Me and Pick are right now on the way."

"You just sit to your seats, my friends," Franklin Saxon said, "both of you big tough brothers. It's a good hour and a half to Sardis, and by the time you got there all you'd see would be a tumped-over Sears fishing boat."

"Bobby Alford," Brent Perkins said, carefully sitting his drink glass on a straw coaster on a chairside table in Franklin Saxon's study. "So he will catch a big one, this fellow."

"He will," Saxon said. "He'll hook a big one, get excited and stand up to land it and flip his little vessel right over."

"And he doesn't know how to swim," Brent Perkins said. "You have it on authority, I reckon, Mr. Saxon."

"He won't be able to," Saxon said. "I know that for a fact."

21

The reel J.W. had borrowed was past needing lubrication. He'd already had it apart twice by eight o'clock, and the second time he'd done a little surgery with a knife blade on one of the plastic parts of the mechanism. That had helped some. Now if he held the baler closed to the last second before he cast and then really got his arm into it, he could get some decent distance about half the time. The whole process was keeping him busier than he wanted to be by about a factor of three, so he began to compensate by not retrieving the line for a longer period after each cast into the bluegreen water of Sardis.

It was working itself out pretty well after a little trial and error, and J.W. began to feel a comforting lull and predictable pattern setting up. He reached into the ice chest, popped open a Schlitz, and ate two cheese crackers out of a plastic sleeve. Feeling the sun begin to poke a little on the back of his neck, J.W. turned up his collar and leaned deeper into a fisherman's slump in his seat. "Let it roll," he said out loud and twitched his plastic bait grub in the water, hoping nothing would strike it for at least another ten or fifteen minutes. He narrowed his eyes and watched the light bounce off the surface ripples of the lake, reflecting through his dark sunglasses almost like fireflies. A light breeze touched him on the face, and he allowed himself another sip of beer, and tried not to think a thing.

It wasn't until the nearest of the three or four other boats he could see on this part of Sardis Lake drifted to within casting distance that J.W. looked away from his fishing rig toward it. The outfit was a blue and white Boston Whaler geared for bass fishing, powered by a 190 horsepower Johnson, and it was being moved along by an electric trolling motor. The man with his hand over the control stood in the rear of the Whaler facing J.W.'s rental, and he appeared to have given up on the fishing for the morning. J.W. noticed that both of the rods sticking up from their holders were rigged with hooks and leaders, but neither had bait attached and both looked ready to unload and throw in the back of a pickup.

When the man operating the trolling motor saw that J.W. was look-ing at him, he lifted his hand from the control and waved. He was wear-ing a blue windbreaker, hot as it was getting to be on Sardis, khaki pants and shirt, and he had an orange gimmie cap on his head covered with print that J.W. couldn't read at this distance. Probably says something witty like "my wife said it's me or fishing, I'm sure going to miss her," J.W. thought to himself and gave his bait two small twitches.

"You having any luck?" the man said, the Boston Whaler now well within the range of a halfway decent cast by even an average fisherman, any closer and somebody was going to have to move his boat.

"Naw," J.W. said, shifting his weight on the seat to get ready to retrieve his line. "You?"

"Maybe you ought to try this," the man said, dropping his hand from the troll motor mechanism and bending over to pick something up from the bottom of the blue Whaler.

As he came back up, his orange cap bright in the sunlight, several things happened in one instant, so many in fact that the moment seemed to stretch on for two or three minutes.

What the man brought up from the bottom of the boat was a twelve-gauge Ithaca pump shotgun, a "Featherlite" J.W. registered, just as something big hit the yellow grub on his line so hard that he lurched for-ward in response upsetting the can of Schlitz on the gunwhale of the Sears rental boat and kicking the ice chest over with his right foot in reflex.

The ten-pound test line sang in the water as whatever had taken the yellow grub headed for the snags and mud at the bottom of Sardis, and the man in the orange cap in the Whaler spun the barrel around toward him.

At the instant the muzzle of the Ithaca was settling into alignment with the part of J.W. visible above the boat gunwale, the trolling motor of the Boston Whaler, still running, collided with some obstruction just beneath the surface of Sardis Lake, and the shooter stumbled and jerked as he got off his first shot.

The sound seemed to hang long enough in the air to be seen.

The misstep caused all of the load of buckshot, save two pellets, to go low and to the left into the lake, kicking up a basketball sized churn of water. J.W. let the biggest fish he'd ever hooked in Sardis Lake have bait, tackle, rod and reel to take with him on his journey into the depths, and he kicked his body free of where he was half-lying across the boat seat and the ice chest into a position parallel to the surface of Sardis and suspended a full four inches above where he'd been.

As he twisted to the left and turned over the side of the Sears rental boat furthest from the shooter and entered the water, feeling the burn of the stray buckshot that had plowed across the top of his neck just beneath the skin, J.W. marvelled at how high he'd gotten on a jump from a prone position. He'd never been able to get over the five-foot high-jump bar back at Batesville High School no matter how hard he'd run at it or what techniques of Western Roll and Fosbury Flop he'd tried, and he had been in shape then.

J.W. thought he heard the Ithaca Featherlite pump action again as he kicked as hard as possible and let air bubbles out of his mouth to aid him on his way to as close as he could get to the bottom of Sardis. There was no mistaking the thud of a full load of double-aught buckshot tearing through the metal of the Sears boat above him, though, and already his lungs were telling him it was necessary to breathe, that it was all right to take in some of the water to see if it would work, come on, take a chance, suck.

Twisting in the cool, dark water, he turned back toward the sunlit surface above him and headed for the outline of the Boston Whaler beyond the rental boat with the bright hole in its bottom where the shotgun load had punched through. He came up at the bow of the boat, close enough to the snag that had fouled the trolling motor and saved his life in the process, to be able to grab the shaft of the motor and slow the entry of his nose and mouth back into the air.

Inhaling a gulp of air as quietly as he could, J.W. waited for the last blow to his face he would ever feel, praying like a Baptist preacher that the shooter would still be focussed on the Sears boat. He was.

Over the edge of the Boston Whaler gunwale, J.W. could see the back of the man's orange cap as he went through the motion of ejecting a spent shell from the Ithaca and lifting the gun again to the ready. The empty shell kicked out by the ejecting mechanism hit the water not two feet from J.W.'s head, sounding as it entered Sardis like a small bass jumping after a dragonfly.

J.W. reached down to the snag beneath the surface and pulled himself back under the water, not stopping his descent until his feet touched the muddy foundation of the lake.

By the time he had to return to the world of air, a full minute after he'd sunk himself away from it, the man in the orange cap with the funny saying on it had cranked the Johnson 190 and raced off down the lake to the east, leaving a silver wake curving behind him.

J.W. hung around the snag that had saved him for another five or ten minutes, keeping all of himself he could spare submerged beneath Sardis, only his nose and mouth barely visible above the surface. The buckshot that had hit his back had dug a shallow trench he could feel opening and closing as he moved in the water, but the trajectory had been glancing and the pellet had not struck bone. J.W. wished it the best of luck in its career and held no grudge against it or the manufacturer of Ithaca Featherlites. He was feeling too much gratitude for a white-oak snag to harbor any resentment against anything except for that son of a bitch in the orange gimmie cap.

Mr. Art Hayes, a recently retired produce manager for Piggly Wiggly in Memphis, pulled his fishing boat up to the half-sunk Sears rental at about the same time J.W. was getting up enough nerve to leave his snag and strike out for the shore two-hundred yards away. Mr. Hayes was surprised to see someone's head pop up out of the water as he cut his motor and drifted up to the Sears boat, now just level with the lake surface.

"Was that you signaling for help?" he asked as he held his boat steady to allow J.W. to crawl up and flop over the side. "Them gunshots? Did you lose your gun in the water?"

"Something like that," J.W. said. "I sure do appreciate your help. You didn't happen to see a blue Boston Whaler going by you in the last few minutes, did you?"

"Yeah, I did. He was sure in a hurry, running like he was in one of these bass tournaments headed for the next hole. That's what I figured he's doing."

"I hope he finds the next one way on down yonder," J.W. said, "and sets up for a long stay at it."

"I'm afraid I can't drag your boat, deep as it is in the water. Afraid it'd burn up my motor."

"Don't worry about that old Sears boat," J.W. said. "I'd just like a ride back to the put-in, if you could lend me a hand."

On the way back to where he'd left the Buick, J.W. kept reaching over his shoulder to finger the path the buckshot had made, wondering as he did just how big the fish had been that had taken everything with him as he sought deeper water. It couldn't have been a catfish, moving the way it did, but if it was a bass, it was a world beater. J.W. did regret not having at least seen it.

22

Y ou did report the shooter to Freddie, didn't you, J.W.?" Major Dalbey asked. "Let him know what kind of anti-social activity's going on in Sardis Lake these days."

"I did," J.W. said, "and the sheriff of Panola County expressed alarm and determination to get to the bottom of it."

"That's good, that's good," Dalbey said, looking at the sheaf of papers J.W. had handed him. "Maybe you was just fishing in the wrong hole, one that belonged to that fellow."

"What I'm beginning to believe," J.W. said, "is that it's just exactly the right damn hole after all, much as I hate to have to tell you."

"Well, Goddamn it, J.W. No fault of yours, you understand, but I thought your little visit to the Delta was going to do me some good. And it looks like it's made everything just a whole lot more complicated."

"Ain't that always the way?" J.W. said. "You stir up a stinkpot, and it just starts smelling worse."

"Tell me about it," the major said. "Ain't nothing happened here with the case, that's for damn sure. What you think's going on?"

"Right now I don't know exactly what to think," J.W. said. "I believe Franklin Saxon's transporting something around he don't want anybody to know about. And I believe he's prepared to take care of anybody that goes poking around asking questions about his business. And I know the name of one man that tried to take care of me, but not the other one yet."

"Take care of you, huh," the major said.

"And," J.W. went on, "I learned that a man named Barry Speed from Baltimore has been driving around the Delta with this fellow Vance Murphy, who works for Franklin Saxon on the farm. Speed is toting coke, a bunch of it, and he's doing some kind of business with Saxon."

"How you know that?"

"Vance Murphy told me," J.W. said. "And I believe he'd a swore on the Bible if I asked him to, at the time."

"You think you can believe what he said?"

"At that particular time in that situation, yessir," J.W. said. "Up and down the line."

"Anything else?"

"I got a few more names to look up, a Louisiana tag, a name on the side of a food truck, the service record of a cropduster, maybe. Enough to keep me and a friend of mine used to be with the DEA real busy for a day or two."

"And you believe Franklin Saxon was behind this fellow shooting at you?"

"I do. Eliminate with extreme prejudice is the way they described it to us in the military," J.W. said. "Way back yonder in the good old days. I can't prove it yet, but I will."

"You gonna keep me posted, J.W., every step of the way," Dalbey said. "Hellfire and damnation."

"Right," J.W. said and left Major Dalbey's office to find Tyrone Walker. Maybe something would have happened with the Bones family business on Baby Street, and J.W. would be able to shake a little of this feeling that lately every way he turned was blocked and that everything he was touching was turning to shit.

Tyrone looked glad to see him and made a big production of coming around from his side of the desk, even offering to shake hands and slap J.W. on the back as part of his greeting. When J.W. made a fist and stepped back, Tyrone laughed.

"Excuse me, partner," he said. "That's right. I forgot somebody said you'd picked up a little shrapnel down yonder in the Mississippi Mekong."

"That's about what it felt like, all right," J.W. said, reaching back over his shoulder to pat his buckshot wound. "I believe that son of a bitch was trying to kill me."

"Now don't go jumping to conclusions, J.W. He's just probably trying to see how you're maintaining your swimming skills."

"I showed the fucker how good I can dive, I flat guarantee you," J.W. said. "I'm still coughing up that mud off the bottom of Sardis Lake. I got in that water so deep and so fast I made Greg Louganis look like a girl scout."

"Who?"

"One of those diving guys. Don't you watch the Wide World of Sports?"

"Not no more. I just watch disposable diapers go in the garbage can. That and my bank account sink."

"The joys," J.W. said sitting down at the desk and retrieving a file from the drawer, "of married life. You ain't picked up Leatherman and that bunch yet, have you?"

"No, but I'm going to this afternoon at about four o'clock. You want to come along with me I'll introduce you to Leatherman and the boys and Ringo Starr, too."

"Ringo Starr? What you talking about? You mean the old Beatle?"

"You ain't going to believe this shit, J.W. But the Bones Family is fixing to go Hollywood. You know Toots Brogan, don't you, the old Stax Record producer back in the seventies?"

"Know of him," J.W. said, searching through the desk for the off-chance of a cigarette. "I know the city give him a bunch of money to set up a studio in that old fire station on Union here about a year ago."

"Yeah," Tyrone said. "Block or two from the old Sun Studio. Well, the boy had managed to talk some folks into backing him in making a music video, like on MTV, and he's hired the Bones Family to be in this thing with Ringo Starr."

"What they going to do? Mug Ringo and take all his jewelry?"

"I imagine they will, but that part won't be on the screen, I reckon. They're setting up scenes to be shot this afternoon down by the Arcade Restaurant across from the old train station."

"Down in there by the Throw Down Lounge? Shit, there's folks down there'll kill that camera crew and eat them, much less carry Ringo Starr off as a souvenir."

"I know it," Tyrone said. "It'll be something to see. Old Toots'll be running around like a blind dog in a meathouse. I figure we'll watch it for a while and then gather up Leatherman and whatever other Bones Family shows up and bring them on back here to the house."

"That'll work, Tyrone. That's real good. Listen, on the way out there I'll tell you what I found out about Franklin Saxon and what I been thinking about it. See can you help me understand it. How in the world do you suppose Toots Brogan talked Ringo's people into bringing him into South Memphis?"

"They must've all been drunk," Tyrone said. "Or high."

"Or crazy," J.W. said.

Tyrone drove them in a blue Dodge from the police department fleet to South Main Street and Pontotoc, and when they got in range, he pointed ahead to a clot of cars, people, vans, and two trucks with booms attached and cables running in several directions. All four corners of the South Main intersection with Pontotoc were roped off with yellow nylon cord, and groups of the local inhabitants of the area, mixed in here and there with obvious outsiders, were collected on the curbs behind the boundary markers.

"Remember when this used to be a street where cars drive up and down and people bought stuff in the stores?" Tyrone said.

"Yeah," J.W. said. "And I remember when Elvis first sang 'That's All Right, Mama' on Dewey Phillips' radio show, too. But that's back when God was a little boy."

"Only time you see anybody out down here now's when some bunch is making a picture show."

"Or scooping up the remains of some fool off the sidewalk," J.W. said. "Park in behind that red Blazer."

"Reckon Ringo Starr's out there in the middle of the street somewhere?" Tyrone said, pulling the Dodge to the curb. "Fixing to sing to the Bones family?"

"I imagine he's in one of them RV trailer houses," J.W. said, "wondering what it is he done so wrong to get dragged down to scuffling around in South Memphis with Toots Brogan in tow."

"You got to pay every bit of your rent," Tyrone said, getting out of the Dodge. "It's somebody somewhere counting up every receipt you signed off on in every minute of your life."

As the two detectives walked closer to the center of the action, somebody in the film area hit a switch, and several banks of hot white lights came on, chasing every shadow away from where Pontotoc crosses South Main.

"There's T-Bird," Tyrone said, nodding toward the group of young black men at the center of the focus of the spotlights. "The one in the blue headrag, the one holding the bugle, or whatever it is, in his hand."

"Looky there beside him," J.W. added. "Ain't that the fucker they call Stone Job?"

"That's my man. And if one of them other ones ain't Leatherman, I'm Mayor Willie Herenton."

"I thought you knew the dude on sight, Tyrone. Be able to pick him out of the bunch quick as you seen him."

"Most of the time that's true, but then most of the time he ain't wearing white makeup all over his ugly face," Tyrone said. "What is that shit they got on them?"

"What that is is art, Tyrone," J.W. announced as the two men came to a stop at the edge of the ring of people crowded up to the barriers surrounding the scene. "I see you don't know much about what's going on with the culture of our nation. I don't expect you ever watch MTV, don't know nothing about Hootie and the Blowfish and all that bunch."

"You're right, J.W. I don't get the opportunities you do to research all the TV sets on the walls of them neat bars you hang out in."

"You want to run with the big dogs, you got to get off the porch," J.W. said.

About then, a lanky man with a four-day growth of beard began talking through a hand-held loudspeaker. Although he was no more than ten feet from the eight young black men with their faces painted a dead white, he addressed them electronically and at great length about what he wanted them to do, sweeping his speaker back and forth in arcs that covered the entire field ahead of him. J.W. admired the blue overalls and the straw hat the director was wearing because they put him in mind of the way his father habitually dressed back when there was still a Ragsdale place in the Mississippi Delta. Wonder where this dude farmed?

"Fellows," the director was saying, "lift your instruments to your mouths and blow as though you were really playing. Don't worry about the sounds, we'll dub later with real musicians. We just want the look. Remember, this is New Orleans, this is a Dixieland jazz funeral, and you're a marching band of the dead. Don't worry about straggling, I want you to straggle. Don't worry about your ranks, I want you ragged. Ready? Let's do it."

With that, the Bones family lifted its instruments, drew a deep breath, and blew a sound not heard in that part of South Memphis before. As they began to move together down the middle of South Main, the crowd parting before them to let the marching band of death proceed, Tyrone turned to J.W.

"Second from the left end, that big motherfucker in the Beale Street T-shirt, that be my man Leather," he said.

"The clarinet player you mean," J.W. said. "Sound like he choking a cat to death, that's the shooter LaQuita named, huh?"

"You got it, Sergeant Ragsdale," said Tyrone, beginning to move at an angle which would intercept the band by the time they reached the end of the block. "I say we wait until the fool with the mike makes them stop and they break up their formation. Then we pick him up when they're mingling around. What do you think, J.W.?"

"Right, and then we grab whoever stays around and wants to get up in our face."

J.W. nodded toward two uniformed police officers on the right side of the street, looking on with little interest at the passing parade. One of them said something to the other who snickered sourly at whatever it was.

"You know either one of them?" J.W. asked Tyrone.

"No, they're still babies, all look alike to me."

"I'll go over there real quick, I.D. us, and get them uniforms ready," J.W. said and started across South Main at a half-trot. One of the men dragging cables said something cross to J.W. as he cut in front of him, but J.W. didn't listen.

As he stepped up on the curb near the patrolmen, he flashed his wallet I.D. and pointed out Tyrone walking at an angle across the street.

"My partner," he said. "Sergeant Walker. We are fixing to bring in at least one, maybe two of these hammerheads on a homicide charge."

"Yessir, Sergeant," said the one who had made the joke, "what do you want us to do?"

"Keep any asshole back who tries to interfere with us when we're cuffing our little friends. That ought to take care of it."

"Right," said the other one, craning his neck and tapping the fingertips of both hands on the array of equipment attached to his belt. "We'll be right there with you. You can depend on it."

"No, you just hang back," J.W. said, reading the name off the patrolman's lapel pin, "Officer Streete. Keep a little distance back behind us with Lanier here, and we'll keep the whole thing low-key. It'll be over before anybody hardly notices."

J.W. looked around at the marching band of death, saw both that they were near the end of the block and that the director in farmer clothes was about to talk into his portable hand-speaker, and then turned to find Tyrone in the crowd of people who had fallen in behind the main procession.

He looks like an insurance salesman on a bad day, J.W. thought, as he caught Tyrone's notice and nodded, looks like he had two big policies pay off and there ain't no way he can find to fuck the beneficiaries out of the money. His eyes are red, his head is down, and he's just dying to meet up with somebody that wants to give him a bad time. Even got his sportcoat all rumpled up in a knot. Give Mr. Walker the ball, and get out of the way.

The man in the straw hat and bib overalls barked a few words through the loudspeaker, and the marching band of death lost its direction and began to mill about as its members lowered their instruments and began to high-five each other. The crowd of onlookers tagging along began to hoot and grunt like the studio audience in a late night talk show J.W. had once turned on by accident when doing a channel sweep, and somebody killed the banks of white lights lining that block of South Main Street.

Tyrone from the far street side and J.W. from the rear converged on Leatherman as he stood holding the clarinet in his left hand and beginning to dab at the thick goo of white cosmetic covering his face from hairline to Adam's apple. Standing in the Memphis heat with the spotlights finally off, Leatherman looked to J.W. as hot as a fresh-fucked sheep in July.

"Here," J.W. said to the Bones family claimer, reaching toward the clarinet, "let me hold that for you."

Still in the MTV acting mode, Leatherman did as the white man told him and moved to hand the beat-up instrument over. As he did, Tyrone

Walker smoothly clamped a handcuff around his wrist, and dipping his left shoulder and stepping under Leatherman's extended arm, moved behind him to end up with the cuffed man in a hammerlock.

"Just lay right down there in the street on your face, Mr. Hollywood," Tyrone said, kicking Leatherman's left foot free of the ground and muscling him forward until he stumbled and collapsed to the pavement. "Give me that other hand now, and I promise not to ruin this one."

"What the fuck going on here?" said another of the Bones Family as Tyrone Walker finished manacling Leatherman's right to his left hand. "Who you motherfuckers be?"

"Memphis police officers," J.W. said as he seized the inquisitive young man in a bearhug and ran him backwards into the side of a GMC van parked at the curb. He was close enough to the man's face to rub some of the white make-up off on his own nose as he spun him around to cuff him. "Just be real nice like Leatherman, and we'll let you ride in our car all wide-awake and perky. Otherwise, you might doze off and miss all the scenery."

"What is happening here?" the director said through his bullhorn, dodging his way through the crowd of Bones Family members, now beginning to flee in the same general direction, back toward the deeper recesses of South Memphis. One of them, a small quick man still carrying a brass trombone, bumped the director as he ran by, knocking off his straw hat and spinning him half-around in passage.

After he'd retrieved the hat, the director, looking like a Delta farmer enraged by a federal cut in cotton subsidies, pushed his way up into J.W.'s face as he was helping his handcuffed Bones Family prisoner back to his feet. The director lifted the bullhorn to his mouth and prepared to speak.

"You say one word to me at this range through that thing," J.W. said, "and I'm gonna stick it so far up your ass your farts are gonna sound like thunder."

Dropping the loudspeaker to chest level and speaking in a normal tone, the director told the camera crew to keep filming. "I want to get all of this on record," he said. "It's a blatant case of police brutality, and I want every blow struck and every kick delivered by these men to be captured for legal action."

"That's all there is," Tyrone said as he and Leatherman stood together watching J.W. and the director. "It ain't gonna be no blows struck or kicks kicked."

"That's right, Mr. DeMille," J.W. said. "Memphis ain't California. It don't take ten policemen to bring in one little murdering shitass like this one. It don't take but two."

"It don't take but one," Tyrone said. "I could have done it by myself."

"Nuh uh," J.W. said to Tyrone, beginning to lead his man toward the Dodge from the carpool. "You know you needed me, Tyrone. Needed me bad."

"Us," said one of the uniformed police, twirling his night stick smartly by its attached leather thong. "You needed us for backup."

"Put that thing up, Lanier, and go give somebody a ticket," Tyrone Walker said. "Come on, let's get going, Leatherman."

"You know one thing, though," J.W. said at the car as they helped the Bones Family claimers climb into the backseat, "I sure wish we'd got a chance to see Ringo."

23

I thought you took care of all your problems in Memphis, Frankie," Barry Speed said. "The last time I made a visit."

"Oh, we did, Mr. Speed," Franklin Saxon said into the telephone, holding the instrument a half inch away from its touching either his ear or his lips. To do less would be like having Speed's mouth somewhere on him. "There are no problems in Memphis in connection with that particular transaction at all."

"Frankie, call me Barry. And hey, when I make a deal, I carry out my end. I'm very well known for that. You ask anybody in Philly. But what's the problem with your share of it now?"

"Let's call it a glitch in transportation. Something's come up to keep things grounded."

"What? You telling me the shipment from New Orleans didn't come in yet? Delcambre ain't delivered?"

"No," said Saxon. "The merchandise came in on time and in good condition, and it's safely stored."

"O.K. O.K. What the fuck? I'm sitting here pulling on my dick, and there ain't nothing coming out. What's the hold up, Frankie?"

"Air transport is presently out of the question. That's the holdup, Mr. Speed. We can't chance air travel."

"Why? Did that crazy fucker that flew me in and out last time finally get his ticket punched? Did you lose your air force?" Speed stopped talking to laugh at what he'd said, and Saxon held the telephone out at arms length until the chortling subsided.

"Nothing as easy as that to solve, I'm afraid," he said. "No, we've had a visitor poking around and asking questions about our cropdusting operation, and Mr. Speed, I am a cautious man."

"DEA?"

"I don't think so, but we're not going to put anything in the air and find out."

"Why don't you have Elmer or Zeke or one of those hillbillies that work for you take care of this putz?"

"That was attempted and did not succeed," Saxon said in a deliberate tone, and both men fell silent.

"Well, then," Speed finally said, "where are we, old buddy? Business can't wait, and you tell me no airplanes, and I tell you no highways north of fucking Tennessee. They are watching the road, the fucking DEA."

"Water," Saxon said. "We go by water. The river up to St. Louis and then by air east to you people."

"A speedboat? One of them cigarette boats the Colombians race around Florida?"

"No, Mr. Speed. Not one of those floating advertisements for drugs. I'm talking about something a lot different."

"Yeah, yeah? What?"

"A vessel no one would ever suspect. The Maid of Cotton's Coronation Barge on its way back to St Louis after the Cotton Carnival is over next week in Memphis."

"A coronation barge?" Speed said. "No shit?"

"No shit," Franklin Saxon answered.

When J.W. eased his way through the door to the Shelby County Courtroom, Second Division, and sat down in the last row of seats at five o'clock, Diane Edge was standing in the well with her back turned. She had just asked a question of the witness on the stand, a large woman with thick glasses and a roil of red hair that stood out all around her head as though it had just been exploded and hadn't yet had time to settle.

The woman was giving Diane the look of someone who had just caught a strange woman in her kitchen pouring motor oil into the cake batter.

"I never said such a thing," the woman declared, her eyes huge enough through her glasses for J.W. to be able to see their whites from the back of the room. "You're just turning and twisting it to make it look bad."

"Mrs. Hall," Diane Edge said, "I can have that read back to you, if you want."

"No, I don't want to hear that mess again."

"They are your words, Mrs. Hall. No one said them but you."

"Objection," the assistant district attorney said from behind her table. She was Fran Forrest, a woman with huge thighs and calves she habitually made no effort to conceal with artfully loose clothing or dark colors, and a prosecuting attorney J.W. had contempt for. She had lost three cases for him that he had dead to rights by screwing up procedurally. Three shitheads got to walk.

"Counsel is arguing with the witness," Fran Forrest said.

"Sustained," Judge David Upton said from the bench, holding his head with both hands. Fran shot a smirk at Diane Edge and shuffled some papers in front of her.

"Mrs. Hall," Diane began, and before she could go on, Judge Upton broke in.

"It's five o'clock, y'all. Court's recessed until 9:30 tomorrow. I'm gone."

With that, the spectators, witnesses, court personnel, defendant, prosecutor and assorted hangers-on scattered like a covey of quail, and J.W. watched Diane Edge gather her papers and turn toward the back of the courtroom. He waited until she had almost reached where he was sitting before he spoke.

"Lady Lawyer," he said, "I be looking for somebody to defend me against false charges."

"Working man," Diane said, stopping at the end of J.W.'s row of seats and fixing him with a fake frown. "Don't be telling me whether them charges be false or real. All I want to know is you got the money up front or not."

"I got it, Mizriz Lawyer."

"Well, pull it out and let's go get a drink."

"My professional advice to you," J.W. said, standing up and taking Diane's briefcase away from her, "is for you to come with me. Go sit by that big window in Captain Bilbo's where you can watch the barges go up the river, and start to pound down as much house gin as you can before they start asking the full price on it."

"Bring that trash you're holding in your hand on out to my car," she said. "We'll go in it. That'll save at least seven or eight minutes."

J.W. counted himself lucky for a change. Just as he and Diane worked their way through the arriving post-five o'clock crowd toward the large windows at the back of the room overlooking the Mississippi River, a couple at a table for two got up to leave and held their chairs until J.W. and Diane reached them.

"You look like you need some scenery," said the man, relinquishing his chair to J.W.

"Buddy, I do," J.W. said. "I appreciate it."

As they seated themselves by the window and J.W. looked around for a waitress, his right hand raised for attention, Diane watched the man who had spoken leave with the woman through a side door.

"You know who that was, don't you?" she said. "That you were swapping polite words with."

"Who?" J.W. said, spotting a little blonde in a short skirt and a river gambler's vest over her blouse bearing down on them with a tray in hand. "Gin," he said to her. "House on the rocks, two."

"Yessir," the waitress said, "it's two for one 'till seven. That means four for y'all, you understand?"

"You talking my language," J.W. said. "I understand it like a native."

"Ringo Starr," Diane said.

"Who? Where?"

"That man was Ringo Starr. The old Beatle. You know, the drummer."

"Well, I'll be damned. I got to see him after all and didn't even know it when I did."

"What do you mean?" Diane said, turning her chair more directly toward the river view.

"Aw, me and Tyrone Walker made an arrest where they were making one of those music videos down on South Main where Ringo was supposed to be. We never saw him, and I thought it was just a rumor."

"Who are you and Tyrone arresting and abusing these days?"

"Bones Family claimers. They mostly go after the Beale Street Boppers or the Gents, but this time they killed a couple of their own, plus a tourist, so it's more interesting. We trying to figure it out."

"It's bound to be crack, isn't it? That's what all the gangs in Memphis are moving these days."

"Well, yeah, of course, but you got to make them say it first."

"Are you violating their rights, Sergeant Ragsdale?" Diane asked and lifted one of the glasses of gin the waitress had just delivered. "Doing anything to deny them the full enjoyment of the due procedures of the justice system?"

"No, we sure as shit ain't," J.W. said, clinking his glass of gin against Diane's and draining a full quarter of its contents with his first sip. "You wouldn't be able to find a mark on either one of the murdering little bastards."

"I believe that. You and Tyrone try to wound only the minds of your victims. You know what John Lennon said in his song."

"No, what?"

"You just can't hide when you're crippled inside."

"I don't like the way this talk is going," J.W. said. "Here's to Mississippi River water, counselor."

"Here's to darkest Arkansas," Diane said, gesturing with her glass toward the green fields across the stretch of water beyond the window of Captain Bilbo's. "May it never be developed."

"You don't have to worry about that," J.W. said, "long as the Old Man gets up every spring and floods out that five miles of flats over there every year."

"Amen," Diane said, putting down her first glass and reaching for the bonus. "One down and one to go."

"Who was that nice lady you were being mean to on the stand there a while ago?"

"That was Mrs. Ellen Hall, the principal of Bedford Forrest Middle School right here in the Bluff City. She claims my client sweet-talked her out of a little over eighteen thousand dollars."

"Did he?"

"Why, no. Mrs. Hall freely and of her own accord advanced him those funds for a business venture the success of which would assure the stability of their coming marriage."

"It cost her that much, did it?" J.W. said and gave the blonde waitress a two-fingered victory sign.

"Yes, it did. She ought to have known you can't trust a man, especially one from Mississippi."

"Hell, Lady Lawyer, us men from the Magnolia State are just so generally admiring of women that we in the habit of losing our minds and saying anything to one of them in the heat of the moment."

"Yes," Diane said. "Either that, or saying nothing at all."

The din of the happy hour drinkers in Captain Bilbo's was rising to another level, one beyond a busy hum and not yet to full voice, the reflection of the sun on the Mississippi was beginning to outline the slow moving barges with halo effects as the vessels plodded upwards against the current, and the two house gins were working in J.W. like a blessing.

"Listen, Diane," he said and touched her hand. "Let's get these next two down, and go get us something to eat."

"O.K. Where to, my captain?"

"The Butcher Block," J.W. said. "Where you cook your own supper."

"All right," Diane said. "Now you're talking. A little salad and a lot of red meat."

After J.W. had picked out the steak he wanted for himself, a sixteen ounce T-bone, and Diane had selected hers, a filet mignon, the choice of every woman J.W. had ever seen grilling her own steak over the huge grill in the Butcher Block, they stood side by side watching the beef cook, and J.W. began to tell Diane about his trip to the Delta.

"So what you want is for me to ask Richard Banks to run a few names through the DEA computer," Diane said.

"That's right," J.W. said. "Isn't your meat about done?"

"No, I like all my microbes killed."

"I've already put in an ask to the New Orleans police department to run priors on Kenneth Delcambre, the guy that owns the truck I saw out on the Saxon place. It's going to get some hits, too. I know, because when I mentioned the name to the New Orleans guy he started laughing."

"He'd heard of him before, huh?"

"I reckon so. They never have got him yet on anything to amount to much, this Delcambre, but he's connected up with the trade, all right."

"Yours is done, J.W.," Diane said, pointing toward the hunk of meat in front of him. "It's releasing all its juices."

At the table, the first fit of feeding over, Diane turned back to the subject of Franklin Saxon and J.W. in the Delta.

"You know what else you could do," she said, "to kind of jog things along is to ask the DEA to make a request of IRS information on Franklin Saxon and his businesses."

"I could?" J.W. said. "That's a good idea. Where'd you learn all those dirty tricks?"

"Where do you think? Working for the master trickster of them all, Uncle Sam."

"Damn, I hope you don't ever get mad at me."

"If I do, you won't know it until the agents come knocking on your door," Diane said. "Of course, they can't do anything fast, I mean the full process of audit, but I could tell them we want Saxon to know immediately it's been requested and to notify him the DEA's going to be talking to the IRS."

"That might could cause him to blow a fuse," J.W. said. "I know it would me. Can you do it tomorrow?"

"Without a doubt. Richard Banks owes me several favors, and I think it's time to call one in just to remind him of the fact."

"Do I owe you any favors?" J.W. said. "Just to be on the safe side."

"Yeah," she said. "Go get me some more salad, and be damn quick about it."

"Cherry tomatoes with that?"

"What else?"

The light from the clock radio on the bedside table was pale green, and by it J.W. could see a stack of books on the floor close to hand. He could tell by the reflection that there were plastic covers on the books, and he knew by that that they had been checked out of the public library. It made him feel sad for some reason to realize that fact. He thought about Diane dealing all day long with the people in trouble who came through her office and ended up in court being questioned and giving lies in response, trying to get away with something and not pay for whatever they'd done. He imagined Diane coming home after dark and sitting down with one of these slick-covered books and beginning to read about people and times that had nothing at all to do with where she lived and what she did for a living.

An image of her lying in bed in a flannel nightgown, all the doors and windows to her little house on Snowden locked tight, one lamp lighting the page, rose up in J.W.'s mind so real that he groaned aloud at the thought of it.

"What's the matter, J.W.?" Diane said from the other side of the bed. "Are you all right?"

"Oh, yeah," J.W. said, coughing so she'd think the first sound she'd heard had been just another different kind of cough. "I'm just fine. Maybe some of that sixteen ounce T-bone I ate is talking back to me."

He turned from his position on his back and put his arm around Diane to lie spooned against her back.

"You ought to be tired out enough to be sound asleep, Working Man," she said, cupping J.W.'s right hand against her throat and mouth, "the way you've been carrying on here for the last little while."

"What do you mean 'little while'?" J.W. said. "There was just so much going on you thought it was a little while. It was more like an hour and a half of hard workout."

"Whatever you say, Sergeant Ragsdale. I wasn't watching the clock myself. Had my mind on other things."

"That wasn't all you had on other things," J.W. said, caressing her face in the darkness and slipping his other hand beneath Diane's head. "Best I remember."

"J.W.," she said. "Can you stay until morning, just sleep the rest of the night here?"

"I don't know why not," he said, taking a deep breath and letting it slide slowly out all the way until he felt himself seeming to sink deeper into the pillow under his head. "I don't imagine my car'll start anyway until the sun gets up. It gets vapor locked down below sixty degrees."

"I'll make you sausage and biscuits," Diane said. "Get your motor running again in the morning."

"I expect it'll turn right over," J.W. said and buried his face deep in her hair on the pillow beside him.

The next morning over breakfast J.W. asked Diane Edge what she could tell him about the history of the Aires Saxon family in Memphis, after the old man had made the move from darkest Batesville. He knew she had had some dealings with the second wife, long after her marriage to Aires had ended and probably knew little or nothing, but he figured it wouldn't hurt to hear what Diane had gathered or was willing to tell him.

"He was in big trouble financially," Diane said, after sitting poised with a biscuit and sausage halfway to her mouth for a few seconds. "I got a look at the books, uncooked, as well as I could tell, and there was a real hole in the middle of all that stuff you see from the outside of the house on Carr Avenue. And that was several years ago when Amanda was getting her share. Far as I know there hasn't been a sudden upswing in fortune."

"What about this big barbecue franchise Franklin has got set up and running?" J.W. said. "They got restaurants all over North Mississippi and on into Arkansas, from what I hear. And like I told you, I have seen the processing plant. Watched a bunch of women pulling meat off the bone."

"You ever eat in one?" Diane said.

"Nuh uh."

"Anybody that does once never goes back."

"I don't have to try it to know it ain't no good," J.W. said and reached for the May haw jelly. "But I am going to cover each and every base and get Tyrone Walker to go eat a sandwich with me in that one on Union later on sometime."

"Most folks aren't religious about pulled pork the way you are, J.W. They need to experience a thing first before rejecting it."

"Oh, ye of little faith," J.W. said. "So the barbecue business don't look like a big money maker for the Saxons. I know cotton ain't for nobody. What else can you tell me, Diane?"

"About the Saxon finances? Nothing. But the DEA asking the IRS for records ought to get a rise out of the son and heir."

"Yeah, buddy," J.W. said. "And you're planning to call Richard Banks this morning about all these names and getting stuff going with the data search?"

"As soon as you leave the house," Diane said.

"Hell," J.W. said. "Now that puts me in a bind."

24

Boyd Hemphill stood on the cobblestones at the edge of the finger of water between Memphis proper and Mud Island and
stared at the rusty barge anchored in front of him with an expression of
deep disgust on his handsome face. Every year it was the same. The
Memphis in May Committee in conjunction with the Cotton Carnival
people came up with some rotting old scow of a barge, fastened it by a
greasy chain to the edge of the Memphis waterfront, and then turned to
Boyd and said make magic.

Here it was again. And this ugly contraption was older and more
dilapidated than any of the ones he could remember from the years
before. God, what cargo had it been hauling up and down the
Mississippi for the past forty years? Pork bellies? Yes, that probably, and
Lord knew what else those stolid Midwesterners up-river had been having shipped in to them in the middle of their cornfields and their char-
acterless cities from all points south.

Well, a luck a day and fuck a duck, Boyd said to himself, lifting a
hand to pat at his hair, tossed as it was by the breeze off the river. I'm
presented again with lead and must create gold of it. There's nothing to
do but make a start. But I swear I cannot fathom what sort of paint or
how much of it I'm going to be forced to slather all over that monstros-
ity. Surely the budget will go bust long before I'm finished, but that will
be their problem and not mine.

"Hello," Boyd called to the young man in tight jeans and a grease-
covered T-shirt who was coiling a rope or strangling a rat or doing
something nautical on the deck of the barge anchored in the back water.
"Will that ramp or gangplank or whatever it's called support me to come
aboard and look around?"

"I reckon so," the young man said. "It done held me up."

"I'm wearing sturdy shoes," Boyd Hemphill said. "I hope I don't slip
on some spilled oil or something."

As he moved toward the long wooden ramp running from the dockside to the deck of the barge, named The Brandon Spencer, he heard a car driving slowly down the cobblestones behind him. He was pleased to see, when he turned carefully on the wet stones to look, that the car was one of the official Cotton Carnival vehicles provided by Pat Hayes Lincoln, and he hoped it was conveying the current Maid of Cotton. It was, and Boyd was pleased, but not surprised.

This new sacrificial virgin, as Boyd called all of them in private with his friends, was proving to be a dream to work with. She was always on time, raring to go and willing to listen. Most of the girls were sweet, or as sweet as a twenty year-old spoiled female could be, all of them were of good family, and certainly Cameron Saxon was, but alas, too many lacked the great dividend the current Maid enjoyed in excess.

Looks.

No agonizing with this one, as Boyd Hemphill too frequently had had to do, over a nose not precisely in the middle of the face, a chin ten or fifteen degrees too weak, eyes set a mite too close together, or skin which had to be attended to far too frequently by the best dermatologists in the land.

Fabric can cover anything, Boyd thought as he watched Cameron Saxon alight from the Lincoln, but it can't cover the face. This child was created to be Maid of Cotton by genes and by background, and the Cotton Carnival was created to showcase her as representative of our best dream of the Delta, Memphis and the South. I will do what needs to be done, Boyd Hemphill silently pledged to himself, to transform that rusty old boat into a coronation barge fit for Cleopatra.

"My dear," he said, beckoning toward Cameron and the older man with her, "come see your barge. Let's go look at the flower before it blossoms."

"I'm so glad you're in charge, Boyd," Cameron said as she approached, a vision in shades of pale green. "You're really the heart of the beauty of the Cotton Carnival. Have you met my brother, Franklin?"

"Cameron," Boyd said to her as he moved toward Franklin Saxon, hand extended, "have I met your brother? Donkey's years ago he was two classes ahead of me at Memphis University School, and I must apologize for not recognizing him. I'm sure he wouldn't remember me. I was the little school drama nerd and Franklin was the Big Man on Campus."

"Anybody who doesn't know Boyd Hemphill hasn't noticed the arts in Memphis for the past thirty years," Franklin said.

"Why thank you, sir," Boyd said. "You're very kind. And your little sister is a credit not only to Memphis and the Cotton Carnival but, of course, to your family."

Boyd reached out to embrace Cameron, and she lifted her face for an air kiss. "Particularly at a time like this for the Saxons," Boyd said.

"She's as brave as a little soldier."

"Yes, she is," Franklin said. "Bless her heart. So this is the barge you'll be working with, Boyd?"

"None other. Isn't it ghastly?"

"You'll do wonders, I'm certain. I'd like to step aboard and check it out structurally, though. Were you about to climb the plank?"

"Yes," Boyd said, "but I'm not going below deck. I shudder to think." Pointing to an area toward the rear of the deck of the Brandon Spencer, he turned and spoke to Cameron.

"Miss Maid of Cotton," Boyd said, "there I'll put your throne, elevated so all may see and marvel. You'll be drop-dead lovely."

25

J.W. Ragsdale was sipping a cup of coffee and peering through the backside of the mirror into Interrogation Room 3 at one Melvin Carter, known on the streets of Memphis as Leatherman.

"You ready to go in there?" Tyrone Walker said. "See if he's ready to tell us something, maybe do a little dealing?"

"We got LaQuita's ID on him," J.W. said. "I don't see why not."

"Better than that," Tyrone said. "LaQuita's going to make it. She's going to have a lot more to say."

"No shit? That's good news."

"You remember Sergeant Ragsdale, don't you, Leatherman?" Tyrone said, after he and J.W. had walked into the room. "From where they had you playing music with your face all painted up on South Main? I believe y'all met up close and personal."

Leatherman opened his mouth as though to speak, but didn't answer. Tyrone sat down in the chair across the table from him and J.W. leaned up against the wall, his back to the observation mirror.

"You may not remember Sergeant Ragsdale, Leatherman," Tyrone said. "But I know you remember Baby Street. You know where that is, don't you?"

"I know where Baby Street is, all right," Leatherman said, "but that don't mean nothing."

"That's where Apple Jefferson lived," J.W. said. "Used to, before you Bones boys took him out."

"I ain't seen Apple Jefferson since last Christmas," Leatherman said. "Naw, take that back. It's before then."

"You might as well give it on up, Leather," Tyrone said. "LaQuita done dropped the word on you. You remember her? She ain't dead. She didn't buy it. She's getting better everyday, and she's talking just as strong as can be, every breath she draws."

"Wait a minute," Leatherman said and pinched the tip of his nose between two fingers. "I didn't do her. She's wrong if she say that. Bitch be lying."

"See which one the jury believes," J.W. said. "Try your luck. It's murder one, Leather, and that big old healthy girl is going to put you on death row."

"You know what we do in Tennessee to people on death row, finally," Tyrone said. "Once the appeals are made and turned down and all that shit. Trip that switch. Put the current to them, that's what."

"Wait a minute," Leatherman said. "I ain't the only one in this. It be others, too."

"We already know that," J.W. said. "We know who they are, too, so telling their names ain't going to do you no good. Idn't that right, Sergeant Walker?"

"Yeah," Tyrone said, elongating the word, "but you know if there was something else Leather could help us on, I mean a thing other than the Baby Street deal, maybe that'd be worth talking about."

"You mean something else the Bones Family had a hand in?" J.W. asked. "You talking about maybe the ATM thing, where that man was killed with the sledgehammer and the screwdriver?"

"Yeah," Tyrone said. "Word is it's a Bones thing. It's just a matter of time before we close that one up, though. Clock's running, you understand, Sergeant Ragsdale."

"I know that," J.W. said. "But maybe Leatherman could speed things up, get that ATM killing took care of. Let us get on to some other stuff. Save us some time."

"It was a white man there," Leatherman said slowly, looking first at J.W., then toward Tyrone. "He's the one told Bones to do it. Told Bones to do Apple, too."

"White man?" J.W. said. "I didn't know you let white folks into the Bones Family."

"He ain't Bones," Leatherman said. "He be a businessman. He wanting to sell to us, we be starting to buy from him."

"What you talking about?" Tyrone said. "Buying and selling what?"

"T-Bird call it the merchandise."

"What kind of merchandise?"

"Crack," Leatherman said, looking in J.W.'s direction.

"What's the white man's name, Leather?" Tyrone said. "Who is he?"

"I can't call his name," Leatherman said. "I ain't never heard it I can remember."

"What's he look like?" J.W. said.

"He be a man wear a suit. Big as you. Drive a big car. His hair slick like."

"Hell, that could be anybody," Tyrone said. "That ain't telling us nothing, Sergeant Ragsdale. Look, we got Leatherman on the Apple thing. LaQuita has done nailed him. Let's just go with that."

"Well," J.W. said. "I see where you're coming from, Sergeant Walker. It's a sure thing. You're making sense, all right."

"Wait," Leatherman said, "wait. What you say if I tell you about the big dude that go along with the white man, the one be with him lots of times?"

"I don't know," Tyrone said. "Give me a hint."

"That real big dude drive the Lincoln," Leatherman said. "He stand outside when they be talking, him and that white man and T-Bird. I see them at Tom Lee Park, Mud Island parking lot, sometimes we go over, meet them on Jackson at the J.R. Junior."

"Who is this big dude you talking about?" J.W. asked, watching the smoke curl up from his Kool cigarette. "You know him?"

"He be Lawrence, T-Bird say. He talk like on TV. He don't sound like he from Memphis."

"Leatherman," Tyrone said. "Tell us some more about this white man in the Lincoln. You say he was there at the ATM?"

"I think," Leatherman said, " I got to talk to my counsel. See how we be doing a deal."

"You do that," J.W. said. "We want to see how you can help us. See, you know, how we can help you."

"You tell your counsel something, though, for me, Leatherman," Tyrone said. "You be sure to tell him about LaQuita, how well she's doing and how mad she is at the Bones Family. See what he tells you to say to us then."

"And, Leatherman," Tyrone went on, "one other thing. You know that video tape from the ATM? You know, what Apple was holding in his house when the Bones Family killed him? LaQuita done told us where it was hid, and we got it. It made some real good pictures, too. Just like Hollywood. I know how the Bones Family been trying to break into show biz. Looks like y'all made it."

Out in the hall, J.W. and Tyrone waited for the Corrections Officer, Grade 2, to come take Leatherman back to the holding cell and stared at each other.

"What's that fucker telling us?" Tyrone said. "Who is this white man he's talking about, and who's Lawrence?"

"I don't know for sure who the white man is, but I can make a damn good guess," J.W. said, standing away from the door to let the jailer enter to fetch Leatherman. "I believe he's a man real heavy into peddling bad barbecue."

"Y'all through for the time being with him?" the officer asked. She was a woman a shade under six feet and a full twenty pounds over two hundred, and her hair was cut so short J.W. could see white skin through it all over her head.

"Yeah, Kay," he said, "the young man's started talking about lawyers, so we won't be able to interview this gentleman no more without a third party along."

"Which means we ain't going to see him again until Ronald Sharp gives us a call," Tyrone said.

"Which ain't going to be long," J.W. said. "You watch."

"I got you," Kay said and efficiently hustled the handcuffed Leatherman down the corridor and out of sight.

"I do know who the driver of the Lincoln is, though," J.W. said, as he and Tyrone began to head out of the Shelby County Justice Center, bitterly and frequently referred to by taxpaying letter writers to the *Commercial Appeal* as the Memphis Sheraton for Criminals.

"Oh, yeah?" Tyrone said. "How you know him?"

"I interviewed the cat. He's the bodyguard for Aires Saxon that didn't do his boss no good the night he got popped on Carr Avenue."

"No shit?"

"Yep. He looks like an outside linebacker for the Chicago Bears, and he talks like a professor at Rhodes College. He acted all broke up about his boss getting his head shot off, too. Just full of self-blame."

"Why'd Aires Saxon even have a bodyguard?" Tyrone said. "Does that make sense?"

"I asked him about that, Tyrone. He said Franklin was concerned about the family way up here in Memphis away from the friendly folks in the Delta and he thought all of them needed a little short-term protection with Aires getting old and Cameron getting to be Maid of Cotton and the media attention and all like that."

"Bullshit."

"That's what you say," J.W. said. "You just don't realize how scary it can be for Delta folks up here in this evil city."

"Like I said," Tyrone said. "Bullshit. But you don't really think Franklin Saxon is running a crack operation through the Bones Family, do you, J.W.? Hell, that family's as about old Memphis as they get. But he was in town, though, that night they did the tourist at the ATM, remember? He told me that himself out at the cemetery. He did that keynote address at the convention there at the Peabody Hotel where Blevins was."

"You don't have to tell me, partner," J.W. said. "But you know I seen some strange behavior with some of these old Memphis family types. Why, Tyrone, when I first joined the police force, I had the chance to be first on the scene of a domestic disagreement involving a lady well placed in Memphis society and a mixed-breed shepherd dog she was deeply in love with. And I'm talking deeply, Tyrone."

"Yeah, J.W., I know. You told me that story more times than I can listen to it. Let's go hit the files one more time."

"They are growing even as we speak, Tyrone. Let me tell you about how Diane's done got the DEA sicced on Franklin Saxon, looking for things to ask. We'll do all this talking at the Delta Pride BarBQ stand on Union," J.W. said as they got into the Dodge from the car pool. "If you got the stomach for it."

"You know something else, J.W.?" Tyrone said. "LaQuita really is ready to sing us a song."

"That's good. But why didn't you tell me about that videotape out of the ATM? That the truth?"

"Yeah," Tyrone said. "You know I wouldn't lie to a suspect. And the reason why I didn't tell you is you been roaming the Delta, out of pocket, and LaQuita just told me about it yesterday. That's what Apple was holding over the Bones Family's heads."

"It got him killed," J.W. said.

"That did, and maybe some other stuff, too. Once that bunch starts jabbering, we're going to hear all kinds of things come out."

"And LaQuita told you about the tape yesterday. You seen it yet?"

"It's being processed. We'll be able to look at it tomorrow. I hope it'll show us something."

"They ought to've made certain to kill her," J.W. said, "when they had the chance."

"Give them some credit, J.W. They did the best they could, under the circumstances."

26

"I'll tell you something, Frankie," Barry Speed said, sitting in the driver's seat of the Buick Park Avenue he'd rented at the Memphis International Airport. "I enjoyed this flight down a whole hell of a lot more than the first trip I made to the Delta."

The car was parked next to an abandoned tenant house just across the Panola County line. It was dusk, the lights were out, and the position of the Buick made the car difficult to see from the road even if somebody drove by, which was not likely. The tenant house was the last structure standing of the original nine it had been one of, and the road in front of it led to the edge of a swamp a quarter of a mile away and ended there, as though the road's last traveler had driven his car on into the mud and water and let it sink.

Franklin Saxon was sitting in the rear seat of the Buick, and Vance Murphy was outside leaning against a porch upright on the house, smoking one cigarette after another. From somewhere beyond the swamp came the deep bay of a hound trailing something in the dark.

"Jesus H. Christ, what's that?" Speed said. "A fucking werewolf?"

"Just a field hand hunting tomorrow's supper, Mr. Speed," Franklin Saxon said from the backseat. "Probably a possum."

"Coloreds holler like that when they're hunting?"

"That's the dog," Saxon said. "I'm surprised to see you here again after our recent conversation. I thought I'd made it clear that the shipment will proceed with no problems. Nothing but a change in the way we're sending it. Not a thing to worry about."

"Hey, you think I'm worried? No way, Jose. It's just, you know, we're talking about an investment here of over two mill. And it's the first time we hooked up with that New Orleans guy, that Delcambre there, on something this big. And you know, I always been kind of a hands-on guy. You know what my boy says about me? My son there, he's in the business school in Philly? I tell you, he said to me, hey, you know what you always do? Listen, he says, you micro-manage. How you like that kid? He learned that there, the business school."

"Don't misunderstand me, Mr. Speed," Saxon said. "It's not that I don't want you to see how and what we're doing. I just wanted to reassure you that everything's under control."

"Gotcha, Frankie, and you know something else? Another reason I slipped off from Baltimore took a real airplane this time? I like it down here. The Delta always calls the blues man back. Listen to some of the stuff the old guys sang after they left, went to Chicago, Detroit, Kansas City. Down home blues, baby, calling them back."

"I'm sure it's very moving," Saxon said. "But what would you like to see? The barge itself in Memphis? The merchandise?"

"Hey, no, Frankie. It don't show up I know who to see. Just tell me. What I want's to get your man Zeke over there on the porch to take me on a little tour again. I need me some more juke house time, some more of that Delta cooking."

"It's simple, and it's foolproof," Saxon said. "Let me explain the transportation, the next step we're going to take."

On the porch of the empty tenant house, Vance Murphy slapped at a mosquito on the back of his neck and let a lungful of cigarette smoke curl slowly out of his mouth. Maybe if he could get enough of it into his immediate vicinity in the still air it would discourage some of these whining bloodsuckers. Damned if he'd get back into the front seat of that Buick Park Avenue again before he had to. It was likely to be a long night hauling that big gutted Yankee fucker up and down these backroads again, and the more delay in having to listen to him the better.

They were going to have to end up sometime during the hours ahead at Big Daddy's Dreamland, and Vance Murphy dreaded having to deal with that. Thinking about the way Big Daddy Monroe was going to look up at them from behind the counter, Vance flipped his cigarette away and walked around to the far side of the sharecropper shack. Suppose that Johnston or Mayfield or whoever he was, the asshole who beat the shit out of him that night at the chicken fights, suppose he told Big Daddy about it? He sure seemed to know Dreamland, the way he talked on and on about barbecue and how to act around it. Vance shuddered and tried to put out of his mind the way he had felt when Johnston had first shoved the barrel of the gun up behind his ear. The fucker was stone crazy. Vance reached into the back pocket of his khaki pants for the half-pint of Jim Beam. Better get a good start now, suck down that first big bubble.

Maybe, he said to himself, the whiskey biting the back of his throat, I won't have to look Big Daddy in the face.

A little after ten o'clock and the hickory fire was hot, and the smoke was rising in Big Daddy Monroe's kitchen. The three boys from across the river in West Helena, Arkansas, were better than they knew themselves, and the guitar work the skinny dark one was doing sounded like it was about to blow out the walls of the main room of Dreamland. The middle one, Moses T he had called himself when he was trying to sell the band to Big Daddy early last week, was singing into the microphone they had brought with them like it was a reluctant woman's ear and he had only a minute to convince her.

Big Daddy allowed himself to move once to the left, twice to the right in rhythm with the music as he worked on plating up the ribs and the inside white and the outside brown of the barbecued pork shoulder on the work table before him. Watch it now, he told himself, don't let these little girls in here in the kitchen see you having a good time. Make them want to slack off and join in, get busy shaking it around too much and forget to move as fast they ought to with all this cooked meat to deliver.

But the boys were good, what they call themselves? Moses T and the Corvettes, and they played a lot of the old stuff, rhythm and blues, not just this rap shit. Big Daddy had told them when he finally agreed to let them come in a couple of nights to play at Dreamland that it was on one condition. No rap. "Mr. Monroe," Moses T had told him, "if we play any rap it be so good you won't even be able to tell it's rap. We that strong."

The boy had told the truth. Even though the song he was wailing away at right now was one that Big Daddy could not recall ever hearing before, it was still true enough and the guitar was sweet enough to put anybody who knew music in mind of the way people used to sing in the Delta. "You're like a picture on the wall," Big Daddy sang to himself under his breath and bumped his hip against the edge of the table twice, "please don't fall"

"Mr. Monroe," one of the waitresses said as she held out both arms to be loaded up with plates of ribs, "Booger Red he say he want to come tell you something."

"What you saying, Boleen?" Big Daddy said. "Tell Mr. Booger Red he got to wait. I'm pulling barbecue as fast as I can move. Ain't got no time to listen to him."

"Yessir, but Booger Red he say tell you he know you going to want to hear what he got to say."

"I can't go out there in the front, girl. You see I'm busy. Here, take this double order of ribs out yonder."

"It ain't me talking, but Booger say he come back in here to see you."

"In my kitchen? Booger Red, do he look cleaned up to you?"

"He wearing a brand new blue shirt. Still got the folding marks on it."

"All right," Big Daddy said. "Get them plates on all them people's tables. Tell Booger Red stick his head in my kitchen for not more than half a minute. I got meat to tend to."

The waitress left for the front room, loaded with ribs and combination plates, and in about half a minute, a small lightskinned man with freckles and red hair pushed the door half-open, blinking in the smoke from the kitchen.

"Mr. Monroe," he said. "That fine little girl carrying all that meat she done told me I could come in your kitchen. Tell you something."

"What do you want, Booger Red?" Big Daddy said, not looking up from the flash of the heavy butcher knife he was using to chop pork shoulder. "You see I'm as busy as a one-legged man in an ass-kicking contest. You looking for credit?"

"No sir," the red haired man said, stepping all the way through the door and maneuvering carefully to avoid touching his electric blue shirt or yellow trousers to any surface in the Dreamland kitchen. "What I got to tell you it be about that man which mess up that Odom girl a while back here."

"Cherene?" Monroe said, looking up sharply.

"I reckon that's her name. He be here again, that white man."

"In my place?"

"Not here yet, no. But he coming for sure. Me and Bo we seen him and one of them Murphy crackers up yonder at the liquor store at Hale's Crossroad."

"How you know they coming to Dreamland?"

"They say they be. That fat white man he say how he be looking for some more dark meat at Big Daddy's. Be buy him a quart bottle of Crown Royal, too."

"When he do that? When you see him at the liquor store?"

"Me and Bo we come right here directly. I come in the door of Dreamland asking to tell you, Big Daddy."

"I appreciate that, Booger," Monroe said. "You and Bo eat you some barbecue, drink you some quarts. You ain't got to give that girl no money tonight."

"I sure do thank you," Booger Red said, moving toward the door. "I purely love them ribs. You want me to tell you when that white trash come in your house?"

"No, I'm gonna know when they come in. I'll be able to tell the minute they hit the door. Go get y'all's order in."

Booger Red stepped back to let one of the waitresses come through the swinging door and then left. Big Daddy motioned to the woman to come to his side of the work table and wiped his hands on a towel hanging from a hook driven into the wall.

"Take over for a few minutes, child," he said, "I got to go over here into my room while you spell me."

He unlocked a door at one end of the kitchen with a key from a ring in his pocket and went into the small room behind it. When he came back into the kitchen after a short time, Big Daddy Monroe was carrying a small brown bottle with a cork in it in his left hand. Moving with care, he reached above his head and placed the container on a shelf filled with spices and condiments and then returned to the chopping table, waving the woman there back to her work in the front room.

As she walked through the swinging door, she spoke to the waitress following her with a load of barbecue orders. "Twanda," she said, "what that Mr. Monroe got in that bottle he put up on that board?"

"Say he did?"

"Yeah, a little bitty old brown bottle he fetch from his room."

"I don't know. Probably 'Match Box.'"

"Uh, uh. Match Box be a oil. This here some kind of a powder, look to me like."

"Child," Twanda said. "Stop worrying about what Mr. Monroe got in a little bottle, and help me get these people something to eat. They done hungry. Listen to them."

"I help you. But I tell you one thing. I don't like that ju ju. It scare me."

"I a Christian," Twanda said. "Don't none of that old magic scare somebody love the Lord."

"Huh," said the other waitress, turning toward a new table of four men and a woman clamoring for quarts of Old Style, "you just ain't seen it work like I has."

Outside Big Daddy's Dreamland, Vance Murphy pulled the Buick Park Avenue belonging to Hertz to the side of Bumble Bee Road and killed the engine. The big bellied Yankee had crawled into the backseat at the liquor store, broke the seal on his bottle of whiskey and directed Vance to take him to the juke house. All the way across half the county, he had crooned one blues song after the other, stopping his racket only to take sips of Crown Royal and brag about what he was going to do to some high-assed black girl tonight.

Vance was sick of that shit. But here he was, back at Dreamland one more time, driving somebody else's big car, at the beck and call of a short, ugly fucker who talked like the people in a gangster movie and who had the power to mess folks up in ways Vance didn't want to think about. It was one thing to hit a man with a tire tool or blow his head off with a shotgun, but Vance had heard that assholes like Speed did stuff with wires and hooks and ice picks and power tools the thought of which made a man's guts crawl.

Nothing to do but hold on, let him do his thing and get him delivered back to Saxon's Hundred by morning, Vance told himself.

"Hey, Homer, are we here yet?" Barry Speed yodelled from the back seat. "Let me in that juke house. Let me get at some of that barbecue, some of that Delta dark meat."

As the two men walked across the clear space in front of the metal-sided building toward the sounds of music, loud talk and laughter coming from Dreamland, Speed threw his head back and allowed a low, baying howl to well up and out from deep in his belly and chest.

"Remember that, Elmer?" he said, stepping up on Big Daddy's porch, "the old Delta blues moan."

"Oh, yeah," Murphy said, opening the screen door, "I know it well."

Speed pushed by him, shoving his way through the door first, and by the time Murphy was well inside, Speed had begun doing a hitching shuffle more or less in time to the music coming from Moses T and the Corvettes. Making a series of huffing, grunting noises deep in his throat, he had worked his way halfway across the area of floor cleared for dancing in front of the band before he turned to look back over his shoulder for Murphy.

"Come on, Homer," Speed said. "Get down. Let your backbone slip."

Jesus Christ on crutches, Vance thought to himself, that sawed-off Yankee bastard is so crazy it makes my head swim.

"You go on ahead," Vance said. "I'm going over here in the corner and sit down at the table, see what's for supper."

A circle of space had appeared instantly around Barry Speed as he had hopped his way into the thick clot of dancers jamming Dreamland's floor, and it followed him perfectly as he moved after Murphy toward the far corner of the room where a table and two chairs sat empty.

"Hey, Cowboy," he said to Murphy. "I'd rather sit at that one closer to the band. I want to study that lead guitar's fingering. You see he's sliding on the frets."

"This'un here's the onliest one open," Murphy said, nodding toward the corner. "See yonder."

"Hell, Zeke, these guys'll trade with us," Speed said, stopping in front of a table where a man and woman sat with two quart bottles of Schlitz before them. "Won't you? I'll buy you another beer."

The man looked at the woman and then back at Speed. He was thin and dark with hands that looked too big for his body, and almost all of his bottom lip was bloodred.

"For both of us?" he said. "Two quarts?"

"Sure," Speed said. "Have a ball."

Boleen watched this transaction from the cracked door to the kitchen and spoke over the shoulder to Twanda. "That fat white man he be making Richard Bartlett and Etta Mae move to another table."

"Richard be doing it?" Twanda said. "He ain't gone to his pocket?"

"Naw, the white man he be looking around like he want something. You better go wait on him. Get more beer in front of Richard Bartlett before he get a bad notion."

"Girl," Big Daddy said from the meat-chopping table, "go speak to Richard, get them all set down listening to the music, waiting on some ribs. Tell them I be fixing some specials. Everybody friendly, everybody share and share alike."

For the next fifteen minutes, Barry Speed pointed out to Vance Murphy from the vantage point of their ringside table the details of slide-guitar fingering. "Watch close now, my friend," he said, pointing toward the left hand of the guitarist and taking a slug from the bottle of Crown Royal he had brought into Dreamland with him. "See how he moves that piece of pipe on his finger up and down. Sounds like a cat in heat, don't it? That'll make you want to tie something down and fuck it. Know what I'm saying?"

"Here comes them ribs, Mr. Speed," Murphy said, watching one of the girls work her way toward the table. "You got the double order."

"You think I don't know that? Hey, give me some room to get at that meat. Red whiskey, old time slide-fingering, and the night is young in the Mississippi Delta. Like they say on TV, Elmer, it don't get no better than this."

With that, Speed reached for the plates of meat Twanda had just sat before him, tore off half of one of the slabs, and began stripping the flesh and sauce so cleanly off the ribs that in less than five minutes nothing but a stack of gleaming bones lay on his side of the table. He cleans them like a fucking cat, Vance Murphy thought, picking delicately at the single slab before him, his appetite gone to zero. It ain't nothing left on them bones but a little bit of grease, and it looks like this son of a bitch is fixing to lick that off.

"You not eating," Speed said, reaching for Murphy's plate. "Let me finish that off for you. I thought you hillbillies could eat some ribs."

"I ain't no hillbilly," Murphy said, pushing the plate of ribs and light bread toward Speed with his left thumb to avoid touching the meat. "And I don't want no ribs tonight."

"Hey, no offense, Elmer. I just call it like I see it. What are you if you ain't a hillbilly? Cracker? Redneck? Ridge-runner?"

"I'm a white man, goddamn it," Murphy said, wondering what would happen to him if this Yankee asshole didn't come back home in his rental car. God, it'd be sweet to lose him in a hole somewhere.

"Yeah," Speed said. "Sure, but who's not a white man? Except for spics, slopes, gooks, jungle-bunnies I mean. You follow me, Jack?"

Picking up the last rib with meat still attached from Murphy's plate, Speed suddenly stopped in mid-motion and stared hard at the chunk of cooked flesh before lifting it the rest of the way to his open mouth. He looked to Murphy like a man who had just discovered a pearl in a Gulf oyster he was about to let slide down his throat and was trying to decide whether to go ahead and eat it or get it set into a ring.

"Christ," Speed said. "There's something different about the taste of this stuff. I can't get enough of it." He thrust the rib between his teeth, chewed and sucked it clean, and then discarded it on the pile on the table.

"More," he said in a strange flat tone, beginning to scrape at the table with both hands.

"All right," Murphy said, looking toward the door of the kitchen. "I'll tell one of them girls."

When he looked back at Speed, the man was finishing up the last slice of bread on the table and was lifting a section of torn-off paper towel to his face. When he got it there, rather than wiping his lips as Vance Murphy expected he was about to do, he instead stuck it in his mouth and began to chew. In about four or five bites he had swallowed it and was looking around the table for more, his eyes darting in his head and a low growling sound coming from his mouth.

One of the young women from the kitchen had started for their table, but before she could get close enough to hear what the tall white man wanted to say to her, the shorter fat one in the purple shirt and flowered tie stood up so quickly his chair overturned behind him, and he began to move in lurching steps toward the table next to his.

He grabbed a handful of outside brown barbecue from a combination plate in front of a large woman named Rose Tulene Shives and crammed most of it into his mouth, what of it he couldn't force in falling from his face like bloody confetti. He chewed two or three times, gagged, spit the whole wad of meat out, and then reached for the paper napkin Rose Tulene had spread across the front of her dress to save it from barbecue sauce. It was a blue polka-dot garment with a large white collar, and everybody in Dreamland could see she cared about it a great deal.

Rose Tulene's napkin seemed to satisfy the fat white man better than her barbecue had, and he chewed the paper until he'd swallowed it. Moses T and the Corvettes had stopped playing right in the middle of Big Legged Woman, and people were standing up from their tables and moving back away from the hungry white man as he began to stagger and hop from one location of barbecue pork and ribs to the other, using both hands to lift food to his face which he would lick at, reject, throw down, and then head for another section of paper towel or napkin.

The low growling sounds the man had started to make after chewing and swallowing the first napkin now began to reach a new level, one loud enough to be heard all through the main room of Dreamland and over the screams and curses of the men and women beginning to flee for the walls and corners.

The first person out of the building, a three-hundred pound man called Heavy Beechum, had taken most of the screen door with him when he'd hit it head-on, and several women were picking their way through the debris he'd created as they followed him out.

"Mister," a thin light-skinned woman in a turban said to Vance Murphy as she pulled at his shirt collar, "that crazy cocksucker has done ruined my supper. You got to get him out of here."

"That's right," said her male companion, "and buy me some more ribs."

"I don't know what's gone wrong with him," Murphy said, standing behind Speed with a hand on each of his shoulders as he tried to prize him away from a table he leaned over, growling fiercely through his mouthful of paper. "Son of a bitch is nuts."

"Get the motherfucker out of here," a man standing near the door said, moving aside to make room. "Get the motherfucker out of Dreamland for good."

"You think I ain't trying?" Murphy said bitterly, struggling to get a solid purchase on Speed's hamlike upper arms. "He's hell to get ahold of."

"Give me some room," Big Daddy Monroe said as he approached from the direction of the kitchen in a half-crouch, each step sounding on the wooden floor like a drumbeat. "Y'all move."

The big man hit Barry Speed chest high, his arms extended in a half-circle like a blitzing linebacker, and the force of his charge drove the smaller man in a stumbling retreat across the floor, through the wreckage of the screen door to the outside, and off the edge of the porch to a resting place on his back in the Delta mud of Dreamland's frontyard.

"All y'all people," Big Daddy Monroe said, climbing back up on the porch and knocking his hands together, "come on back in the house. I'll give everybody what got their supper ruined a fresh plate. Get that guitar to howling, Moses T."

While Vance Murphy worked outside to get Barry Speed up and off the ground where he had discovered he liked the taste of Mississippi Delta dirt by shoveling a handful into his mouth, Big Daddy Monroe stood in his kitchen at the chopping table, steadily repairing the damage to Dreamland's supper hour.

"Mr. Monroe," Boleen said as she waited for a load of heaped-up plates, "what kind of a hex you done put on that evil white man?"

"Girl," Big Daddy said, knife flashing in his hand, "I never put no hex on that piece of garbage. I just give him a little something bound to make him more so of what he already is. It ain't no such of a thing as a hex. All ju ju can do is just encourage people to be theyselves."

"That poison gonna kill him?"

"I just told you, child, I ain't give that man no poison. It just be a road opener. Let his mind do exactly what it bound to do."

"That fat white man gonna get over it, then? Be just like he was?"

"It ain't gonna kill him, that what you asking," Big Daddy said, beginning to layer plates of ribs and barbecue on her outstretched arms. "I tell you one thing though, and it's something you can tell Cherene Odom, too. That sick white man from now on ain't never going to get no more suption from his food, no matter what he take a mind to eat, no matter how much he try to get it down."

"Say he won't?"

"Uh uh, not never no more. Now, honey, 'fore you go get them tables served, I want you to dial me a long distance number on that telephone hanging on the wall. It's gonna be the Memphis Police Department and the onliest one I wants to talk to he be Sergeant J.W. Ragsdale in that homicide bunch of policemans they got up yonder."

"Dial the telephone," Boleen said. "Long distance."

"Hanging on the wall," Big Daddy said. "We got us ribs to get out, girl."

27

S o you plan to let him see you?" Tyrone Walker said, looking first down at his wrist and then up at the wall clock that was part of a Busch Beer advertisement featuring running water and snowcapped mountains. The display had long served as the artistic centerpiece of the Owl Bar and had survived several direct hits of thrown bottles of beer over the years. J.W. considered it restful and would sit directly in front of the scene when he was drinking alone at the bar and admire the bubble effect in the water.

"Not exactly," he said to Tyrone. "He's done talked to me before tonight. I plan to let him see you. You're gonna be the dog that flushes him. Why you looking at the damn time so much?"

"Because it's after seven and I'm through for the day and I got something at the house to go home for," Tyrone said. "Other than that, no reason. Why you want me to be the one to get Lawrence Glide moving? Think you can't scare him enough?"

"The way I'm feeling these days," J.W. said, "I couldn't scare a girl scout troop if I was to flash them with no britches on." He stopped to take a measured sip of Schlitz, holding the bottle up to the light to see how much he'd left himself for the next fifteen minutes. This one had to last him until 7:30.

"What I figure is Mr. Lawrence Glide ought to be feeling by now as nervous as a pregnant nun at a church picnic. I want to see where he goes when he feels like he's got to move. I mean he's got to want to talk to somebody with that story in the *Commercial Appeal* about us busting them Bones Family claimers on the ATM deal."

"You think he had to wait to read about it in the newspaper, J.W.? I guarantee you word went out to the brothers like a lightning bolt striking."

"I know it," J.W. said. "But he's going to be sure everybody's heaved their guts about everything, and there was that pretty picture of you in the paper, looking like Bo Jackson in a pin stripe suit. And that's what he's going to remember when you knock on Mr. Glide's door in about thirty minutes."

"You think he's still staying at Aires Saxon's house on Carr?"

"I know he is," J.W. said and finished the Schlitz a full seven minutes before his schedule called for. "He's too smart to move out yet, and besides, I done checked it out today. Lawrence Glide is still in residence in Central Gardens."

"What you want me to say to him?"

"I leave that up to you, Tyrone," J.W. said. "Just get him to want to see some people. Make him feel like everything's getting tight all around him. The walls're fixing to close in, and he's got to find out if his business associates are still dependable. You know, make something up. Hell, you're used to dealing with a wife."

"I might can lie to a Big Ten college graduate and get away with it, but I learned a long time ago not to try that shit with Marvelle."

"We all got our cross to bear," J.W. said. "Make him think we planning a serious conversation with him for tomorrow. After that, get on back in your car and go home to the little lady and them twins. I'll pick it up then."

"You don't suppose he was there at the ATM with the white man Leather was talking about, do you?"

"Could've been. I believe one thing for sure. The way Leatherman's positioning himself to dodge the murder one for Apple, I expect he's telling the truth about Glide being in on the crack dealing that's been going on with that bunch."

"Oh, yeah," Tyrone said. "Hell, he knew Glide's first name and the way he talks. We could take him in now, stick him in a line-up, get Leatherman to pick him out."

"I don't want to, yet," J.W. said. "I want to let him take us as close as he will to some other folks first."

"I think that's the way to go, all right," Tyrone said. "See what happens. You ready to go?"

"In a minute, " J.W. said. "Let me tell you about my phone call I got first from down in the Delta."

"Oh, yeah? Who called you?"

"Big Daddy Monroe, that's who."

"The Dreamland guy you told me so much about, right?"

"Yeah. He called to tell me that Vance Murphy and that fat fucker from points east showed up there again. I don't know exactly what Big Daddy did, but both of them left Dreamland a lot less pert than they was when they got there."

"I bet you that means they're moving stuff now," Tyrone said, "if that guy's back. He was the man with the high-grade shit first time, according to what that poor boy you abused told you. He's in business with Franklin, Murphy said, didn't he? That man from Baltimore's probably carrying the payroll for the folks on this end."

"I 'spect so," J.W. said. "But whoever he is, he ain't in no shape to keep his mind on business, according to what Paul told me."

"Paul?"

"Big Daddy to you tourist types, Tyrone. I knew him way back when, long before Dreamland."

"Where'd this Barry Speed and Murphy go when they left?"

"I don't know," J.W. said. "But they'll show up here in Memphis in the next day or two, if I don't miss my guess. You wait and see."

"Everybody's coming to the party. There ain't nobody don't want to be at the Cotton Carnival once it gets cranked up in Memphis."

"That's always been my experience in the Bluff City in the month of May, Tyrone."

"All right, then," Tyrone said. "Are you ready to go now?"

"No, I ain't," J.W. said and nodded toward the Busch mountain scene on the Owl Bar wall. "See the hands on that clock by that pretty picture up yonder? They're telling me it's time to buy that last beer for the night."

"You mean the last one for the night in this location."

"Well," J.W. said. "With the right hand holding the bottle."

"God," Cameron Saxon said, walking briskly toward the dressing table and beginning to search through the cosmetics, combs, brushes and adornments stashed there. "Larry, you are so spooked."

"I'm sorry," Lawrence Glide said from the far side of the queen-sized bed. "I don't know what it is. I guess I just got a lot on my mind."

"There's where you're going wrong," Cameron said, her face about a foot from the mirror as she carefully lifted a brush to the right side of her head. "This is not a mind thing. Never was, never can be. If I had listened to my mind instead of what I did listen to, you'd have never laid a hand on me."

"It never has happened before," Lawrence said, reaching for a pair of pants on the floor between the bed and the wall of the room. "It's a brand new experience for me."

"That's what every man always says," Cameron said in a singing tone, "every time the deal goes down. Would you look at this fucking hair? Just when I had it looking halfway decent, in struts Mr. Hot Stuff ready to do the wild thing, and fifteen minutes later my hair looks like I just played two sets of tennis. Goddamn it!"

"Cameron," Lawrence said. "Cammy, please."

"Don't 'Cammy please' me, Larry. Tomorrow night's the Grand

Procession and the Coronation and I have five million things to do before then. And I have got to get this fucking hair to lay down in two minutes before I get picked up for the King of Cotton's Ball tonight."

"But, Cameron..."

"Look, you," Cameron said, spinning around from the mirror and fixing Lawrence Glide with a stare that could have brought blood, "it's time for you to move on. Get out of this room and don't make any noise in the hall. Not even my mother's so dumb she couldn't see your big ass sneaking down the stairs."

"All right, all right," Glide said, buttoning his shirt and moving toward the door in his stockinged feet. "Will you be back here tonight?"

"I'm not ever going to be back here again for you, Larry," Cameron said. "The time has come, I believe, for bigger and better things for me, and I want you to fade away. And for Christ's sake, put your goddamn shoes on."

As he stepped out into the hall and softly closed the door behind him, a huge pair of Bass Weejuns in his hand, Lawrence Glide felt like he had just been blindsided by a trapping guard. Flying sideways through the air, a generalized pain down all one side of his head and body, a sound of something big and solid and unaccommodating ringing in his ears, and a sense that he had brought all this grief on himself by not being careful to keep looking in both directions at once.

It had all seemed so easy and sweet at first, like sliding into a hot whirlpool after a hard workout. Spend a little time down South after that business in Chicago, when he'd let himself get tied up with Barry Speed and his urban outreach crack business. Just a little time to get the head straight and take the money from Franklin Saxon to "protect" his old man who didn't even realize who he really needed to be protected from. Just keep one hand from knowing what the one's doing, that's all the Glideman had to do.

And then the girl, oh, God, then the girl. And it had been so easy and oh so sweet. Just kick back, let it flow, let it take him to a place where nobody could lay a finger on him, nobody would think to raise a question, nobody would dare disturb the Glideman. The easiest part of the day had been a cloud float, and the hardest part was not taking too many bites of a sweet, sweet thing.

Fooled around, though, he said to himself as he moved soundlessly toward the stairs to the first floor, fooled around and fell in love. How could I let such a dumb, evil thing happen? I know better, I've always known better. Like Ray Parker, Jr. says in the song, I know the scene, you supposed to hit it once and get away clean. But now, I'm in love with the other woman. My life was fine, until she blew my mind.

Just let me get into my room, crawl up onto the bed, stick about half a pillow into my mouth and scream into it until I can't draw another breath. I got to holler, I got to move, I got to run, I got to flex every muscle and bend every bone until the body collapses and the mind shuts off.

Reaching the door and fumbling in his pocket for the key with his eyes squeezed shut so hard he could see purple stars and white galaxies exploding in his head, Lawrence suddenly realized that part of the sound pounding in his ears was coming from outside the narrow Glideman universe into which he was driven and enclosed. He opened his eyes and looked up.

Mrs. Aires Saxon, newly widowed, stood before him. She was dressed in a dark, flowing garment which extended from the hardwood floor to her throat where it was fastened with a series of small silver buttons. Her face was stark white, her lipstick was bright red, and her eyes looked as though someone had given her a controlled and expert beating while wearing four-ounce boxing gloves. In her right hand she held a crystal water glass two-thirds filled with a yellowish liquid.

"Lawrence," Mrs. Saxon said in a querulous voice, fixing her eyes on a spot just above his head, "I swear I have been calling you from the foyer for the last two minutes. You seem never to hear my entreaties. You didn't before my dear husband was taken from me, and I'm certain there's no reason to expect any closer attention now that he's gone."

"Yes, ma'am," Lawrence said, keeping his hand on the key but turning to face Mrs. Saxon. "I'm sorry I didn't hear you calling. I think we all have so much on our minds now. I'm just preoccupied. I do apologize."

"Nevertheless, Lawrence, we mustn't allow standards to lapse. Lord knows that Mr. Saxon wouldn't have wanted any of us to slacken in the performance of our duties."

"No, ma'am," Lawrence said, thinking I've got to get in that room and find a way to holler, else I'm going to pick up this old woman by her arms and yell into her face until I bust a bloodvessel. See how she'd like 260 pounds of black man two inches from the bridge of her sharp old nose, hollering like a Ubangi on the warpath.

"Regardless of that," Mrs. Saxon said, lifting both hands to poke gently at the puffy, blue flesh around her eye sockets. "The reason I was summoning you, Lawrence, is that there's a man at the door who says he wants to speak to you."

"Oh, really?" Lawrence said, withdrawing the key from the door and turning toward the front of the house. "Did he give you his name, Mrs. Saxon?"

"Oh, yes, but I've forgotten it. Sergeant something. I assume he's a friend of yours. He's a Negro."

"Not necessarily," Lawrence said.

"I did see him. He is black."

"Yes, ma'am. I didn't mean that. Is he still at the door?"

"Just inside it. Waiting for you."

All thoughts of a feather pillow to shove profoundly into his face left Lawrence Glide instantly, and he started for the entranceway to the house, his heart rate elevated and adrenalin beginning to pump to all its assigned bodily stations. What the fuck does this spook sergeant want? And what the fuck does he know? And why did I let myself get between Franklin Saxon and a bunch of punks with their heads full of crack? Why did I ever let myself get stuck in one spot? I never have made that mistake before. But he knew the answer to that one, and to why he had stayed around when his whole world had gotten mixed up with the universe of a paranoid honky, and the answer was a woman's name he couldn't bear to say. He could not make himself go, no matter how right the time had come to be to leave Memphis and everything in it behind.

The man waited just inside the foyer, head down and eyes fixed either on a large porcelain vase or the pattern in the Oriental rug on which it sat. Like most of these local blacks, he was very dark, but much better dressed than any plainclothes police officer Lawrence had ever seen before, and he was built like a cornerback, a good set of shoulders, no hips and long, quick looking legs. The kind of a son of a bitch who would hit a man high just as the ball touched his fingertips, trying to take off a head in the process. "Mrs. Saxon said you wanted to speak to me," Lawrence said and stopped just out of range. "I'm Lawrence Glide."

"Mr. Glide," the officer said, extending his hand, "I'd recognize you even without the numbers on your shirt. I'm Tyrone Walker, sergeant with the Memphis Police Department, Midtown Division. I'd like to ask you a few questions, clear up a matter in which your name arose."

"We have to talk here?"

"We could go somewhere else. My office over on Union, if you'd like."

"No, no," Lawrence said and pointed toward the door on the left. "I'd rather stay here. Mrs. Saxon won't mind if we go into the study."

"The room where Aires Saxon was shot, right?" Tyrone said, following Lawrence through the door.

"This is about Mr. Saxon's death, then. I've told everything I know to lots of officers. It was a bad, bad thing."

"Uh huh," Tyrone said, looking around the room and then choosing a leather covered sofa to sit on. "No, this matter has to do with a bunch of asshole brothers call themselves the Bones Family. Couple of them claim to know you."

"Gang members?" Lawrence said, making himself sit down in a hardback chair across from the sofa where the police sergeant reposed and thinking goddamn having to work with stupid punks doped to the gills. "I don't know any gang members. Lots of kids know me, of course, or at least they used to back in the old days."

"Nuh uh, not this bunch. No, they don't watch the Rose Bowl, and they sure never tuned into the New England Patriots. What they say is that your relationship with the Bones Family was more of a business transaction, you understand, and didn't have nothing to do with spectator sports."

"A business transaction? What kind of dealings would I have with a bunch of teenage hoods?"

"Hoods," Tyrone said. "That's a word I haven't heard in a long time. These Bones claimers are saying, see, that you've been selling merchandise to them, not the other way around."

"A complete and utter lie," Lawrence said, staying seated well back on the straightback chair and telling himself not to lean forward or clench up. A look of surprise and disbelief, now, that would be appropriate and called for. "Am I being charged with something because of a street gang lying to the police?"

"No, Mr. Glide, I'm not ready to charge you with anything at this point," Tyrone said. "He was right over yonder, huh, up against the wall behind the desk?"

"What? Who? You're talking about Mr. Saxon?"

"Yeah, the bossman. I see it's a new panel of wallpaper been stuck up over there on that wall. I guess the lab guys done dug out everything they needed to. Now it's business as usual here at the old home place. Back to chopping that cotton and lifting them bales, huh?"

"Who was it said I was involved with the Bones Family? What's his name?"

"You know, brother, kids like that ain't even got real names. They just slap labels on each other from what they see on television and hear on rap tapes. Hell, he was probably named something like Dante Washington by his mama, but they call him on the street some shit like Too Cool or Peachie Blue."

"I never heard any of those names before," Lawrence said. "I don't know any of them."

"They ain't real. Just theoretical. Tell you what, Mr. Glide. I'll be getting back to you soon as I find out a little something else. In the meantime, you want to take this card of mine and give me a call, case you think of anything you think I need to hear?"

"I won't think of anything," Lawrence said, letting himself rise from his chair and move toward the door. "I've got nothing to think about in connection with lies somebody's been telling about me."

"Well, here," Tyrone said, handing a card to the other man, "put your mind to it. I'll be talking at you probably tomorrow, the next day. And hey, that USC game in '85, wasn't it? You really laid a whipping on them two poor old boys across from you. Man, I could feel it all the way through the TV set."

"That was a long time and lots of cartilage ago. But, thanks, sergeant."

"Hey, no problem. Long as you can remember something, it wasn't too long ago. Know what I mean?"

After the plainclothes police sergeant left the house and Lawrence Glide started back toward his room, he could hear Mrs. Saxon calling from halfway up the stairs.

"Lawrence," she said, "have you finished your conversation with your friend?"

"Yes ma'am," he said, opening the door to his room and aching to go inside and shut it behind him. "He's gone now."

"Did you make plans to go out? You know after Cameron's gone to her ball, I'll be alone here."

"Not for long, Mrs. Saxon," Lawrence said. "I'll return well before it gets late. I've got a little business to tend to. It won't take any time at all."

Two blocks up Carr Avenue, J.W. sat in his '78 Buick in front of a house where the people inside were having a dinner party. It was a small one by Midtown Memphis standards, and not more than ten or twelve people had parked around him and gone inside the red brick Colonial behind the groupings of flowering bushes and trees which covered its front lawn.

J.W. had recognized one of the guests, Morris Mossbaugh, a judge of the Third District Court of Tennessee. He had gotten out of a tan Mercedes and helped a woman out of the passenger seat who must have been his wife, a lady who looked to J.W. like she had had her head expertly retooled and remounted with a new, tighter model of skin. You touch just the edge of a table knife to the surface of her cheek and it'd pop open like a ripe peach, he thought to himself as he slunk lower behind the steering wheel. And that nose has been so whittled away at, you look at her head-on and it looks like she's got a snakebite right slap in the middle of her face.

The judge and his remodeled lady seemed to have been the last guests to arrive, and after J.W. watched them being received at the door and vanishing behind it, he sat for a full ten minutes before he spotted Tyrone cross the street and climb into the police-pool Dodge parked facing his Buick. Tyrone drove up, slowed the car to a stop and spoke through the window.

"What you doing sitting here, you vagrant-looking white trash?"

"You lost, boy?" J.W. said. "You better get your ass out of Central Gardens or else pick up a yard tool fast and start clipping some bushes."

"Glide is wound so tight I thought any minute he was gonna jump up and slam a forearm into my mouth," Tyrone said. "He is one nervous motherfucker."

"He's gonna move, then?"

"In less than two minutes by the clock. You can write it down in your little book. He is ready to leave the territory. He's got people to see and things to do."

"What'd you tell him?"

"Told him his name had come up in a little talk with some Bones claimers."

"That did the job, I do expect. I'll be right behind the man. You better go play with them twins of yours."

"Wipe their butts, more like it," Tyrone said and pulled away.

Down Carr Avenue the black wrought-iron gates to the driveway of the Saxon residence swung open, and the taillights of a red Mazda Miata came smartly into view as the driver backed onto the street. The car drove away to the east and turned left toward Peabody Avenue, and J.W. fell in behind, wondering how in the hell a man as big as Lawrence Glide got into a car as small as that one. He must put it on like a pair of tight shoes, holding his breath and keeping his toes all scrunched up the whole time.

The red Miata was proceeding west on Peabody toward downtown Memphis by the time J.W. got to the turn off Willett onto the Avenue, and he had to gig the Buick a little to avoid getting caught at the light. No reason to scare any citizens, though, he told himself, it ain't gonna be hard to find that vehicle even if he does get out of sight for a spell. All I got to do is look for rubberneckers leaning forward to see what just went rolling by.

J.W. didn't pick up the red car again until Peabody doglegged onto Vance. There Lawrence Glide had caught a light, and he was just pulling away as J.W. lumbered up in the Buick, careful to let a couple of vehicles stay between him and the Miata. The traffic thickened almost instantly once J.W. made the turn onto Vance, the stream of cars, pickups, and light trucks slowing steadily the closer in to downtown South Memphis and the Cotton Carnival it approached.

J.W. remembered the first time he had made the trek up from Panola County to see the goings-on at the Carnival. He was accompanied by two other Mississippi eighteen year-olds looking to get drunk and hang around women who took money for doing it, Wayland Austin and Donald String, and they achieved both of the major goals of their jour-

ney. Donald String in particular had been moved by the events of the festival, getting shitfaced drunk twice in a twenty-four hour period, throwing up and becoming sober, and sometime during the might falling in
love with a caramel-skinned young woman named Lou Anne.

The next morning, driving back south into the Delta in a smoking '52
Plymouth, heads pounding in the waves of heat off Highway 51, J.W.
and Wayland Austin had been subjected to Donald's declarations about
the woman in Memphis who had taken him so far at the Cotton Carnival.

"I love that girl," Donald String had stated, "I don't care if she is colored."

"Colored?" Wayland said. "Since when you started calling them colored when they ain't listening, String?"

"Don't you never say that other word around me no more, Austin,"
String had said. "You do, and I'll make you eat a knuckle sandwich."

Things had changed now with the Cotton Carnival, though, since the
days there had been a separate weeklong party for black Memphians to
parallel the brunches, dinners, dances, balls, coronations, costume parties, adulteries and moonlight cruises on the Mississippi that formed the
backbone of the Cotton Carnival for the white folks.

Back then, as J.W.'s English teacher in the eighth grade at Batesville
Junior High School told the class when describing the Middle Ages and
Shakespeare's time in England, the colored people in Memphis at the
Cotton Carnival were acting just like the serfs and commoners in Merrie
Olde England. "They are aping," she told her forty-five eighth graders,
"the habits and customs of their betters. It makes for a richness and a
highlighting of the pageantry of the real Cotton Carnival."

What would Mrs. Margaret Pritchard think now, J.W. wondered,
about the black people having their own krewe in the Cotton Carnival
Procession and their own representative in the Maid of Cotton's Court,
much less the fact that they had a hell of a lot better music and barbecue
at their party? Good thing the poor old lady died when she did, J.W.
thought as he strained to see around a Ford Econoline in the clot of cars
between him and Lawrence Glide's red Miata. Mrs. Margaret would
think the serfs had done rose up, killed all the kings and queens and
princesses, and had got heavy into the royal wine cellar, if she could see
what he was observing down Vance on the way to South Memphis.

Stopped at a light, J.W. watched the swirls and eddies of people
headed downtown, the cars of many already abandoned and the buses
some of them had ridden this far now stalled in traffic. This early in the
evening there were still bunches of older people on the move, many of
the men still wearing the kinds of hats that J.W. associated with his
father's generation and the women in dresses and only occasionally here
and there in pants outfits. The youth was in evidence, certainly, but they

were mostly pre-teen, and some were even hanging on to the arms and hands of adults, well in control.

After it got good and dark and the street lights that had not yet been broken out came on, the bulk of the action would show up, J.W. knew, and most of the people he was watching now making their way toward the noise of the amusement park rides set up on Beale and the smell of the barbecue and popcorn would find their way back to a place where they could lock a door behind them and wait for daylight.

The Cotton Carnival might have come into being to satisfy the good-time urge of people who had once held a hoe in their hands and stooped over for twelve hours a day in picking season to fill a bag with white gold, but now it belonged almost entirely to brothers and sisters whose only connection with the land and the seasons was Saturdays at Overton Park listening to boom boxes and riding around in circles in somebody else's car.

Who is Lawrence Glide needing to see at the Cotton Carnival, J.W. asked himself as he pulled through the intersection three cars back from the Miata. The Bones Family claimers would be hard to find this early at night. Most of them'd be cribbed up, snorting, smoking, sucking, pounding those controlled substances into every possible orifice and making new openings in their bodies when the old ones wouldn't do. You might think Glide would be wanting some magic powder himself, but I doubt he's a user, or if he is, or ever was, that he'd be such a short term planner he'd have to hunt down the kind of crackhead who'd be dealing on the biggest night of the Carnival in South Memphis. Only the ones really on the edge, the kind with veins closing all up and down the system, would be needing to roam around, sniffing like a blue tick hound on trail tonight, crazy to score.

Just ahead, the red Miata took a sudden dive left on Abel Street, and J.W. found himself squeezed toward the right by the bloat of a late '60s Cadillac DeVille. He leaned on his horn, stuck his left arm straight out, and goosed the Buick, finding himself a crack of daylight to run his nose into. That move set off brake lights, bleats from horns both standard and customized, and a series of shouts and curses from all drivers in earshot, but it gave J.W. room to move, and he did, swerving left onto Abel in front of a Ford pickup that stood on its nose to avoid a collision.

"Rave on, friends," J.W. said out loud, grinning widely and waving his hand slowly back and forth as he looked into the rearview mirror. "Thanks for your attention."

When he looked back for the Miata, J.W. could see it turning to the right up an alley between the backsides of two rows of abandoned buildings, and as he eased the Buick down Abel Street and peered up the narrow space Glide had entered, he could see the rear of the car just disappearing through the double doors of a warehouse at the end of the short drive. By the time J.W. had found an empty space up the street large enough to get most of the '78 Buick into it and had walked back to the row of buildings to look up the alley, the doors to the warehouse were closed. From the broken sidewalk where he stood, he could see that they had been fastened with a large padlock as well.

J.W. thought about going back to the Buick to repark it in a more off-the-road location, said fuck it, and walked back to Vance Street to join the crowd working its way in the direction of the river. Halfway up the block to the next street where he planned to turn back left and find the front side of the warehouse Glide had disappeared into, J.W. spotted an entrepreneur who had set up a jungle juice stand beneath the marquee of an abandoned movie theatre, the Old King Cole.

The owner and operator working behind the plank set up between two City of Memphis barricade markers was doing a good business, filling paper cups with different colored liquid from three separate containers and making change from a carpenter's apron tied around his middle.

"What flavors you got?" J.W. asked after the man finished a transaction and turned toward him.

"Got your red, your blue, your yellow. Fifty cents."

"That red, now, that's the original jungle juice, ain't it? That's the true flavor?"

"Yes sir. Ain't what the kids want, but the older peoples, now they do."

"That's the ticket," J.W. said, putting his money down and pointing toward the stack of the largest cups. "Give me a double."

By the time he'd turned the corner of the next block toward where the front of the warehouse building should be, J.W. had drunk about a third of the jungle juice, enough to make his ears begin to ring from the sugar overload. Goddamn, that tasted good, but it sure was bad for you. It was like biting down on a sore tooth. It hurt, but you couldn't keep from doing it because it hurt so damn good and made your ears ring so loud, loud, loud.

The warehouse dated from the early part of the century, and it had been a cotton factor's storage facility. It had also contained offices on the street side and according to the faded signs painted across the face of the brick above the boarded-up windows, Hirsch and Downing were prime factors to the Mississippi Valley from St. Louis to New Orleans. Glad the old boys can't see what's been going on in the board room and the bossman's office for the last twenty years, J.W. thought, sipping at his jungle juice, a little different clientele and a little different kind of dealing behind those walls these days.

The front door to the building began to rattle from the inside, and

J.W. stepped back behind two women who were facing each other at close range, both talking at once about somebody called Brother Dennis. Through the small space between their faces, J.W. watched Lawrence Glide step outside the building, turn back and lock a deadbolt on the door, and then stride off across the street, angled for the intersection with Vance. He was carrying a small leather case, and he was moving at a rate quick enough to cause people to look up and step out of his way.

J.W. killed the last two fingers of the jungle juice, set the empty cup on the window ledge of Hirsch and Downing's dead business establishment, and took off after Glide. He had no trouble keeping the man in sight, tall as he was, and Glide wasn't bothering to look around to see if anybody was dogging him. No reason not to step along real lively, then, J.W. figured, and he did, dodging in and out of the steady stream of folks headed for Beale Street, W.C. Handy Park, and the heat and crush of the Carnival. I'll blend right into the crowd, since I'm the only white man in sight for two blocks. Good thing Mr. Lawrence Glide ain't used to looking back over his shoulder.

When he reached Main Street, his huge head bobbing up and down in the press of people around him a block further on, Glide didn't turn right toward Beale, as J.W. had expected he'd do, but instead kept moving straight ahead, passing Front and Wagner and then turning left on Tennessee and entering an alley that led toward Chester and the row of warehouses lining it.

Hey, Glide, J.W. felt like yelling, you missed your turn. The fun's all over here on this side, where all the smoke's roiling up and the hollering's coming from. Instead, he stepped between two cars parked nose to tail at the head of the alley off Tennessee and strained to keep Lawrence Glide in sight as he walked out of the streetlights into the darkness between the buildings.

His silhouette emerged at the other end of the alley, outlined by the light from Chester, and J.W. watched it vanish as Glide moved to the left out of sight. He's headed for one of the warehouses that's got a dock on the river, J.W. thought, just past the old marina, I bet you two dollars and a half, and I'm going to cut across shorty and save me the long trip.

J.W. had just started on his diagonal path when a woman stepped in front of him, forcing him to stop to avoid running into her. She had bright red hair, she swayed slightly from one side to the other, and she reached up and put her right hand on his shoulder.

"Sugar," she said, "where you running off to? I'm right here. Can't you see me?"

"Ain't no doubt about that," J.W. said. "Take a blind man not to see you, standing there. But I tell you what. I can't spend no time talking right now, much as I'd like to. I got to see a man about a boat."

"A boat?" the woman said, stepping back and giving J.W. a long look up and down. "Uh oh. Shame on me."

"What's the matter?"

"I just seen them shoes. Please officer, don't be taking me down tonight."

"You're right," J.W. said, glancing down at the one-inch soled black brogans to which he'd become addicted right after he'd joined the force. "These boys are gentle on the toes, and they just seem to ease my way. But don't you worry none. I ain't that kind of knocker. I don't care who you spend your time with and what you do with him, long as you don't kill the dude."

"I ain't never would've done nothing like that," the red haired woman said, lifting both hands in the air. "I cross my heart to Jesus."

"Stay sweet," J.W. said. "I got to roll."

"Mr. Glide," Franklin Saxon said, looking toward the top of the ladder into the hold of the vessel. "What a pleasant surprise. Welcome to the coronation barge. Or should I call it the Brandon Spencer resurrected?"

"Oh, he is one of yours," Boyd Hemphill called over Lawrence Glide's shoulder into the rusty dimness below the deck. "I had no idea whether to believe him or not. Everybody wants to get into the act before the curtain goes up."

"Don't worry, Boyd," Franklin said. "He's one of our stalwarts, just dropped by to see how our safety measures are shaping up. Thanks for being so careful."

"Don't mention it, Mr. Saxon," Boyd said and hurried back to make certain the work crew was following directions on balancing the lines of sight from each side of the queen's dais in the bow of the barge.

"Come see what the welder is doing to strengthen these supports, Lawrence," Saxon said, gesturing toward a man with a welding machine and several flat sheets of metal, kneeling well forward in the cargo hold. "Got to make certain my little sis, the Maid of Cotton, doesn't go kerplunk in the Father of Waters."

"Sure thing," Lawrence said. "I know you're a real worrier about whether things are going to float or sink. This is where you're going to put the flake, huh?"

"What are you talking about? If you mean the support beams to make sure that Cameron's craft is seaworthy, the answer is yes. If you mean otherwise, you've got a wild imagination."

"I've got to talk to you," Lawrence said. "I had a visitor tonight."

"Oh, yeah?" Saxon said and pointed toward the opposite end of the hold. "Who might that have been?"

"A cop," Glide answered, following Saxon across the rusting metal surface. "A Midtown station homicide cop, that's who."

"You've seen plenty of those. What's different this time?"

"The Bones Family, that's what. The police're putting the squeeze on some of those retards, and they are about to bust open and start puking up all they know."

"They don't know shit," Saxon said. "All they've ever done is hand somebody money and pick up packages."

"The Bones Family knows you, Franklin, and they know how to tie me to the people who've been selling them the merchandise, and I'm not about to wait around to see if the police can start linking me up to the brains up on the wall in your papa's study."

"How could they? You weren't involved with that break-in."

"Time's past for being cute, Franklin. Once that Bones bunch starts cutting deals with the DA, they'll tell everything they know about what things happened when and who did the arranging and the set-up and organized that whole affair that night in your papa's house. They'll name me and that retard Leatherman faster than they'd light a crack pipe."

"Calm down," Saxon said. "This cop, what did he look like? Pale eyes, sandy hair, just on the edge of being a redneck-looking son of a bitch?"

"No, fuck no. He was a brother. Black as midnight, built like a cornerback."

"Did he say his name?" Saxon said. "Was it something Walker?"

"Yes, it sure as hell was," Glide said. "Sergeant Tyrone Walker from the Midtown Division."

"That is something to consider, all right," Franklin Saxon said. "He tried to talk to me at the funeral, but he never followed up on it. At least it wasn't that cropduster from the Delta."

"Who? A cropduster?"

"Never mind. Just a fellow poking around in the Delta, asking things he ought not to a few days ago. We were supposed to have introduced him to some catfish in Sardis Lake, but he hasn't bobbed up again yet. So I had a sudden little intuition when you described your visitor. Thought he might have surfaced in the wrong place."

"I don't know what the fuck you're talking about," Glide said, "but I do know it's time for me to move."

"It'll all shake out," Saxon said, beginning to bite at a thumbnail. "It's no time to lose concentration now. One step, then another. Then we'll be through it on the other side, home free."

"What I know is I can't run now they're watching me. I know they'll put somebody on me."

"You mean now?" Saxon said. "Is there a chance somebody knows you're here?"

"No, I don't mean now. There's no way anybody could have stayed with me in among all these happy darkies at their cotton party. Not the way I came down here."

"Why, Mr. Glide, I'm shocked. You malign your own people at their play."

"My people are not in Memphis, Tennessee, Mr. Saxon," Glide said in a flat tone. "They're in Chicago, and I intend to get back there as soon as I can. I'm not going to hang around here another day."

"Look, Lawrence," Saxon said and pointed toward where the welder was tacking one of the flat sheets of metal between two ribs of the barge's structure. "I've got an idea. What you can do after the whoopde-do tomorrow night is do a reverse Huck Finn."

"What do you mean?"

"This loaner barge is slated to be pushed back up the river after the Cotton Carnival is finished with it. The story is they'll eventually fill it with soybeans in St. Louis, and all you've got to do is go along for the ride. You can even help the Murphy brothers watch our merchandise get delivered."

"That's an idea," Glide said and paused. "It should work. Nobody'll be watching for me on the river."

"Sure," Saxon said. "Put you in work clothes, who's going to check you out?"

Saxon stopped for a beat.

"Were you going to say something insulting, Frank?"

"Hey, Lawrence," Saxon said. "Don't get me wrong. I'm just talking books. I always figured you for a great admirer of our nation's literature."

As Glide emerged from the hold of the Brandon Spencer, moving with care but at a good clip among the crowd of people fastening bunting, cotton bolls, and paper flowerets by the gross to all parts of the deck, J.W. Ragsdale stepped further back into the mass of revelers watching the proceedings from the landing area. He turned his back, put a can of Budweiser up to his lips, and when he looked back over his shoulder, he saw that Glide had already moved down the gangplank and was plunging into the crowd to head south back up the bluff. In less than a minute Franklin Saxon came up from the hold of the boat and began to speak to Boyd Hemphill, who was standing near the dais under construction for the Maid of Cotton and her court.

J.W. finished his beer, watched Boyd gesturing grandly toward all points of the compass as he talked to Saxon, and then thought about the trek back in the direction of where he had left his Buick. I hope nobody's broke into it, he told himself, and I hope Lawrence Glide and Franklin Saxon had a nice little nerve-calming talk this night on the river. If things don't get fast and furious now, eggs ain't poultry, grits ain't groceries, and Mona Lisa was a man.

28

Major Dalbey sat behind his desk with his chair rolled back as far as the wall would allow it, the laces in both his shoes untied and the cinch in his belt eased two notches. He held a metal letter-opener in his right hand, and was using it to scratch a point on his scalp just beside the bald spot on the top of his head. He was looking at J.W. Ragsdale with an expression J.W.'s father would have called that of a bull studying an orphan calf.

Tyrone Walker leaned against the wall behind the chair where J.W. was sitting, pensively turning his left hand from side to side to watch the reflection of a beam of sunlight play off the wedding band on his ring finger.

"What's Captain Willis say about this notion?" Dalbey said. "You did check it out with him, didn't you?"

"Oh, yeah, Major," J.W. said. "The captain said me and Tyrone had his complete support."

"Within appropriate and prescribed limits," Tyrone said from his lean against the wall of Major Dalbey's office, maintaining his surveillance of the flashing sunbeam.

"He said that, yeah," J.W. agreed. "That's why me and Tyrone came to you. For appropriate and prescribed."

"Damn it, J.W. You and Tyrone don't know what you're asking," Dalbey said. "This here's the Cotton Carnival, boys. Y'all do something to fuck that up, give it some bad publicity, go running in there without good reason with your heads up your asses, you know what that would mean for y'all's jobs? You know what it would mean for mine? Hell, I'm fixing to retire here in eighteen months with a full major's stipend. That'd put me and the old lady on Horseshoe Lake with a Garcia casting rod in my hand until I keel over with either a stroke or a heart attack."

"Could be cancer that finally gets you," Tyrone said. "Depends on the genetic background and all that shit. You can't ever predict."

"Well, yeah, Tyrone," Dalbey admitted. "But I'm sticking with this diet. Gonna make a breakthrough here, anytime now, too."

"We know all that about the Carnival and the International Barbecue Festival," J.W. said. "The kind of stink it could raise. And we think we're about to be able to get two or three things took care of at the same time that'll give us all some relief. We don't want you to think we hadn't studied over all this stuff beforehand, because we have. Ain't that right, Tyrone?"

"That's right, Sergeant Ragsdale," Tyrone said, fixing Dalbey with a long look. "Tell the Major what you seen."

"All right," J.W. said, leaning forward in his chair, placing both hands on the edge of Dalbey's desk, and beginning to speak in an earnest tone. Just listening to him, Tyrone thought to himself, and not knowing who he was talking to, you'd think J.W. was trying to persuade some woman who'd been divorced twice and knew every trick in the game to let him come on in the house after midnight just to get a glass of water because he's thirsty. Ma'am, he's saying, I don't want nothing but to wet my whistle before I get directly back on the road and go home for a good night's sleep before church in the morning.

"Franklin Saxon," J.W. was saying. "That's right, Major. Yeah, and I know he's got a right to talk to whoever he wants to, and no I didn't actually hear a word they might've been saying in the hold of that barge that's all prettied up for tonight, but, see after Lawrence Glide came back up on top and left, Saxon followed him in a minute or two, and I hung around and just watched some more."

"Didn't nobody make you?" Dalbey asked.

"No, hell, they's two or three hundred people swarming around that barge, up and down that gangplank, carrying this and that, seeing and being seen. It looked like halftime in the Pyramid at a Memphis basketball game against Louisville. Besides, I had a Bud Dry beer can stuck in my face two-thirds of the time. Protective coloration, you understand."

"Ain't nobody gonna look at J.W. with all them pretty young folks around," Tyrone said. "Less he tried to grab one of them and run off."

"It was a couple of them I would have liked to, all right," J.W. said. "Seeing that kind of shameful display makes it awful hard on an old man."

"Hard as arithmetic," Tyrone said.

"Y'all ought to go on cable television, one of these stand-up comic shows that comes on late at night," Major Dalbey said. "What else did you see, then, after Glide took off?"

"A man dressed in overalls," J.W. said. "Him and another fellow came up from below deck with Franklin Saxon a little after eleven o'clock. The other one was carrying a welding torch and a tool kit, but only one of them had been working down in the hold of that barge."

"So what?," Major Dalbey said. "They getting that thing ready to haul the Maid of Cotton up and down the waterfront tonight. I imagine those fellows were plugging holes, working on the sound system, something like that."

"Thing of it is," J.W. said, "the one in the clean clothes is the same cocksucker that cut down on me with that twelve gauge on Sardis Lake last week."

"Huh," the Major said and sat forward in his chair. "What would he be doing there?"

"He sure wasn't welding," J.W. said. "I expect he's there to see what the layout is in that barge. See what working conditions are going to be like for a man who uses shotguns for tools."

"You're sure it was that same fellow that took the shot at you on Sardis?" Dalbey said. "Maybe it just looked like him."

"Listen. Last time I saw that face was behind the muzzle of an Ithaca Featherlite. Something like that'll focus your attention. If I was an artist, I could draw his picture right now on that piece of paper lying in the middle of your desk, and his own mama would recognize it."

"Mean old thing that she probably was," Tyrone said.

"All right, now," Dalbey said. "What y'all think is going on, again, and what you asking for? But before you answer that, I'm telling you I'm not going to commit more people than you two to any operation involving the Cotton Carnival and all that stuff on the river tonight. It's got to be low-level."

"First of all," J.W. said, "that welder wasn't just patching up the rust holes in the Brandon Spencer. What he was making down there up in the front of the hold looked to me like storage compartments. And he had them fixed to look like just part of the structure of the damn boat."

"You got down in there in the barge then?"

"Yeah," J.W. said, "after Saxon and his boys left, I walked on up the gangplank and got Boyd Hemphill to let me see down below the deck."

"Boyd Hemphill," Major Dalbey said. "I knew him in the third grade. He sure could color good. Tell me, J.W., what kind of a deal did you have to strike with Boyd to get him to let you see below his deck?"

"Nothing," J.W. said. "I just asked him about the decorations, and he was proud as a peacock to show off what all they'd been doing on top and down below. He showed me how to get in the barge from the river side, too, where they cut holes out for the loudspeakers. All I got to do is be there early enough at the right time before they load the Maid of Cotton and her Court and all that bunch on the deck."

"Ain't Boyd Hemphill curious about you wanting to crawl up in his boat, J.W.?" Dalbey said. "I know I would be."

"Now an ordinary man might, Major," Tyrone said. "But when J.W. starts talking to him, Boyd just loses all judgment. His eyes get real wide and kind of wet-looking."

"So what's going in them compartments?" Dalbey said and then answered his own question. "Dope, I reckon. But what's that got to do with you and Tyrone and the homicide division?"

"Number one, that son of a bitch on the barge tried to kill me," J.W. said, giving Tyrone a hard glance out of the corner of his eye. "Number two, a friend of mine who used to prosecute for the DEA has done me a favor and had some names run through their computer. Let's start with the man who operates the cropduster for Franklin Saxon, a fellow who's gone by several names, one of which is Ray Hubley. He's spent a stretch for flying in dope to Florida from Jamaica. Kenneth Delcambre, the man who owns the truck with Louisiana tags I saw on the Saxon plantation when I was down there, is a known drug distributor for stuff up from Colombia. They hadn't nailed him yet on anything big, but they will, they're claiming. The New Orleans people say they getting close. The DEA has requested for an audit report from the IRS on Franklin Saxon's business dealings with the farm and this Delta Pride BarBQ. They notified Franklin yesterday that they fixing to do it. I imagine he's as nervous as a cat with kittens."

"Well, I would be, too," Dalbey said. "What else?"

"Number three, I guess it is, this Vance Murphy redneck that works for Saxon has been driving around a man named Barry Speed, toting coke all over North Mississippi. This Speed fellow is also in the DEA data banks for drug trafficking on the East Coast and also in Chicago. He's served a stretch in Illinois back eight or ten years ago, and Vance told me Speed's doing a business deal with Franklin Saxon."

"You think Vance Murphy was giving you a straight story?"

"I didn't give him no selection," J.W. said. "He answered every question I put to him, and if I knew then what I know now, I could have got him to tell me a whole lot more before I was finished talking to him that night."

"You got a lot out of the DEA quick," Major Dalbey said. "How'd you do that?"

"He's got a real close working relationship with this former DEA prosecutor, that's how," Tyrone Walker said. "Do anything for J.W."

"Number four," J.W. said, refusing to look in Tyrone's direction, "this Bones Family killing, the Apple Jefferson thing on Baby Street, is busting wide open. We got a eye-witness ID on Melvin Carter AKA Leatherman, who's ready to deal that for the ATM killing of that tourist down on Front Street."

"Blevins," Tyrone said to the major. "Tollman Blevins, that conventioneer they popped."

"Leatherman is ready to tie Lawrence Glide to the white man who's just started supplying the Bones Family with crack to move. And the Bones bunch offed Apple Jefferson, because for one thing he was holding the video tape from that ATM the night the killing happened."

"What does it show?" Dalbey said. "Anybody you'd recognize?"

"Oh, yeah," J.W. said. "A bunch of Bones Family claimers and a car over across the street. A Lincoln Continental with somebody leaning up against it. Looks like a white man, dark as it is. He's the man, I expect, that wanted that tape back after Apple Jefferson had tried to use it to make some headway with him. Apple, he wanted in the game, too. LaQuita Jackson, our eye-witness for Baby Street, she told us about the deal her old man Apple was trying to make with this white man."

"Where'd he get that tape?" Dalbey said. "Somebody give it to him?"

"He took it out of the ATM where the Bones bunch left it in a culvert off of Jackson where they got the money out of the machine," J.W. said.

"That white man beside the Lincoln, that wouldn't be Franklin Saxon?" Dalbey said. "That what you telling me?"

"Glide'll help out with that ID when the time comes," J.W. said. "You watch, Major. It'll be worth his while."

"Is that the last of it, then?" Dalbey said.

"Almost. Aires Saxon was killed in his house in Central Gardens," J.W. said. "I ain't got nothing to tie that to this other stuff directly yet, but I'll lay you odds once we get people to talking and dealing with us about what we do know's been going on, we're going to find out who did the old man, too."

"Preach it, Reverend Ragsdale," Tyrone said. "Tell it on out."

"You think you can show all that?" Dalbey said. "You better be able to."

"Give us the chance, Major," J.W. said, "and I could show it to a nun."

29

The International Barbecue Festival had begun as a small adjunct party to the historic Cotton Carnival and the Memphis in May Celebration, the latter a Chamber of Commerce sponsored idea of the mid 70s. After the 1968 riots had erupted at the death of Dr. Martin Luther King, the city fathers had taken the ax of urban renewal to downtown and ripped out a good portion of it, hoping that response would calm things down as the white power structure moved east away from the river.

It was during that period that J.W. Ragsdale had gone to work for the police department and got to witness the outcome of this social engineering: empty buildings, a well-developed drug trade, a dying waterfront, and an unlimited opportunity to sharpen, practice and expand his law enforcement skills.

What had begun as a thin dream to prop up the Cotton Carnival for the old families of Memphis, had by the '90s grown to be the huge tail wagging a small dog. By the night of the Grand Procession on the River of the Cotton Carnival and the Coronation of the Maid of Cotton, smoke from the fires of the hundreds of barbecue teams competing in the International Barbecue Festival lay over Tom Lee Park, the Mississippi River and downtown Bluff City like the clouds of a small war after a successful bombing run.

So that when J.W. had made his way down to the river in late afternoon, he saw close to a half million people occupying a ten-by-four city block space of ground between the river and Front Street by eight o'clock and moving in a slow tide between the rows of tiny plots of earth allocated to the teams of pork barbecuers from all over the Western world. The Chemical Basters of Buckman Laboratories were carefully pouring a secret mixture of liquids over pork shoulders next to a team from St. Louis which would parachute two hog carcasses in from a light plane later that night. Back-up hogs, they called them, and the crowd had come to see the annual pork drop as a highlight of the festival.

Two booths down from the Buckman Chemists, J.W. said hello to four men dressed in undertaker's clothes working on meat cooking over a fire contained in the rear compartment of a Lincoln hearse converted to a barbecue cooker. Next to the whole hog turning slowly on a spit, a woman dressed in a Miss Piggy outfit and a mourning dress dabbed at her eyes as the meat sizzled on the bone.

One booth down from the mourning Miss Piggy, J.W. stopped to examine the Delta Pride BarBQ exhibit which had a plate of sample pulls of pork shoulder for passersby to taste. There were no takers, even though two young women in red bikinis leaned over the counter ready to discuss the merits of their ware to anybody who made any sign of slowing to look. "It's yumlicious," the blonder of the two said to J.W., but he waved a hand and moved on.

He spotted a team of bankers wearing matching Union Planters T-shirts as they fed hickory chips to a blaze beneath a cooker and hammered away at Jack Daniel's, Bombay gin and beer in green bottles. The Swine Lake Ballet, four overweight men in pink tutus and toe-shoes, last year's winners in the Pulled Shoulder category, fussed over this year's offering. Heat rose, the sun steadily sank into Arkansas, an insistent mumble and roar mounted into the sky, and Memphians black and white, old and young, rich and poor, straight and twisted, settled ever more solidly into their play.

The pork sandwich J.W. had eaten at the Delta Pride BarBQ franchise on Union Avenue earlier in the day when he had had lunch with Tyrone lay in his belly like a stone, and J.W. promised himself he would never again try barbecue in the line of duty rather than as a matter of choice. The meat between the dry bun of the sandwich had been gray in color and tasted as though it had been parboiled before smoking. "That there," Tyrone had said, pushing away his plate in the dining room of Franklin Saxon's franchise, "is not fit to eat. I got to admit, though, that Franklin Saxon has figured out a good way to move crack right into the middle of town wherever he's got a franchise set up."

"Yeah," J.W. said, "haul it in in a barbecue truck. Who's going to think to check that out?"

"Especially with this stuff," Tyrone had said, staring at his partially-eaten sandwich. "Who wants to touch it?"

"We had to find it out firsthand," J.W. had said. "Be able to make a scientific study of why there ain't no profit in Delta Pride."

"Next time, do it on your own," Tyrone had said.

That was around noon, and by now J.W. had made his way unobserved to the water-side of the Brandon Spencer and found his way into the barge.

Back on the bluff, up on the stage especially erected in Tom Lee Park each year next to the granite obelisk in memory of "the good and the faithful Negro" who had used his small boat to save eighty white people after a steamboat explosion sometime in the last century, the Memphis Symphony Orchestra was finishing up a medley of popular favorites, and James Highlander was readying himself to go on.

Each year at this moment in the unfolding of the ceremonies, the sun across the river a red ball of flame plunging into the Land of Opportunity and hundreds of thousands of Cotton Carnival and Barbecue Festival participants about two gins, or beers, or whiskies, or rums, or nosefuls, or injections, or tokes over the line, the huge black man with the tremendous bass voice would ascend the stage, bow toward the conductor and orchestra, lift one hand toward the Mississippi flowing by, turn back to face the masses flooding down from the high-dollar condos on the top of the Bluff, all the way across the Illinois Central railroad and the pounded dust of Tom Lee Park, and begin to deliver in song "Old Man River."

As the first phrase would boom from the banks of loudspeakers, the rich dark tones of James Highlander's bass caressing the first announcement of the politically incorrect distinction between the black and white dwellers along the Father of Waters (Darkies all work on the Mississippi, Darkies all work, and the White Man play), the deep shout of welcome from the cotton and barbecue crowd would mount up between the water and the bluff so loudly it could be heard almost to Forrest City, Arkansas.

"It is so incredibly camp," Boyd Hemphill said to Cameron Saxon, reaching up to adjust an errant curl on the left side of her head as she sat on the Maid of Cotton's throne in the center of the bow of the transformed Brandon Spencer, "that it is truly wonderful. James Highlander's 'Old Man River' gig just simply transcends category."

"God, I hate to have to spray this gunk on my hair," Cameron said, "it feels like stiff meringue on a gooey pie."

"Hush, Cameron. The breeze demands it," Boyd said and pulled Cameron's hand away from her head. "The wonderful thing is that it is not racist, in the slightest."

"My hair?"

"Ol' Man River. Despite what my chi chi New York friends might say, James' performance of that number is a uniting experience, not a divisive one. It's so Memphis. How many encores do you think he'll have to do this year?"

"Oh, I don't know. Do you think the light display will be on time? It was terrible in the run-through."

"Trust me, you lovely Maid. Bad rehearsal, great performance. I remember back in eighty-three, James Highlander did it seven times, every word. And then did the chorus twice."

"I will be blown to pieces by the wind if I have to wait more than another ten minutes on this water."

"Not to worry," Boyd said. "The pageant people are much more in control of the schedule these days. You'll arrive at the dock at the peak of perfection. You'll be luscious when you step off the Coronation barge to be received by your public. Count on it, Maid of Cotton. Show me those teeth."

By the time the captain on the tug boat set to push the Coronation barge got word on the short-wave radio to crank it up, James Highlander had sung "Old Man River" completely through four times and had done the chorus alone twice. The festival crowd had toted that barge, lifted that bale, gotten a little drunk, and landed in jail enough times to satisfy for another year, and had returned with new dedication to its consumption of mood-altering substances.

Across the Mississippi River, Arkansas had gobbled up the last vestige of the sun, and true darkness descended upon the multitudes of the combined Cotton Carnival Coronation and International Barbecue Festival. The tugboat Miss Audrey Jane settled into a steady push against the stern of the Maid of Cotton's barge in a progress toward the floating dock at the foot of Tom Lee Park. Boyd Hemphill maintained a hawk-like surveillance of the Maid's throne and of the four young women of her court at the compass points around her. And below decks, half-lying behind a barricade of large cardboard boxes, J.W. Ragsdale sweated buckshot-sized drops in the stifling darkness of the hold and wondered why the shit every breath of air he drew smelled like rotting meat. No, he thought, sniffing twice in a measured and analytic way, not just rotten meat exactly. Pork shoulders. Pork shoulders way yonder past their prime of aging.

About two-thirds of the way through James Highlander's fourth singing of "Old Man River," J.W. had imagined himself scrambling up the ladder to the festooned and beribboned deck of the barge, jumping overboard into the river, swimming at Olympic speed to Tom Lee Park, and choking the best bass singer in the Midsouth until he'd never be able to do that song again. Instead, he'd lit one of the five Kools he'd allowed himself to pack for this job and smoked it right down to where he began tasting burning filter. He had then stuck the filter, cool end first, into his right nostril to match the one he'd already inserted into the other side of his nose.

When a little later J.W. heard the bump of the Audrey Jane against the stern of the barge, he felt something like the same elation he'd experienced when he'd read the orders posting him stateside over twenty-five years ago in Vietnam. Movement at last, life ahead somewhere in the future. Now all he had to do was get through the disembarking of the Maid of Cotton and her court from the sheet of steel above his head, and soon after that took place, the good stuff ought to start, and he'd be able to suck in a breath free of the stench of expired pork shoulder.

I gets weary, J.W. said to himself, and sick of trying, I'm tired of living and feared of dying. But Old Man River, that son of a bitch keeps rolling along.

30

I t'll take almost two days," Franklin Saxon said into the rear of the blue step van with the words Delta Pride BarBQ painted in three places on its panels. "Once the push gets started, they only make fifteen miles an hour, and ten of that's canceled out by the current."

"By the current," Pick Murphy repeated.

"Up river, my friends, remember. St. Louis, the last time I consulted a map, is still north of Memphis. So you got some opposition to overcome."

"It'll be three of us going all the way, then," Vance Murphy said.

"Not counting the football player," Pick said.

"All the way, I said," Vance said to his brother. "If you was listening to me."

"I don't believe I'd call Mr. Lawrence Glide anything but Mr. Glide to his face, Vance," Franklin said. "Not even in jest."

"Oh, I won't," Vance Murphy said, "but just the one time. Right before he gets off that barge."

"I'll leave it to you to amuse yourself in the way you like best, Vance," Saxon said, "so long as the job gets done."

"You just set your mind at ease about that," Vance said. "He ain't going all the way."

"It'll get done, all right," Pick said. "For damn sure. That boy'll be sucking mud."

"Bobby Alford will be waiting for you when you get to the barge, around ten or so. Now, you both know him when you see him, and he'll be at the floating dock, wearing that welding company shirt, when you get there. Drive right up the ramp, just like we did when we put in that first little load this afternoon, and transfer the pork shoulder boxes into the barge. After everything's down below, take out the merchandise and put it where Bobby'll show you."

"It'd be some surprised folks that ate what's in them barbecue boxes, huh?" Pick Murphy said.

Franklin ignored him.

"Now, Vance, the push will start as soon as Bobby tells them everything's ready. He's in charge until you get to St. Louis and those people there take over. One other thing now. You say Ray Hubley has flown the Stearman up to the field in South Memphis and has it in the hangar. You've seen it, right? Actually put your eyes on it?"

"Yessir. I have eyeballed it. Ray's gonna be by the phone if you was to need to call him."

"And you're going to call me immediately when the last box is unloaded."

"Yessir," Vance said. "On the money. I got a back-up phone, like you said, if the first one don't work."

"And you understand if I don't hear from you by midnight, I'll act accordingly."

"Yessir," Vance said, thinking what's the asshole going to do if I don't call him, give me a good talking to?

"Is Glide gonna be at the barge already?" Pick said.

"He will, but you won't see him above deck until you get well up river."

"We gonna see him above deck one time anyway," Pick said. "Somewhere, sometime, somehow."

"Well, we won't be seeing that Yankee blues singer waiting for us in St. Louis," Vance said. "He has found hisself a permanent home in the Delta in among all that blues music he's so funny about, it looks like."

"I never have got straight what happened to him," Franklin Saxon said, stepping back from the door of the van. "Did he overdose on something? Was he using, Vance?"

"No sir. He acted plumb nuts. He wouldn't even try to walk after we got out of Dreamland. I got him over to Saxon's Hundred to the landing strip and that's when he took off. Just running fulltilt back into them marshes toward the river, once I got the car stopped. Never even slowed down after he got his feet on the ground."

"The people in Baltimore didn't seem the least bit bothered by it after I told them how he'd acted," Saxon said. "They just said they'd make other arrangements at the St. Louis end. If he shows up, he'll show up, they said."

"Yankees is funny," Pick Murphy said in a thoughtful tone. "They don't care nothing about nobody."

"For once, I think you might have said something worth pondering, Pick," Saxon said. "But I'm probably wrong."

"All I can say is I expect Mr. Speed ain't never coming out of that swamp," Vance said. "I do believe he's lost for good."

"You think he is, for sure," Saxon said.

"Uh huh," Vance said. "Yessir, yeah."

"Fuck him," Pick said.

"All I know is Baltimore called," Saxon said, "and gave me a different name for the man in St. Louis. The man that did the talking didn't ask me anything more about Mr. Barry Speed. I suppose he's not our problem anymore."

"Fuck him," Pick said.

"We heard you the first time," Saxon said.

31

The revels now were all ended, except for the parachute drop of the back-up hogs from St. Louis. That event would occur at midnight to allow the pork to be slow-smoked all night and the next morning for the farewell lunch for the award winners. The last cluster of Memphis Symphony Orchestra members, the percussionist backline, had wrestled their instruments into the final truck, the ultimate limousine filled with Cotton Carnival clout had headed for the Peabody Hotel, and the stage where Miss Cameron Saxon of Midtown Memphis had been formally crowned Maid of Cotton was empty of all official parties. What occupied it now were between forty and fifty young men moving in highly stylized steps to the beat of music booming from a portable cassette player the size of a child's coffin.

Lawrence Glide worked his way through clumps of people in the thinning crowd toward the right side of the stage beyond which he could see the white bulk of the Coronation barge, once again simply the Brandon Spencer waiting for a load of soybeans or cottonseed oil and no longer the royal conveyance for the most heartbreaking trim he'd ever run across.

Thought I was sneaking something I wasn't supposed to have, Glide said to himself as he observed the scattered flower petals, flecks of sequins, burst cotton bolls and yards of white ribbon festooning the abandoned throne on the barge's deck, and it turned out I was being sneaked up on myself. This one here's going to take a while to get over and a whole lot of distance between me and it. At the time it seemed like that gash in Jamaica was the one going to wake me up nights in a sweat, put that need for something chemical in my head to get me past it, but put it up against what's blindsided me here in Memphis and it shrinks and shrivels up to a nothing. Just like my heart, he told himself, just like my heart.

Nobody challenged Glide as he walked up the ramp between the dock and the barge, and by keeping his gaze fastened on the colored lights flickering on the water, he was able to get past the spot where Cameron's throne sat empty without having to let his eyes actually fasten on it. It wasn't until he had reached a spot near the center of the deck, well behind the bow where most of the decorations were centered, the broken and forgotten debris which had served the Maid of Cotton in its time and was of no further use now forever, that someone spoke to him.

"You got a reason to be here, friend?"

The words came from the stern of the boat, about as far from the row of lights on the ramp to the dock as a man could get and not be in the river. The speaker stood up from where he'd been sitting on the deck in the shadow of the railing and took a step forward. He was wearing dark overalls with lettering across the chest. Glide couldn't see his hands.

"I'm afraid I do," Glide said, turning his head slightly from side to side to try to get a better look in the reflections off the water. "Franklin Saxon must have told you about me. I'm here to ride this boat to St. Louis. Name is Lawrence Glide."

"It ain't a boat," the man said. "It's just a barge. No power of its own at all. That's the difference, see. But, yeah, Mr. Saxon did say you'd be showing up, needing transportation. Rest of them ain't here yet. You better go on down in the hold and start waiting. They'll be along directly."

On the way down the ladder, Glide misjudged the location of the edge of the hatch he'd just climbed through and banged his head sharply against the metal edge. "Motherfucker," he said out loud and then reaching the foot of the ladder, he began to move slowly through the darkness and into a stench of rancid meat, away from the circle of lighter sky visible through the hatch overhead, rubbing at the sore spot just above his right temple with the heel of his hand. "Isn't there a light in this fucking rustbucket?"

"Naw, there ain't," J.W. Ragsdale said, jamming the muzzle of the nine millimeter Glock into the point on the left side of Lawrence Glide's head where the lower jaw hinged onto the skull. "We got to do all this shit in the dark, and it's making me real nervous. Don't do nothing to make me jump, now."

"Wait a minute," Glide said, forcing the words between his lips which seemed suddenly to belong to somebody else. It felt like he was working his mouth at a distance with his hands. "It's all right. I'm employed by Mr. Saxon. Didn't they tell you I was coming down here? Ask the man upstairs. He'll verify it."

"I think the man upstairs has done forgot about you. What it is, partner, see," J.W. said, turning Glide to the left with his free hand and then putting pressure on the back of the huge man's neck until he began to sink to his knees, "is I ain't who you think I am. You and me, we wearing different colored uniforms, and if you don't lie down there in that nasty old water on your face and put your hands up behind your head, the center's going to snap that ball. He's listening for somebody to holler hut."

"I got permission to be here," Glide said, lying down on the rusty metal, a rib of the barge's floor construction cutting him across the chest and forcing him to let his face touch the two inches of foul water sloshing back and forth in the steel trough beneath him. It tasted like what came out of a South Chicago tap. "Ask Franklin Saxon. I'm here for the ride."

"There you go," J.W. said, clicking the second cuff shut on Glide's wrists. "I knew to bring along them oversized ones. But don't you worry none. You going to finish out your ride all the way to the end of the line. I flat guarantee you that. But one thing you got to do on your own, because I run out of filters. You got to breathe this nasty old air without a bit of help. I don't know why Franklin Saxon would want to do it, but it smells like to me he's been dipping his plastic bags of crack down into his bad old barbecue. Suppose he's trying to scare off drug-sniffing dogs? It'd drive me away, if it wasn't my job to stick my hands down in nasty places and root around for stuff. I find the damndest shit some-time."

"Wait," Glide said. "Crack? I don't know anything about crack."

"That's not what the Bones Family says, Mister Glide," J.W. said. "But you're going to get a chance to match stories with lots of people here in a little while. There's all kinds of folks want to say things about you and what you've been doing here in Memphis. Working with under-privileged gang members. Guarding people in their houses in Central Gardens and letting them get killed anyhow. All kinds of funny things."

"I didn't have anything to do with Aires Saxon's death," Glide said, trying to lift his head high enough to keep the bilge water from touching his face. "I don't know what you're talking about."

"I don't know if you actually pulled the trigger on the old man, yet," J.W. said, leaning forward to speak to the man who was lying in the darkness before him and beginning to tremble as though the water touching him were cold rather than at body temperature. "But if you did-n't, you helped somebody else do it. But don't you worry. We'll have plenty of time to find out just the way it went down, now that every-body's busted open and starting to tell each and every last thing they know. Meantime, you just be quiet and try not to think about barbecue."

32

Y ou ever see so many porch monkeys all in one place before in
your whole damn life?" Vance Murphy said, easing the nose of
the Delta Pride BarBQ van through a clot of people struggling up the
bluff from Tom Lee Park toward what remained of the Cotton Carnival
on Beale Street. "Ain't but every fourth one of these assholes white."

"Not just a counting heads, no," Pick said. "But I seen a higher concentration of them before in one spot."

"Yeah. You get out and herd them kids out of the way. And you don't
got to show no ordnance to them, neither. Hear me now, numbnuts."

By the time Vance had swung the company van around in a half-circle and begun backing the vehicle down toward the ramp to the Brandon
Spencer, Pick had opened up a lane through the crowd of young people
still gathered on and around the stage. A rap band, screaming at full volume through the speakers of a giant boom box, held most of the group
fixed in a trance of robotic movement near one end of the structure, so
Vance guided the van with relative ease until the rear wheels hit the
incline up to the deck of the barge.

"Hey, Vance," Pick said, walking up to the side of the van. "I see a
fellow up on the boat with one of them uniform shirts on."

"Well, go talk to him while I back this fucker up these boards."

"All right," Pick said. "Hey, you know what that song is saying them
punks is listening to?"

"No, and I don't give a shit," Vance said, tapping the accelerator.
"Tend to business, now, goddamn it."

"It's saying 'whip that cunt on me,'" Pick said. "Over and over.
'Whip that cunt on me.'"

Damn a fucking retard, Vance said to himself as he carefully maneu-
vered the van out over the gap of water and up onto the deck of the
barge. My brother's mind is just as scattered as a crazy woman's shit.
Daddy must have been drinking whiskey run through a lead radiator
when he put that dummy in mama's belly.

Look at him now. Down there at the foot of the ramp still on the dock. Talking to one of them people instead of getting on the boat like I said for him to do. I reckon Pick'll make Bobby Alford think we're both as dumb as my little brother looks.

"Pick," Vance Murphy said, killing the motor and climbing out of the van. "Come on up here, and let's get this thing unloaded."

Pick said something else to the black man standing near the end of the ramp on the dock and then turned and trotted up onto the barge.

"That big tall one that stopped me," he said to Vance and to Bobby Alford who had moved up to the side of the van, "he says he knows me. Used to work in the Delta and seen me on Saxon's Hundred. That one I was just talking to. See him down yonder?"

"You don't know how happy it makes all of us that you run into one of your old buddies, Pick," Vance said. "Now cut out the shit, and let's tend to business." He turned back to face the man in the welding company shirt.

"Ready for us to unload these here boxes of barbecue, Mr. Alford?" he said. Alford nodded and gestured toward the open hatch in the center of the deck.

"Has your passenger done showed up?" Vance asked. "The one Mr. Saxon's so worried about?"

"He's down in yonder," Alford said, looking again at the hatch. "Just as quiet as a mouse."

"I don't expect he's gonna give nobody no trouble," Pick Murphy said, pulling down the handle on the rear door of the Delta Pride BarBQ van.

"How heavy is these boxes?" Alford said, "that y'all are going to have to unload?"

"They weigh the same as that first few we put in there this afternoon. How much does a kilo weigh?" Vance said and reached for the metal container nearest the door. "It's about four of them in every one of these cardboard boxes."

As he leaned over to pull the first one to him, Vance felt the forty-five caliber that he had stuck down in the back of the waistband of his pants cut into the soft flesh in the area of his right kidney. He had to straighten up and rearrange the fit before he continued. "Here," he said to Pick, "you take this first one and I'll follow you. We got a shitload to tote down into that hole."

Vance turned and looked back at Bobby Alford, standing off to one side with a jacket draped over one arm, hot as it was that late in May in Memphis under the river bluff where the breeze didn't reach you.

"I reckon you going to watch the van while we fetch and carry this shit back and forth," Vance said.

"You can bank on it," Alford said and shifted the coat and what it was covering to his other hand. "Just do what you got to do."

By the time Vance had wrestled the second box out of the company van and up onto his shoulder, Pick had begun to climb down the steel ladder into the hold of the barge, his burden balanced between his head and one arm as he descended from step to step, grumbling at the trouble he was having in the process.

"This here's too hard to do this way, goddamn it, Vance," he said, "trying to stay on these stairs and carry this thing at the same time. Why don't you bring all of them over here like we did with that first few and then hand them down to me at the bottom, so I can catch them one at a time?"

"I believe," Vance said to his brother, leaning over the edge of the hatch to look down into the dark hold, "you showing a little sense for a change. Why don't you wake up the football star down yonder and get him to give you a hand while I tote the rest of them fuckers over here."

"All right," Pick said. "Ain't it no lights down in here? Where's the wall switch? It wasn't dark this afternoon."

"It's night now, fool. We don't need a lot of light. I'll bring a flashlight from the truck."

Vance could hear Pick beginning to call Lawrence Glide's name as he started back to the van for the next barbecue box with the white letters on a green background stating "It's Yumlicious, Y'all!" Pick's voice sounded metallic and booming in the empty cargo hold of the barge. I bet my little brother's scared shitless, Vance thought as he reached through the van door, down in yonder in the deck with that big black man he can't see. Wasn't for that other fellow here to shame him, he'd a come boiling up out of that hole by now with his hair standing, running like the devil was at his heels.

At the first scream from the hold of the barge, a sound that began low and then worked up higher with an abrupt break somewhere in the course of its progress, Vance jerked his head up abruptly and banged it against the edge of the van's roof as he stepped back and spun around. That little fucker's sure on edge down there in the dark. Mr. Glide the Midnight Man must've tapped Pick on the shoulder from behind and scared the pure dee shit out of him, Vance told himself as he rubbed the sore spot on the back of his head. Son of a bitch, that hurt.

When the second yell came, it began in the higher register when the first one left off, and it lasted only a fraction of the time it took for the first, chopping off abruptly as though somebody had just pulled the plug on a radio with a volume that had been set too high. The sudden silence after the stoppage of the shrill sound seemed louder than Pick's scream itself had been.

"What's going on, Pick?" Vance Murphy yelled, dropping the cardboard box he'd been ready to lift and starting for the open black mouth of the hatch. "Is it something wrong?"

He reached behind him as he ran and dragged the .45 from his pants, snagging it on the waistband and having to pull at it again before the weapon came free. Behind him Bobby Alford shook his left hand, slinging the jacket loose from the sawed-off Ithaca Featherlite it covered, and followed Vance toward the hatch at a slower pace.

"Murphy," he said. "Stop. Don't run up there."

"It's my brother," Vance said, leaning toward the opening in the deck like a bloodhound fighting the leash, but obeying Alford's command. "That bastard's killing him. I'm going to shoot the motherfucker."

"You damn fool," Alford said, pumping a shell into the chamber of the shotgun, "that fellow down below ain't done nothing to nobody. It might be something else going on down there. Go get the flashlight."

"Don't shoot down in there at him while I'm getting the light," Vance said. "You liable to hit Pick."

Alford didn't answer, but instead lay down on the deck of the barge about four feet from the open hatch and began to move his head up and down and back and forth as he tried to see into the darkness below. Keeping the shotgun free of contact with the deck, he began to hitch himself on his belly to the left where he thought he might take advantage of the shaft of light coming from the stage area on shore and penetrating about two steps down on the ladder into the hold. He held his breath, listening for sounds from beneath, but all he could hear was Vance Murphy walking around to the back of the van and fumbling with things in the back of it. I'll make him the spotter, Alford thought to himself as he eased his body a half-foot further along the circle of his path, he's too dumb to know the first thing they'll shoot at's the light.

Vance had just found an eight cell flashlight in among the scattered wrenches, pieces of pipe, boxes, coils of wire and empty Coke cans in the floor of the van and was checking the switch when he saw from the corner of his eye a man step from the ramp up onto the deck, not ten feet from him. It was the man Pick had been talking to at the foot of the ramp. He had a big grin on his face, and he was holding both hands out in front of him with the palms down as though he was trying to quiet a crowd. He pushed them down, down, down as he approached Vance standing at the open door of the van.

"Hidy," he said, "how you this evening?"

"Get the fuck out of here," Vance said, "or I'll knock you off this boat."

"The other gentleman," the black man said, pointing over Vance's shoulder and coming a step closer, "he done told me y'all need some help unloading your truck. He say you pay me five dollars give you a hand."

"Look, piss-ant, if I wasn't scared of breaking this flashlight, I'd wear it out on your head."

"Yes sir," the man said and began to turn away, seeming to slip a little on the surface of the deck. When he caught himself, he stepped forward, coming up from a crouch in a coordinated smooth movement, and hit Vance Murphy in the middle of the face with a straight right so hard his feet flew up and he fell backwards into the storage area of the Delta Pride van, banging his head on the sore place against something unmoving and very hard.

Vance tried to fight off the great white burst of light that had bloomed before his eyes, shaking his head and trying to yell past the obstruction that was filling his mouth and throat, but the man was all over him, one hand pinning the flashlight he still held against the floor of the van and the other, the left, where was it? Even as he asked himself the question, forcing it through the ball of light so he could see what it was he needed to find out, Vance found the answer, the left painlessly landing at the joint of his jaw and tipping the white ball of light over into a dark well where Vance watched it fade into a tiny speck that winked out into nothing.

"Where's the flashlight?" Bobby Alford called from his location near the hatch, scrambling to his feet and swinging the shotgun back and forth in short arcs, covering the van and two-thirds of the deck of the Brandon Spencer. "Where did you get to, you peckerwood son of a bitch?"

Tyrone Walker finished fastening a set of handcuffs on Vance Murphy, rolling the unconscious bulk back over to be sure he had room to pull all of himself into the rear of the van in case the man with the shotgun started checking for visible body parts dangling out of the vehicle. He jammed Murphy's .45 under a pile of loose cardboard and cans making sure it was well buried, and began to ease himself over the stack of stinking barbecue boxes between him and the front of the van. He pulled one open, then another, and could see a sheen of thick plastic wrapped around with wide strips of tape. It's here, he told himself, the stuff we've all been waiting for. As he worked his way between the two bucket seats, having to turn sideways to squeeze his shoulders through the tight space, he lifted his head for a quick look through the window on the driver's side.

The man with the shotgun was leaning forward in a crouch, the weapon aimed into the open hatch, and just as Tyrone glimpsed him, he pulled the trigger, sending a load of buckshot into the darkness of the hold. The muzzle flash looked two feet long to Tyrone as he scrambled his way into the driver's seat of the van and brought the nine-millimeter Glock into firing position.

The first slug took Bobby Alford high up on the right arm, spinning him around and away from the open hatch and causing Tyrone's second shot to miss completely and end up somewhere in the Mississippi River a third of the way to the Arkansas shore. Alford fell to one knee and reached with his left hand to pump another shell into the chamber of the sawed-off Ithaca, but before he could complete the action, Tyrone saw J.W. Ragsdale's head abruptly appear above deck level as he charged up the steel ladder into the open air.

Alford had just finished jacking the new load of buckshot into firing position and was swinging the shotgun down to touch it off when J.W. shot him through the throat and then ran over him, his momentum carrying the kneeling man to a position flat on his back, his left leg twisted beneath him.

When Tyrone got there from the front seat of the van, J.W. was standing over Alford with one foot pinning the shotgun to the deck and the muzzle of his handgun a foot from the bridge of the fallen man's nose.

"Don't do it, partner," Tyrone said, putting his hand on J.W.'s shoulder, "you ain't wearing no condom. Why didn't you wait? I was about to get me some more."

"Goddamn it, I ought to do it," J.W. said. "This son of a bitch has shot at me twice in the last eight days with the same damn shotgun. And both times he has put pellets through the top skin of my shoulder, and I don't even know the cocksucker. And the reason why I didn't wait no longer is because it stinks like a hog's been dead for a week down in there."

"He does act like he knows you, though," Tyrone said, leaning over to look at the bloody bubbles breaking out of Alford's nose and mouth. "He knew what he wanted to do, for a fact. He knew what he thought you needed."

"I feel like if I don't go ahead and off the bastard, the next time he's going to get serious with that shotgun and blow a hole in my ass."

"Nuh uh," Tyrone said. "I believe unless I get back to the car and call this in damn quick, this fellow has done pumped his last load into the chamber."

"Well," J.W. said and picked up the shotgun from the deck, "I reckon it's his lucky day. It ain't often I got somebody following me around saying please don't do it once I get my mind set on a thing."

"Maybe I ought to just stick to you day and night," Tyrone said, "keep telling you how to lead a decent and upright life. Point you in the direction of righteousness for a change."

"Yea though I walk," J.W. said. "Reckon how Mister Lawrence

Glide and that country asshole are doing down yonder in the hold?"

"I imagine they're enjoying that smell you been talking about. What you think it is? It stinks the same way in that Delta Pride van where the rest of the crack is."

"I'm afraid it might be pork shoulder. Shit, I hope not. If it is, it's about put me off of barbecue for good."

"Maybe this fellow hit you with one or two of those buckshot somewhere you don't know about," Tyrone said. "You're starting to talk out of your head. Look, why don't you see about our friends down below, and I'll give Irma Ray a call on the radio and get some folks out here."

"All right. Tell them to send me a bandaid or else a drink of whiskey. I expect Lawrence Glide is mad as hell down there lying in that nasty old bilge water breathing that stink," J.W. said, starting for the ladder into the hold.

"He's going to be a real tattletale, too, I imagine," Tyrone said. "By the time he thinks about things for a spell. We got to see where Mr. Franklin Saxon has done got off to."

"I imagine he's propping up the bar in one of these country clubs," J.W. said. "Or doing the boogaloo at one of them Cotton Carnival balls."

"You are so resentful," Tyrone said and started toward the gangplank.

As J.W. climbed back down the ladder, he could hear Tyrone ordering some kids off the ramp up which they'd ventured in search of the reasons for the gunfire they had heard earlier. They were hoping to find somebody down, he figured, unable to guard his pockets. Maybe next time, children, J.W. thought as he worked his way toward the bow of the barge where he'd fastened his two prisoners, but not this night on the big river.

33

"You were the most lovely Maid of them all, Cameron," Mrs. Aires Saxon said, standing by a window in her daughter's room and watching the younger woman contemplate a triple bank of footwear. "And I should know. I've seen thirty-seven coronations over the years. I've missed only one. Twenty-one years ago the night you were born in Methodist Hospital on Union Avenue."

"Yes, mother," Cameron said. "I know. Where is Franklin? I should be arriving at the University Club in four minutes, and I haven't seen my official family escort in days."

"He's here, darling," Mrs. Saxon said gesturing vaguely toward the window. "I talked to him not thirty minutes ago. He was in the study waiting for a telephone call. I don't believe it came, and then he said he was going to take you to the midnight reception in your papa's car, and that he would go out to the garage to fetch it."

"Why, for God's sake? He knows the pageant people have a limousine waiting in front of the house."

"I would imagine," Mrs. Aires Saxon said, "for sentimental reasons, young lady. Your brother is taking the place of your dear father as the elder male family member, and I presume he thought transporting you in your father's automobile would lend a touch of tradition and heritage and continuance to the process. I apologize for your brother's being a romantic and a gentleman."

"Jesus Christ, Mother," Cameron said, stepping into a pair of beige shoes and moving to the window. "Well, where is he then?"

"You speak like a merchant's daughter," Mrs. Saxon said. "He's there in the garage with the Lincoln. Perhaps he's having trouble getting it started. It's not been driven since it happened, you know."

"Thirty minutes?" the Maid of Cotton said, turning and beginning to run toward the door to the hall. "You said thirty minutes?"

"Yes, at least that," her mother said. "What are you doing? You're going to ruin your hair before you even get near where you're going.

Stop running like that."

On the way down the stairs, the heels of her shoes ringing against the hardwood risers like rifle shots as she ran, Cameron spoke to herself the way she always did before any competition, whether at a ball or a sorority election or before a panel of pageant judges or meeting some man for the first time. Keep your head, she told herself, eyes up and back straight, no detectable expression for anyone to interpret, lips relaxed just on the edge of a smile.

He's done it, she thought as she went through the hall to the rear door and across the pavement to the carriage house converted into a garage for three automobiles, the whole thing has come apart and he's checked out leaving me holding the fucking bag. Franklin Saxon, my big brother always acting the same, never staying around to even acknowledge the mess he's made, much less helping to fix it.

Cameron could see that the door to the garage was open and that the Lincoln was gone before she was halfway to the old carriage house. He didn't want to take his own car, she said to herself, and I know what that means. It went down, it's over, and he knows it, and they'll be here in a few minutes, the fucking police and the reporters from the *Commercial Appeal* and the goddamn TV people and, God, Central Gardens, Central Gardens, Central Gardens.

"Goddamn you, Franklin," Cameron said, peering into the empty garage where the Lincoln had been as though it could be hidden somehow from view and knowing she would never see any space ever filled up again. It was always going to look like everything had just left for good from now on, wherever she turned her eyes. "You were always scared to do anything by yourself," Cameron Saxon said to the empty space which was her brother. "You have always had to have somebody with you in the dark."

One thing I will do, she thought, stepping back through the door and pulling it locked behind her before she started for the side of the house and the street with the limousine parked waiting in front to transport the Maid of Cotton to the Midnight Reception at the University Club on Coronation Night of the Carnival, I will have another dance before they show up. Everyone in the room will stand and applaud when I come in. I will smile and smile, and they will clap and clap and clap until my ears ring.

34

The fools in the rear compartment of the twin engine Beechcraft had been chugging Budweisers and shots of Old Granddad from the minute Bob Llewellyn got them into the air in St. Louis, and by the time they were within ten miles of the Memphis drop zone and closing fast, they had set both of the hog carcasses up beside them on the metal benches bolted down the sides of the fuselage. They had stuck cigarettes into the hogs' mouths, tied scarves around their necks, fastened opened cans of Bud to their right feet with rubber bands, and when Bob stuck his head into the compartment to tell them to get the carcasses ready for the parachute drop into Tom Lee Park on the river where the festival was drawing to its end, he could see that Dick Stark was trying to give one of the hogs a light for its cigarette.

"Fun's fun," Bob said, observing Stark having difficulty getting a match lit, leaning forward toward the uncooperative hog, and maintaining his balance all at the same time. "But you got to get ready to throw them hogs out of this Beechcraft in a few minutes here now."

"You want we should hook them up," said Dick Stark, giving up on the cigarette and turning to yell in Bob's direction, "or are we going to let these back-up hogs pull their own rip cords?"

Bob didn't bother to answer, but the other two drunks laughed so hard at what Dick Stark had just said that they had to lie down on the benches beside the hogs to do it.

It was to be a five thousand-foot drop, about one-fifth higher than Bob Llewellyn wanted to make it, but the St. Louis barbecue team had insisted on that extra thousand. "We want folks to have time to watch them back-up hogs tumble out of the sky," Robert Black had said. "We want the colored smoke to have plenty of room to make a pretty red, white and blue design in the air all the way down."

Bob Llewellyn had pointed out that it was going to be dark anyway and that the spotlights positioned below to pick up the back-up hogs in their descent wouldn't be a factor until the last couple of thousand feet anyhow.

"Still," Black had said, "still, that's the way we want it. I want to know it's happening right, even if I can't see it all the way down. I want folks's first sight of our St. Louis hogs to be of the national colors of Budweiser beer."

Everybody in earshot had hooted and yelled at that pronouncement, and Bob Llewellyn had given up trying to talk sense to a bunch of men spending thousands of dollars to parachute two dead hogs into a river-side park in Memphis at the hour of midnight.

Just fly the plane, he told himself. Make it a good run, and put that meat right on target.

Though he knew all three of the drunk crew had fastened themselves into harnesses connected to the flanges welded to the supports of the fuselage, Bob still crossed his fingers that none of them fell out when they tumped the hogs out of the jump door, and he eased back on the throttle, checked airspeed and altitude and began his approach toward the pattern of orange lights he had insisted be arranged for the mission. Robert Black had thought it was an unnecessary precaution, but he had backed off when Bob had stood up in the executive office of Black's Sports Vehicles Unlimited of St. Louis and began to walk toward the door.

"Jump in one minute," Bob Llewellyn said into his mouthpiece. "Ready jumpers."

Up ahead around a deep bend of the Mississippi, the lights of Memphis and the concentration of smoke rising from a thousand barbe-cue fires came into view. Behind him in the Beechcraft, Bob Llewellyn heard the clunk of the jump door being opened and fastened back and in a few seconds the words of Dick Stark in his earpiece saying that's a roger on the cargo.

"Ten," Bob began counting into the headset, his gaze flitting back and forth from the instrument panel to the scene ahead, one that might have involved an ammunition dump in the Mekong about to go, judging from the glare and smoke.

"Hog away," came the announcement in his ear, and a count later, its repetition. Bob felt the Beechcraft lift in the old familiar way as jumpers left the aircraft, and his heart and viscera mounted in sympathy, as they always did at the sensation.

"Chutes open," Stark said. "Oh, looky at the red and blue smoke coming off their heels. Idn't it pretty?"

Cheers mounted in the compartment behind him, and Bob Llewellyn banked his craft toward Arkansas across the river, heading for the land-ing strip in South Memphis, mission successfully completed.

* * *

The Stearman's angle of ascent was not really that steep, even though Franklin Saxon kept urging it to be by pounding on the back of the pilot's seat where Ray Hubley sat at the controls guiding the aircraft up into flying space about two thousand feet above the river, so Ray knew that whatever was happening was not because of undue stress he was putting on the engine.

The sky was clear, and the Stearman was percolating, and suddenly it wasn't anymore. The collision with whatever it was, when it came, caused the craft to seem to hesitate and then pause in the air, as though a huge hand had abruptly reached out and tapped the single-engine craft on the nose. The propeller made a high-pitched squalling sound, as if it had been wrapped in a hundred yards of gauze, ceased revolving, and the engine coughed deeply and stopped. Instantly, the controls seized up and then suddenly relaxed, the stick as loose as a baby tooth falling from the gum of a five-year old when its time had come.

Ray did not lose all composure at that point, even though Franklin Saxon had begun to scream in the rear seat and tear at the roof of the Stearman as if by ripping through the metal that enclosed him he would find a way out to a place of stability in mid-air.

Ray Hubley's surrender to panic came when the craft yawed savagely to the right and, engine dead, began to plunge toward the surface of the Mississippi shimmering below in the lights reflected from Tom Lee Park.

Falling back into his seat and twisting to the left with the momentum of the Stearman's descent, Franklin Saxon stared through the plane's side window directly into the face of a dead creature, upside down and not a foot from his nose. The eyes were half-open, and the jaw was set in a grin, and spots of blood marked the teeth in front, and Franklin began to scream at a new level, the countenance of his dead father pushed up against the glass between them, the old man riding him down, down, down as what had been conveying him out of Memphis with all he was carrying plunged into the dark blankness of the Father of Waters on his journey toward the Delta and the sea.

At four thousand feet, in the aircraft above the Arkansas flats, leaning out of the jump door of the Beechcraft secured by his safety harness, Dick Stark, picking out only one chute in the spotlights of Tom Lee Park, complained bitterly at not being able to see both back-up hogs float safely all the way down into Memphis where all that good barbecue was being smoked and cooked.

35

"U h huh," said Tyrone Walker, leaning over to kiss his wife on the cheek as he saw the door to Big Daddy's kitchen swing open to let the waitress through. "Here come them ribs J.W.'s been talking about all these years. How can that little bitty girl carry so much?"

"You act as excited as a kid at Christmas," Marvelle said. "These people are going to think I don't cook for you at home."

"Speaking of kids," Diane Edge said, "how are those twins J.W. has told me about? They must be a handful."

"Don't mention those boys," Tyrone said. "We trying to forget about them for a few hours. I just hope they haven't got the babysitter gagged and locked up in a closet by now."

"They are just fine," Marvelle said to Diane. "Do you want one of them?"

"We rent them out," Tyrone said. "Fact of the matter is I'll pay you to take them off our hands. You name the price."

"Tyrone wouldn't no more give up them boys than I would Big Daddy's ribs," J.W. said, reaching for a slab on the plate the waitress had just put on the table in front of him. "He just talks big. He got a weakness there."

"Wait a minute before you dive in, J.W.," Diane said. "I want to propose a toast to you and Tyrone in honor of your latest triumph over crime in the Bluff City. Everybody grab a bottle of Schlitz."

J.W. and Tyrone clinked quart bottles against the glasses the two women were holding up, and everybody took down a good bubble or two.

"Tell me something, J.W.," Marvelle said, watching as her husband's partner began addressing serious attention to the barbecued pork ribs before him. "What you think was really going on between that crazy old man and his children there in Midtown?"

"You mean other than the household budget? I tell you one thing, Marvelle. There wasn't no way the Saxons were going to make a living off of canned barbecue. But don't ask me more than that because I don't know. I don't try to figure out why people do what they done. Me and Tyrone just want to find out enough to catch them for it and then let our fine justice system deal with the perpetrators." He cut his eye over at Diane Edge and then pulled another rib loose from the slab. "Ain't that right, partner?"

"I'll tell you one thing," Tyrone said. "That paratrooper hog sure gave me and J.W. a hand in this whole business."

"What the hog did," J.W. said, talking around some rib meat, "was he made what we called in Nam a pre-emptive strike on that Stearman. People all up and down the river are still fishing out pictures of Benjamin Franklin from Mr. Hog knocking them boys out of the air and spilling Saxon's overnight bag in the water."

"One thing I want to know, J.W.," said Tyrone, "is why you gone back on your word. Remember you said you was off barbecue after spending that three or four hours down there in that barge with that first helping of Franklin Saxon's old combination plate, that crack cocaine and pork shoulder casserole."

"That was true," J.W. said, "and I'm glad I didn't have to spend time with all of it at once. Big Daddy done brought me back to the faith, though. I'll never sin against barbecue again, as God is my witness."

"All that's fine," Marvelle said, "but I still want to know what you think was going on in that family. What was it with those people? I mean the son hiring people to kill his own father. Lord have mercy."

"The human heart," Diane said before Tyrone or J.W. could try to answer, "is dark, mysterious, and impossible to know."

"Only thing dark I'm ready to try to figure out is this outside brown barbecue that Big Daddy cooks," J.W. Ragsdale said, peering hard into his plate. "Here in Dreamland."

"Get down on that barbecue, Eagle," Tyrone said. "Get down on them ribs."

ENEMY WITHIN
Phillip Thompson
0-9664520-2-X • $11.00

After a successful career as a Marine Corps officer, Wade Stuart, an ATF special agent, finds himself working undercover in his home territory, the Mississippi Delta, infiltrating a militia unit with lofty goals. When Stuart uncovers a plot to assassinate the governor of Mississippi and take over the state as part of a people's revolution, Washington plans to send in the 2nd Marine Division to attack the militia. Stuart sees a bloodbath coming, begs for more time to quash the plan, but the president sees this as a good opportunity to set an example. Isolated and unsure of the decision out of Washington, Stuart must race to shut down the militia before the military arrives. *Enemy Within* rushes forward at breakneck speed, and only one man can stop these domestic terrorists...Wade Stuart!

"Extremely intriguing...the book is so well written that it is easy to forget the story is fiction."
—*James B. Woulfe*, author of *Into the Crucible*

Available now at your favorite bookstore.

To order a copy direct from the publisher, send your name, address, and a check or money order for $11.00 for each book ordered, plus $2.00 for postage and handling payable to Salvo Press, to:

Salvo Press
61149 South Hwy 97, Suite 134
Bend, OR 97702
www.salvopress.com